OPPORTUNITY FOR DEATH

OPPORTUNITY FOR DEATH

BY

E M ELLIOT

For Mum

Following in your footsteps…

2006

Chapter One

Bella Sparkle nosed her metallic blue VW Golf into the gravelled parking area beside the house, turned off the engine and sat gazing at what was to be her home for the next six months. The mellowness of the aged brick basked in the late spring sunshine and the pale pink climbing rose weaved its way up the front wall and draped itself over the top of the doorway. The quintessential English country cottage, she thought smiling to herself as she hopped out of the car and walked up the path to the front door. She breathed in the sweet scent of the roses, whilst taking in the twee, white, picket fence, neat parcel of lawn on either side of the path and abundance of lavender which enveloped Bella in a cloud of heady scent as she brushed past it.

From appearances, there was nothing remarkable about Bella. If you were to pass her in the street she probably wouldn't even register in your mind, her average height of 5'5", her average size of 12 to 14, her long browny/blonde hair scraped back into a ponytail. But, if you looked closer, looked deep into her eyes, you would be struck by their azure blue colour, the depth of which shone brightly, and realise that, here, was a person who was exceptional. You could not help but be drawn to her, open up to her, tell her things which you could not bring yourself to tell anyone else, even though you may never have met her before. She exuded a quiet calmness, confidence and serenity, even when she did not necessarily feel it herself.

So, here I am, she thought fitting the key into the lock. This will be such fun she told herself, six months in the country, close to my best friend. She tried to ignore the ambivalence which niggled within her, opened the door and stepped into the light, spacious hall of the semi-detached cottage. The stairs rose in front of her and she glanced through the door on the left to a spotless dining room with mahogany table and chairs for six, which gave the impression of never having been used. To the right of the staircase was the sitting room. Bella pushed open the white painted door and smiled approvingly, the room ran the depth of the house, a large window over-looked the front garden, an open fireplace held a small wood burning stove which waited patiently for winter to come and its chance to burst into life again. It had a warm, cosy, lived-in feel, a bookcase full of books, television, DVD player, coffee table, lamps, paintings on the walls and half a dozen china ornaments. The sunshine outside reflected off the creamy walls and into the room, the cream and green striped curtains added a touch of colour without dominating. Best of all were the two French doors which led out into the garden. Bella fumbled with the bunch of keys in her hand until she found the correct one, unlocked them and pushed the doors open onto the south facing garden and stepped out onto the flagstone patio.

Nice. Very nice, she thought, wandering across the lawn admiring the well stocked borders which were bursting in a riot of colours and perfume.

Keen to get unpacked, Bella had a quick whizz round the rest of the house; the immaculate, wood based, granite topped kitchen, three bright and airy bedrooms and one clean, functional white bathroom.

She'd been lucky to get the place. Having sold her house in Norfolk, and desperate to get away for a change of scenery, her best friend Mia Thurgood had persuaded her to rent somewhere near to her and, having persuaded Bella to do so, set about finding somewhere a bit more special than the usual practical rental property. As luck would have it a couple she knew were off to Hong Kong for at least the next year. Keen to rent it out just to friends, or friends of friends, they happily agreed to rent it to Bella, once the usual checks had been carried out, then the contract and deposit had subsequently been dealt with. So Number 2 Church Cottages, The Green, Monhurst, Kent became Bella's home for the coming months.

It was a beautiful location looking out over an expansive green, the lane off the main road through the village looped round the green to enable access. The ancient Norman church was off to the right at the top of the green and the barn-like Village Hall was on the far side, far enough away for noise not to cause a disturbance from the many events held there. Further down, and directly opposite the cottage, was The Old Rectory, a magnificent Georgian property of generous proportions.

It all seems so peaceful and quiet, thought Bella as she unpacked load after load of luggage and boxes that had been shoe-horned into every available space in her tardis like car. Hope I won't be bored though, she mulled ambivalently, doesn't look like anything goes on here.

As dusk drew in, Bella finally flopped down onto a comfortable wooden garden chair with a glass of perfectly chilled Sauvignon Blanc and relaxed. All she had to do now was to come up with a plan to keep herself occupied for the next six months or so. A sense of unease rippled through her. Making herself snap out of it, she picked up the village magazine and local paper, which Mia had given her earlier at lunch, and flicked through them – Farmers' Markets, Village Fêtes, Open Gardens – there seemed so much to do, but she wasn't sure if she'd be able to adjust to the change of pace having just left life in an urban environment.

Giving herself a telling off and to be positive, and not be negative, she ran a relaxing bath, soaked for an hour, sank into bed, snuggled under her duvet and fell straight to sleep.

The morning sun slanted through the gap in the spriggy Laura Ashley curtains. Bella yawned, stretched, and rolled over to look at the clock. 9 o'clock! She couldn't remember the last time she'd slept right through the night, let alone to such a late hour.

With a burst of energy she leapt out of bed and trotted into the pristine white bathroom for her morning ablutions. Those completed, she dressed herself in a pair of mid-grey, loose-fitting linen trousers and a plain, pale blue, semi-fitted, cotton top with three-quarter length sleeves. She glanced at herself in the full length mirror and sighed at the reflection. Who would believe that two years ago I was a size 8 with incredibly toned muscles and a stomach that most women would die for? It seemed a long time since she'd been that person; the one who took pride in her appearance, exercised religiously, ate a healthy, well-balanced diet, and was happy, she thought sadly. She didn't feel that the person in the reflection was really her. Hair, which needed a good cut and highlights, skin that should be having more than a touch of moisturiser slapped onto it and, worst of all, the muffin top. That bane of most women's lives, particularly in middle age, the roll of fat that hung over the top of the waist of trousers or skirt.

She mused that maybe now was the time to start doing something about it? The daily runs and weight sessions were a long way off. 'I'd probably keel over with a heart attack if I tried to do that now,' she muttered to herself.

But perhaps brisk walks and a bit of cycling might be a good start – she'd noticed a bicycle in the garage when she put the car away the previous night - and there were always the weights, which had found their way mysteriously into the car and not into storage with the remainder of her possessions that she'd not sold or given away. My subconscious trying to tell me something, she wondered.

Well, today will be the first day of my new exercise regime, she decided, running downstairs to the kitchen. A brisk walk around the village will help me orientate myself and perhaps discover whether this place is really as quiet and inactive as the first impression has given. Muffin top no more! There was nothing wrong with being a size 12 to 14 or larger, in fact a lot of men seemed to prefer women with a bit of shape to them, but having been the same size and weight her whole life up until two years ago, psychologically Bella just didn't feel herself with the extra weight and also worried about long term health problems if she kept piling on the pounds.

Bella opened the cupboard, took the half eaten box of sugary cereal out and banished it purposefully to the bin, then reached for the more healthy, unopened muesli box that she'd bought. As she poured the boiled water into the cafetière, deemed old fashioned by some, she caught the delicious aroma of fresh coffee wafting through the air, the telephone rang. Bella frowned. No one knew the number, as she had not got round to sending out change of address cards. Must be for the owners, she concluded. Deciding that whoever it was would only ring back, and she'd have to get used to answering it for the owners of the house, she picked it up and pressed the answer button.

'Hello?'

'Bella. It's me. How are you?'

'Hi Mia. I wondered who'd be phoning. I'd forgotten that you had the number. How are you?'

'Good thanks. You settled in?'

'Yup. Just working out my plan of action. How about you?'

'Wading my way through Fred's accounts at the moment - always a joyous event: not! Anyway, I was ringing because Fred and I are going to some friends for lunch on Saturday, and you've been invited too. Sophie and Harry have invited about a dozen friends. Should be fun, they're great, really nice people. I think you'll get on well and it'll give you a chance to meet some local people. I suspect you'll find it rather interesting... it certainly won't be boring!'

Bella could feel her friend grinning down the phone. 'That sounds lovely, I'll look forward to it. But what do you mean, "I think you'll find it rather interesting"? I know you don't say things like that without meaning something!'

'Ah, well you'll just have to wait and see! They live up at Beacon Hill Farm. Turn right from the green, follow the road along and take the next right. After a short distance the house is off to the right. You can't miss it - there are no other houses near it. Sophie said about 12 o'clock. I'll see you up there. Don't forget to call if you need anything and don't forget our trip out next week!'

Bella laughed. 'As if I'd forget! Well, I'll see you on Saturday. Have fun with the accounts!'

'Thanks. You're too kind! Bye.'

Bella smiled to herself as she munched her cereal in the morning sunshine. It was good to have her best friend so close, knowing she could drop in and see Mia anytime, but also knowing that she didn't have to live in Mia's pocket during her stay in the village.

True to her word, after breakfast Bella slipped on her canvas shoes and set off for a brisk walk round the village. She turned left at the bottom of the green and walked along the lane, leaping unnecessarily into the hedge every time a car went past; she may have been brought up in the country but living in a small town for the past 18 years had de-sensitised her from village and rural country living. Fifteen minutes into her walk she was puffing and panting as though she had run a marathon. Sense overcame her keenness to get fit, after all Rome wasn't built in a day, she persuaded herself as she crossed the lane and turned to walk back towards the village.

Bella revelled in listening to the gentle peacefulness of the countryside; birds tweeting joyously, full of lots to say for themselves, bees humming, bugs buzzing. As her mind drifted off she was startled by the distant roar of a vehicle, which suddenly hurtled round the corner swerving in all directions. Bella leapt into the hedge, this time justified in doing so, and gaped as the cumbersome beast of a Range Rover roared past her. All she could remember when it had gone was a flash of green and the number plate W1NE. Idiot! she fumed. Some people just shouldn't be on the roads! Bella tried hard to quell the anger that rose in her and by the time she'd reached the centre of the village she was slightly calmer, but still muttering to herself.

Bella pushed open the door to the village Post Office, making the bell tinkle announcing her arrival. 'Morning,' said the middle aged woman in her late fifties who was behind the counter.

'Oh, er, morning,' replied Bella, looking around to locate the newspapers. She picked one up and went to pay.

'Lovely day out there isn't. Shame I'm stuck in here on a day like this. By the time I have a day off it'll be raining! Usually does,' the shop assistant chattered on. 'Passing through are you?'

'No.' replied Bella, fearful that if she were too chatty the woman would want her life story.

'Local then?' The woman seemed oblivious of Bella's reluctance.

'Renting a house in the village.'

'Oh, lovely. You must be renting 2 Church Cottages?'

How on earth does she know that?

'Yes, that's right.'

'Friend of Mia and Fred's aren't you?'

She nodded mutely. Was there nothing that this woman didn't know? Bella fervently hoped that village life wasn't going to be a claustrophobic prison of nosiness.

'I'm Sharon and that's my husband Ron,' she said waving in the direction of the Post Office section of the shop. Unaware that there was anyone else in the shop Bella turned and smiled in the direction to which Sharon was waving her hand. A small, thin, grey-haired man smiled back at her; he had kind eyes and looked hen-pecked.

Probably enjoys being shut in the Post Office section, provides some sort of barrier to his wife, mused Bella. No! I mustn't be nasty, they're only being friendly, thought Bella.

'I'm Bella. Bella Sparkle.'

'Bella. What's that short for? Isabella?'

Really?! The inquisitiveness of the woman was astounding. Bella did her best to quell her grumpiness, after all it wasn't Sharon's fault that she was in a bad mood because of some lunatic driver. 'It's short for Christabel,' she replied evenly.

'Ooh, I say! Very posh name,' giggled Sharon. 'Don't you like it? I think it's lovely. Do you mind if I call you Christabel instead of Bella?'

What was the point? thought Bella admitting defeat; she'd probably call me that no matter what I said.

'Most people call me Bella,' she attempted weakly.

'Christabel it is then,' said Sharon cheerily. 'Now, would you like me to have that paper delivered to you every day? The Times Monday to Saturday, and would that be the Sunday Times on Sunday?'

'Er. No, thanks. I'd quite like to walk down myself. Thanks anyway.' She didn't want to make any kind of

17

commitment to this woman, imagining the drama that would unfold if she fancied a different paper one day. A thought suddenly sprang to mind. If Sharon was so nosy, it was likely that she would know everyone in the village. 'I don't suppose you happen to know who owns a green Range Rover with the number plate W1NE, do you?'

Sharon laughed. 'That'll be Rupert. Why d'you want to know? Almost get run down by him did you?'

'Well. Yes as a matter of fact.'

'No surprise there then.' At that moment the door opened and someone, who was as chatty as Sharon, walked in allowing Bella the chance to slip away before introductions were given and her life story expected.

Carefully she crossed the road and strolled back up to the cottage, intrigued to know more about this Rupert person who would appear to be a well known character. Must ask Mia on Saturday, she's bound to know, Bella thought, making a mental note to herself.

Bella slowed as she arrived at the gate to the cottage. It all looked so perfect. Just how one would imagine an English country cottage to look like. Who'd have thought, six months ago, I'd now be living in such a pretty little cottage, she mused? Inwardly she made a note to cut some roses and lavender to bring into the house, they were so fragrant and bright and chirpy. Just looking at them, and breathing in their heady scent, made her spirits lift. Unlocking the front door, Bella tried studiously to ignore the pile of boxes she'd abandoned in the sitting room, and which still needed unpacking, their heavy presence trying to guilt her into doing what she knew she had to. After her first flurry of enthusiastic unpacking the day before, she'd convinced herself that it was too late to carry on last night, when really she just wanted to sit back and enjoy being at the cottage. Reluctantly she set the newspaper down on the kitchen table, opened the windows up throughout the house to allow the warm breeze to flow through, and braced herself.

The first box was full of just a small selection of her favourite books A few classics in the form of Thomas Hardy, Charles Dickens and Jane Austen, along with a few chic-lit books and a lot by her absolute favourite author – Agatha Christie. She sat on the sofa and picked each one out individually, turning it over and reading the back as though she'd never read the book before. There was something about a book which she found seductive. It had the power to fill you with so many emotions, take you away from your own life, make you reflect on how little people ultimately change over the centuries. Consistently there was greed, hate, love, fear, passion, adultery, murder, jealousy. Without exception there was always a book to suit her mood.

She often felt empathy with the authors. Their observations about human behaviour and life in general reflected her quiet observations of those she met and what happened around her. The likes of Miss Marple and Poirot fascinated her and secretly she felt that, although they were fictitious characters, she was a little bit like them, observing what most would miss.

The books she had before her now were her stalwarts. Her loyal companions who were there through thick and thin, unwavering in their ability to whisk her away from her own life, to distract her from the past two years, the worst two years of her life. She knew that, no matter what, she could dip into any one of the books and they would comfort her, cushion her temporarily, and distract her from her own emotions.

Bella got up and removed three shelves worth of books from the bookcase, which belonged to the owners of the cottage, and ferried them backwards and forwards to the dining room, placing them carefully on the dining room table which she knew she would not use. She was intrigued by their collection of books, which indicated total opposites in terms of taste: Jackie Collins to thick, non-fiction, tomes on history. Neither was her normal literary fodder, but she thought she might dip in and venture outside her usual taste should the mood take her. With the shelves clear, she set about lovingly placing her own books on them. Bella stepped back, she admired, with satisfaction, her selection, the room felt much more like home already.

Next up was a box filled with what she classed as "useful bits": a sewing kit, knitting needles and wool (though it had been several years since she had last attempted to knit), note pads, pens, sticky notepads to put by the phone, small spanner set, a set of screwdrivers, candles and matches, a torch and other such assorted paraphernalia. She buzzed round trying to find homes for them all, resorting to either one of the spare bedrooms, or in a cupboard in the kitchen. The next box had some paintings in it which she decided not to put up, and staggered upstairs with it to the spare room she had designated for the overflow of her things, and which was now no longer looking like a spare room but more like a storage unit.

Finally, and hesitantly, she opened the last box. Gingerly she removed the first photograph and unwrapped it from its protective paper, aware of the apprehension rising within her as she did so. She turned the photo over and gazed lovingly at it, feeling the tears well up in her. Her fingers traced the outline of the couple staring back at her. A familiar tear splashed down onto the glass and she wiped it away with the clean, white handkerchief she'd retrieved from her pocket. Though she could not live without having the wedding photograph of her and Hugh somewhere in the house, it still brought such raw pain when she saw it, that sometimes she wondered whether she would be better off hiding it away and keeping it in a drawer. Every time she glimpsed it, she wondered why? Why on earth had it had to happen to her? To them? She wasn't sure if she would ever understand. The happy smiling couple in the photograph, taken twenty-two years ago, seemed a lifetime away.

Bella stood up and tried to decide where to put it. If she left it in the sitting room visitors would no doubt ask questions, and she wanted any information about her private life given on her terms, not as and when anyone enquired. Ruling out all the rooms downstairs, she wandered up to the spare bedrooms, putting it down on bedside tables and chests of drawers in turn and standing back to observe each time. None of them seemed right. She'd had it out in the sitting room at her previous house. It had seemed right there, always there, but here it was different, she'd come to Kent for a change, for an escape. Eventually she walked into her bedroom and put it on the bedside table. Though it evoked pain in her when she saw it, for some strange reason it felt right to have it there. Satisfied, she went downstairs. Maybe it would help her if it was more visible? Deciding she'd had enough unpacking for one day, she folded the top of the box over, pushed it behind a chair and spent the rest of the day pottering around, familiarising herself with the kitchen and its many utensils and reading the paper quietly in the garden, enjoying the peacefulness of it all. She looked forward to the lunch on Saturday and felt a gentle, light contentment begin to settle on her.

Chapter Two

Saturday dawned as another gloriously sunny pleasant day. Clear blue skies, without the hint of a cloud, and brilliant warm sun glowing high, would provide the perfect backdrop to the lunch party. Bella was eager for it to come round, keen to meet all the, she anticipated, interesting people who would be there, but also slightly nervous, after all, if they're so fascinating she was sure that she would seem boring to them.

Bella was ready by 11.45 and itching to go, but etiquette dictated that she wait a while to ensure arrival at about 12.15 to 12.30. She smoothed her flowing, pale green and white, spriggy, floral dress down. Whilst not exactly shapeless it hung loosely off her frame and, in her opinion, hid her well padded shape. The upside of having put on weight was that her breasts had ballooned simultaneously to the rest of her body, giving her a generously proportioned bust which rippled lusciously above the scoop neck of the dress. Low heeled, soft green, suede mules completed the outfit, and Bella felt confident that if the lunch was either casual or more formal she would fit in at one end of the scale.

She waited until 12.05pm, locked the door and got into her Golf and drove cautiously up the road, turning right as instructed and then, eventually, right again into the drive of a fabulous period farmhouse. A perfectly manicured circle of lawn centred the drive, four cars were neatly lined up off to one side. Bella pulled in next to a blue VW Beetle that looked distinctly like the one which was often parked outside the detached cottage just up from Bella's cottage, next to the church. With relief Bella saw Mia and Fred's silver Volvo estate sitting in the row of cars and, with a flutter of nerves, picked up the hand-tied bouquet of flowers from the front seat, and headed to the front door. Before she could get there a smiley-faced woman in her mid thirties, with long curly blonde hair came round the side of the house clutching an equally smiley six month old baby.

'Hi! You must be Bella. I'm Sophie and this is Jemima.' On cue the baby beamed even more brightly and giggled.

'Hi Sophie. Here these are for you,' she said proffering the flowers.

'They're beautiful! Thank you, but you didn't need to bring anything!'

'It's a pleasure. Thanks for inviting me. Would you like me to carry them for you?'

'Please. If Jemima gets close to those she'll be pulling them out and tweaking the petals off before I can arrange them. Come round the back and meet the others.'

Bella dutifully followed her through a wrought iron gate and round to the back of the house, gasping at the stunning view. From the terrace you could see for miles, across the village and to the distant hills.

'It's beautiful! You have such a lovely house and what amazing views.'

'Thanks. We're very lucky. Bella, this is my husband Harry. Darling, this is Bella.'

A short, slim man with short, blond, grey-splattered hair, turned to greet her. His eyes, like his wife's, were green and sparkly and he had laughter lines which crinkled as he spoke. 'Nice to meet you Bella. What can I get you to drink? Wine? Pimms? A soft drink?'

'Something soft would be lovely thanks. Whatever you've got.' Harry disappeared off into the house leaving Bella to greet Mia and Fred.

'Good to see you,' kissed Mia. Fred engulfed her in a hug.

'You too. Thanks for this.' Her best friend looked as elegant as ever in a simple cream linen shift dress. Though they were the same age, at 42, Bella always felt that Mia looked younger than her years, and certainly more youthful than herself. They were the same height but Mia was slimmer and her cropped, glistening, brown hair was always perfectly kept, never a hair out of place. It framed her petite face, with small button nose and full lips, which looked as though she'd had collagen injected into them, but were actually as nature had created them.

'Come on. Let me introduce you to the others.' Offered Harry, who had returned with a tall glass filled with elderflower pressé and ice bobbing on the top.

'Thanks,' she said as he and Mia led her over to the other invitees who'd arrived.

'This is Jennifer. Jennifer this is Bella. Bella's renting 2 Church Cottages. Bella, Jennifer lives in Willow Tree Cottage up by the Church.'

'Hi Bella, I thought I'd seen you in the village. Certainly Sharon in the shop has been announcing your arrival! Though she keeps talking about "Christabel" do you prefer that or 'Bella'?' She grinned at her.

Bella rolled her eyes and laughed. 'Bella is just fine. No one has called me Christabel since I was a little girl. It seemed futile arguing about it with her.'

'Very wise, there's no point, just admit defeat where Sharon is concerned.'

Bella instantly felt like she'd found a new friend in the tall young woman who stood in front of her, despite the fact that she was the sort of woman most females would be jealous of. Jennifer exuded a sensuousness that many men found irresistible, her lengthy rich glossy chestnut hair curled seductively down, mirroring the curviness of her body. Long, slim, shapely, tanned legs were revealed below a knee length, pale yellow, fitted skirt and a fitted white cotton blouse which clung snugly to her breasts and was unbuttoned to reveal a hint of what nestled beneath.

'Have you settled in then?'

'Pretty much. It's a lovely village. Quite quiet though.'

'Never judge a book by its cover! I think you'll come to realise that all is not as it seems…', she smiled mysteriously.

'Really? I don't suppose you'd like to expand on that?' Bella's curiosity was roused.

'Oh, I think that would spoil the fun,' she laughed, 'wouldn't you agree Mia?'

Mia nodded and grinned.

'Hi,' said a skinny, ferrety-faced man joining their group. Though gaunt and with a razor sharp slender nose and smudges of dark under his eyes, Bella could see that his soft brown eyes exuded a warmth and gentleness. His blue and white checked cotton shirt was fraying around the collar and cuffs and his pale beige chinos looked well lived in.

'Bella, this is Seb. Seb, this is Bella,' introduced Jennifer.

'Ah! You're Mia and Fred's friend who's renting the cottage,' he smiled warmly at her. Bella liked him immediately. She didn't know him, but she wanted to. There was something vulnerable about him which appealed to her. 'Settling in well? Suppose I shouldn't ask as I imagine this lot have already grilled you? Must be getting tedious having to keep offering the same response.'

Bella laughed. 'I don't mind. Everyone's been so friendly. How do you all know each other?'

'Mia, Sophie, myself, Cressa - who's over there talking to Sophie - Kimberley (who we all call Kim) and Florence all play tennis together. Jack plays at the club too with Harry and Fred, and when we all get together the husbands or wives come too, that's how it started,' replied Jennifer. 'Though some of us go back a lot further than that.'

'So is Cressa your wife then Seb?' asked Bella politely. Jennifer sniggered. Seb shot her a filthy look.

'No. I'm not married, never have been and shouldn't think I ever will.' Bella felt a twinge of disappointment. What was his story? There was an air of them all seeming to know something, but also that they weren't going to divulge the secret. 'Cressa is married to Jack. You see that short, rotund chap talking to Harry, that's Jack.' Everyone chortled except Bella. Wasn't it a bit rude to describe him like that? Still, they obviously knew each other well, besides he wasn't that fat. At that moment Jack turned slightly and Bella caught sight of his rather expansive stomach which eclipsed Harry. She could see what they meant.

'Hey! Cressa! Come over here and meet Bella,' called Jennifer. Another very tall, slim, elegant woman glided serenely across to them despite the cocktail-stick-thin, towering spikes of her heels sinking into the grass with a little 'pop' at each step. She was the polar opposite in appearance to her husband.

'Pleased to meet you Bella.' She proffered her hand with long elegant fingers, which Bella shook accordingly, noting how soft it felt.

'Likewise. Jennifer was just telling me that you play tennis together.'

'We certainly do.' There was a reserved air about Cressa, slightly aloof, as though she wasn't quiet comfortable in the presence of her friends. Bella's brow wrinkled slightly in puzzlement.

'And this is Florence,' announced Sophie, joining the swelling group.

Bella's head was starting to swim with so many rapid introductions. She'd never remember all their names at this rate! Out of all the women, Florence was the one who looked misplaced and the dowdiest. Bizarre, considering the fact that she must be the youngest observed Bella. Florence wore a plain, pale blue, cotton skirt, which didn't fit properly and a slightly over-sized white shirt, which was left untucked. Bella felt that she looked like an ugly duckling waiting to blossom into a swan. She was very petite, and had a beautiful heart-shaped face with rose bud lips, and the most perfect and clearest complexion that Bella had ever seen. Her eyes were a deep emerald green, flecked with gold, which were enhanced by the rich goldenness of her lengthy, rather unkempt, straight, blonde hair. A change of clothes, and a good hair cut, and she would be stunning, by far the most beautiful woman here. Peculiar then, that she should dress like that. There was something about her which puzzled Bella. Something she couldn't put her finger on, but given that she had only just met her - and the others - it was hardly surprising.

Bella was distracted from greeting Florence by a commotion coming from the side of the house. Raised voices could be heard but though she strained to catch a few words she couldn't hear precisely what was being said, however she could feel a subtle shift in the previously jolly atmosphere. She noticed Seb clenching his jaw and his hands were screwed up into a fist. Hmm, intriguing, mused Bella.

Jennifer rolled her eyes. 'Here they are, no doubting that.' She saw Bella's enquiring look. 'Rupert and Kim,' she added.

Rupert, trailed by Kim, made a beeline for the group, shaking Harry's hand on the way. Suddenly he stopped short. Observing, Bella could see his face pale almost imperceptibly but not the cause. Curiouser and curiouser. He recovered quickly and pounced on Jennifer, giving her a squeeze and a long wet kiss on each cheek. Bella shuddered. In his mid forties and well over six feet tall he towered over the rest of the group, which was fortunate for him because with his height he could carry off the substantial weight around his middle and get away without looking too portly. His face was puffy with large dark circles under his dull, brown, bloodshot eyes, his nose was bulbous and red with broken capillaries fanning out over his face. Bella was convinced, by the look of him, that he was an alcoholic. There was something decidedly slimy about him, which made her dislike him instantly even though, as yet, she had not been introduced. His slicked back, black greasy hair added to his unappetising appearance.

Having extracted herself from his clutches, Jennifer introduced Florence to him, as this was the first time Florence had met him because she had only joined the tennis club a few months beforehand.

'Have we met?' barked Rupert peering intently at her. 'You look familiar.'

'No,' replied Florence meekly. 'We definitely have not met, I would have remembered.'

He stared intently at her before his lecherous eyes alighted on Bella. 'And who do we have here?' he said leering at her.

Bella shivered in repulsion. 'Bella Sparkle,' she replied making a huge effort not to grimace when his chubby fingered, clammy hand grasped hers.

'Now I know we haven't met, or I would have remembered,' he licked his lips surreptitiously. Bella felt like a helpless rabbit caught in the talons of an eagle.

Mia stepped in to save the moment. 'And this is Kimberley, Kim to us, Rupert's wife,' she said pointedly looking at him.

A much younger woman, at least ten years, thought Bella. What on earth is she doing with a lech like him? Kim was quite tall, skinny - bony even - with short, blonde, stylishly cut hair and very pretty. Her skin was clear, but there were bags and dark circles under her dulled blue eyes. The stress of being married to Rupert reflected in her face.

'Hi Bella, nice to meet you. Mia told us you were going to live in the village for a bit. D'you play tennis?'

'I haven't for several years.   I'm not very good I'm afraid.'

'Not very good!' snorted Mia.   'You used to thrash me!'

'That was a long time ago.   I am definitely not as fit as I used to be.'

'I don't know about that, you look pretty fit to me,' oozed Rupert.

Bella mentally vomited, but smiled politely.   How on earth did Kim put up with him?   Or perhaps more importantly, why?   Perhaps he has hidden qualities, ones which no one else sees?   Or possibly it's the size of his bank balance?   Maybe he's really rich?   Don't be so judgemental and cynical, Bella chided herself.   You don't know them and apart from that nobody's perfect.

'You must come and play with us!   We have a lot of fun!' continued Kim.

'Thanks.   I'd like that, as long as you keep your expectations of my ability on the court low,' she grinned.

Harry discreetly topped up glasses, whilst Sophie disappeared into the kitchen to complete the final preparations for lunch, leaving Jennifer holding Jemima.   'She's so cute isn't she?' Jennifer said jiggling the little tot in her arms, making her smile and giggle the cute infectious giggle that only babies do.

A few minutes later Sophie called everyone to the exquisitely laid table, under a wooden arbour covered in a honey scented honeysuckle, providing much needed shade out of the now scorching sun.   It was laden with poached salmon, a riot of multi-coloured salads, and an interesting selection of breads.

'This looks delicious Sophie. How on earth have you managed to produce such a banquet whilst looking after Jemima?'

Sophie smiled, pleased that all her hard work had not gone unnoticed. 'I just prepared things while Jemima had a sleep, and did a lot last night, and Harry's looked after Jemima this morning.' Harry in the meantime had taken Jemima off for her nap, with her having already been fed with pureed carrot and parsnips and some milk before everyone arrived. Two additional seats remained empty.

'Who's missing?' asked Kim.

'Ariadne and her friend,' replied Sophie.

'She's always late, never turns up on time. We could be waiting until supper time and she still might not turn up,' whispered Seb to Bella who was seated on her right. 'Just wait until Ariadne arrives, then the entertainment will really start…' He grinned broadly at her and raised his eyebrows.

Chapter Three

Mid-way through the meal, the noisy chatter and laughter was suddenly silenced by the dramatic arrival of the much awaited Ariadne, who swept in blowing kisses to everyone, as though she were accepting an Oscar.

'Darlings! It's so wonderful to see you,' she breathed.

Sophie jumped up and hugged her friend. Bella was struck by how different they appeared. Ariadne was like a beanpole in both height and physique, and so thin that Bella thought that if she stood sideways you wouldn't see her. Her hipster cut-offs were excruciatingly tight, there was no way she could have got into them other than by being literally poured in. Matching was an equally tight white top, which stretched so tightly over her surgically enhanced breasts that it was surely only a matter of time before the fabric ripped under the strain. In every way she seemed perfect. The perfection, it has to be said, that the fashion and film industry tried to brainwash ordinary mortals into believing is the only way to look. Ariadne's skin was flawless and wrinkle free, despite being 35 by which time most women have a few fine lines beginning to appear. Her nose was perfect. Her chin was perfect and her lips were an apparent luscious perfection. Her golden blonde hair was iron-straight down to her mid back, with not a single hair out of place. Her sapphire blue eyes sparkled like an oasis in the perfectness which was Ariadne. She looked totally perfect, but completely unreal thought Bella. Bella was roused out of her Ariadne-esq trance by the flourishing introduction of the guest whom she had brought with her.

As her eyes swept round to look at the guest, Bella did a double take at Rupert, who had momentarily stopped pouring wine down his throat in order to dribble and lech at Ariadne, managing a quick grope of her bottom whilst he greeted her. But Rupert's face was turning as white as a sheet, even whiter than earlier. Bella shivered. As the guest approached him he hesitantly held out his hand to receive the one which was offered and shook it. Bella pushed her attention back to Ariadne who was announcing that the guest was Kit, her agent, who was an "absolute darling", and she couldn't live without him.

'Nice to meet you,' said Kit giving Rupert a firm shake and, to Bella's observation, what appeared to be a rather intense stare. Am I imagining it, thought Bella, or do they already know each other? Rupert seemed to relax, relieved even, at these words and muttered a greeting in return.

Bella focused on the exceptionally handsome man that was Kit. Again, he seemed to exude a similar perfection to Ariadne. He was exceedingly tall, well over 6'4", she guessed, slim with perfectly toned muscles she imagined, but not too muscular. Short, trim, chocolaty brown, perfectly groomed hair framed his face. He looked incredibly attractive in his faded jeans and white shirt which exuded casual expense. Bella felt her stomach flutter as he took her hand in his, and smiled at her as though she were the most beautiful, and only, woman in the world for him. Her legs turned to jelly and she was glad she was sitting down. She blushed at her silliness, berating herself for responding like a teenager at her age, over him simply because of his looks. She glanced furtively around, relieved that no one seemed to have noticed. He slid lithely into the chair at the end of the table and, feeling her eyes upon him, glanced up and held hers for just a moment. Bella melted.

'Trust Ariadne to bring an Adonis with her. She always does this,' muttered Seb to her, oblivious to the fact that Bella was smitten by the said Adonis.

Bella munched cautiously on her food, now even more highly aware of her size in comparison to Ariadne, who must be at least a Size 0 if not a Size 00. And how on earth can anyone wear white and keep it looking so blindingly pristine? She herself had given up on white a long time ago. It didn't seem to matter what she did, she only had to breathe and there would be dirt on it and, though she never normally spilt her drink, you could guarantee that as soon as she was wearing white, her first sip of coffee would end up all over it. Yet there was Ariadne sitting, chatting, laughing gaily as the centre of attention, sipping wine, picking at a lettuce leaf and not a hint of anything ever having been dropped or spilt onto the blinding whiteness. Had she had lessons in how to wear white? Is this what they learnt in Hollywood? Bella gloomily felt more and more dowdy as the minutes passed.

Sensing a little cloud of dejection over her, Harry – who was sitting on her left – whispered to her.

'You okay?'

Bella nodded.

'You sure? Don't let Ariadne spoil things for you. The others have all got used to her, but you should have heard them after Sophie had first introduced her to them. The girls spent weeks mauling Ariadne to bits. But don't be taken in, because although she may look "perfect", as others would tell us, she's not a very happy person.'

'Really?' Bella tried to suppress the glee which popped up.

'Not a happy bunny at all.' Bella felt too embarrassed to ask why, as she hardly knew Harry, but was grateful for his attempt at cheering her up.

Kit in the meantime was gazing intently into Jennifer's eyes, his honey voice whispering things to her that, no matter how much Bella strained, she could not hear. Jealousy nudged at her and she wished she were Jennifer. Bella looked round the table as the lunch continued like a play unravelling itself before her. Rupert was drinking copious amounts of wine and glaring at Kit as though he could kill him. Kim was chatting quietly to Fred, with the occasional nervous glance in Rupert's direction. Cressa was listening intently to Ariadne, who was in turn trying to command everyone's attention. Sophie was dividing her time between Jack and Rupert. It was an interesting set up with Ariadne sitting next to Harry, Harry next to Bella, then Seb, Jennifer, Kit, Mia, Rupert, Sophie, Jack, Florence, Fred, Kim and Cressa who had Ariadne on her other side. Bella could only assume that Sophie and Harry had spent a long time devising the seating plan in order to keep certain people away from one another, as it was obvious there was a lot of history simmering away beneath the eclectic mix of people.

Seb was an affable chap who chatted away to Bella and, whilst she enjoyed their conversation, she got the feeling that his mind was elsewhere. Every so often he surreptitiously glanced at Kim and regularly, without hiding it, glowered at Rupert who was becoming more and more drunk as the minutes ticked by. Perhaps Sophie and Harry hadn't organised a seating plan after all, if the filthy looks Seb was giving Rupert were anything to go by? Wonder what the history is there? And it wasn't just Seb who had a problem with Rupert, Jack too was wincing and scowling every time Rupert's monotonous, drunken monologue became too loud. Maybe it was just because Rupert was so drunk? The more he drank, the more of a bore he became and the more self-righteous and self-opinionated he became. And the more lecherous.

He was making Bella feel queasy at his lewd behaviour, and not so subtle suggestive language towards, mainly, Jennifer but also Ariadne. Both were doing their utmost to ignore him. In fact, everyone seemed to ignore Rupert as though this were a regular occurrence and something which just had to be endured and they wouldn't allow to spoil their lunch. His face became redder and Bella was convinced that his bulbous nose was growing before her very eyes. Drops of spittle flew in all directions as he spoke, and his eyes now had a glazed look about them. Mia caught her eyes and smiled, raising her eyebrows as if to say "I told you it'd be interesting". Bella grinned back. Mia was going to have a lot of explaining to do. She wanted a full run down on everyone in the group.

By mid afternoon as the heat of the sun was starting to wane they all moved to sit on the terrace in the sunshine. Bella estimated that by this time Rupert must have imbibed at least three or four bottles of wine. Anyone else would have been paralytic but he still managed to stagger up from the table, admittedly bumping into it as he negotiated his way around it, but nevertheless he made it across to the other side of the terrace, where he dropped his heavy load onto the wicker double seat next to Jennifer, who immediately looked panic stricken. Rupert leaned towards her, put an arm around her shoulders, and pulled her to him. Jennifer did her best to struggle out from his clutches, but was thwarted as his other hand slid its way surprisingly swiftly up her legs and under her skirt, his head lolling over her breasts. Enough was enough and Harry and Fred extricated Jennifer from his clutches.

'Come on Jen,' slurred Rupert, 'you know you want it. Stop playing hard to get and let me give you a good seeing to.'

She ignored him and moved to a seat as far away from him as possible, smiling apologetically at Kim, who looked resigned to this kind of behaviour. Poor thing, thought Bella, why on earth does she stay with such an odious specimen of a male, it's so humiliating for her.

Seb, who had been standing silently beside Bella, could restrain himself no longer. 'Can't you at least show some respect for your wife?' he snapped.

Rupert looked at him and swayed gently; a malicious sneer coming over his face. 'Don't be such a bad loser Seb. She's my wife, not yours.' This was followed by a phlegmy cackle.

Seb leapt forward, but Harry and Fred, anticipating this move, grabbed him, both muttering to him. 'He's not worth it. Let it go.'

Curiouser and curiouser, mused Bella.

Kim subtly slid beside Seb, squeezed his arm and just as subtly went back to where she'd been standing. 'Here's the coffee,' chirped Sophie, setting the heavy tray down on to the large wicker table. She poured and passed out fine bone china cups and saucers until she got to Rupert, who was given a large sturdy mug.

'Don't give me that rubbish!' he snapped. 'I want a proper drink.

'Think you've had enough Rupert. Have the coffee and this glass of water,' said Harry setting them down in front of him.

Ariadne, sensing trouble brewing, glided onto the sofa beside Rupert and purred, 'Come on now Rupert, you know I don't like it when you drink too much.' She gently stroked his face with the back of her hand as though she were trying to soothe a troubled child. Rupert's demeanour changed instantly, turning on what he believed to be charm but any sane woman would see as lechery. Ariadne picked up the mug and passed it to him. 'Come on, drink this for me and then I'll pass you the water.' She made the simple act of drinking coffee and water a seduction scene. But whatever it was it worked. Rupert meekly took the mug and drank it, his eyes wandering over her breasts as he did so. It made Bella cringe just to watch, but there was an imperceptible sigh of relief from the rest of the group, at Ariadne's rescue of the situation.

'He is such a jerk,' muttered Jack. Cressa kicked him to shut him up, not wanting the situation to be inflamed again.

'Here she is, all bright and awake from her lovely sleep,' announced Sophie returning with the beaming Jemima.

'She's such a cutie, here let me have a cuddle,' requested Mia putting her hands out to take the bundle from Sophie.

Momentary peace settled over the group until Rupert, realising that he was being placated rather than onto a promise with Ariadne, got up to go. 'Sophie, Harry, fun as ever, see you around.' He rummaged in his pocket until he found his keys. 'Kim, I'm sure you'll find your own way home. See you,' he called to everyone, waving his arm in the air as he walked in a zigzag towards the drive.

'He's not going to drive is he?' asked Bella aghast.

Harry and Fred looked at each other. 'Suppose we should try.'

'Of course you should!' shrieked Bella.

Everyone looked startled.

'The thing is, every time someone tries to stop him they get hurt,' said Cressa. 'Oh! Like that,' she continued as Fred staggered back having been punched in the face by Rupert. Mia leapt up to see to her husband and Sophie raced off to get some ice to put onto the undoubted bruise which would shortly be appearing.

Bella meanwhile was open-mouthed, not sure whether she was more shocked at what she had just seen, or the fact that this was a regular occurrence when anyone tried to stop Rupert drink driving. 'But he could kill someone! He can't be allowed to drive in that condition!' she shouted, tears pricking at her eyes. 'We should call the police.'

'We've tried that and everything else,' murmured Kim sadly. 'By the time the police arrive Rupert's at home and denying ever having been out. They're too busy dealing with other crimes to come out every five minutes to see Rupert. Sooner or later they will catch him drink driving, it's just astounding that he's not been caught yet.'

'But it's a disgrace! It shouldn't be allowed to happen,' snapped Bella.

By now the others were raising their eyebrows and wondering how a stranger could have the audacity to pass judgement on them? All except Mia and Fred. Fred whispered something to Mia, who left nursing her husband and came over and put her arm around the distraught Bella.

'Hey. It's okay. We're doing our best to stop him,' she whispered.

'But it's not okay.'

'And who are you to judge us?' snapped Cressa in response, 'you don't know us.'

An uneasy silence followed. 'You should tell them,' whispered Mia, 'they'll understand.'

Feeling cornered, but of her own doing, Bella reluctantly spoke. 'I don't mean to offend you, and you're right I don't know you and I shouldn't judge you, but my husband was killed by a drink driver, so I know all too well what the consequence can be.' She gazed miserably at her lap and fiddled with her fingers.

'I'm so sorry,' murmured Sophie squeezing Bella's shoulders and kissing her on the top of her head. 'It must have been so awful for you.' The others sat looking stunned, a reality brought to the scenario they had been allowing to play out for years, that Rupert could be the cause of someone else's death.

'I didn't want to spoil the day. I'm sorry.'

'You haven't spoilt it. I think we've become too complacent about Rupert, something really needs to be done and it's me that needs to do it,' replied Kim. 'I have tried, it's not easy and it won't be, but he has to be stopped.'

So taken up were they with Bella's revelation, that they had not heard the crunching and scraping coming from the drive as Rupert attempted to depart, damaging most of the cars in the drive as he did so.

Shortly afterwards Bella decided it was time to go and let them enjoy the rest of the day without her dragging them down. She thanked Harry and Sophie profusely and promised the girls that she would attempt to play tennis with them in the next few weeks. 'See you next week,' she said softly to Mia, 'sorry for upsetting your friends.'

'You've got nothing to be sorry about. I'll call you later.'

Bella didn't notice the slight dent in her bumper as she got into her car, she was too busy struggling with her conscience. Should she leave it to Kim to deal with her husband or should she take matters into her own hands? It was a decision she had made by the time she'd got home. She would never forgive herself if Rupert killed someone and through her disinclination had let it happen. She picked up the phone and set the wheels in motion.

Chapter Four

Sunday morning dawned as bright and beautiful as Saturday had the previous day. Bella lay in bed listening to the church bells chiming away, calling the village to its doors. She toyed with the idea of going to the morning service, but decided she wouldn't be ready in time. Maybe next week, she thought, lazily stretching in bed before getting up.

The day passed peacefully. Other than purchasing a paper in the shop before breakfast, Bella did not stray from the house, spending most of her time reading in the gloriously warm sunshine, the birds tweeting enthusiastically in the trees as though communicating some major gossip to one another. She did a good job of not thinking about Rupert but eventually she couldn't help it, it was niggling away at her. Had he been dealt with yet? Had the route to him permanently being stopped from drink-driving been set in motion? She hoped so.

With only a shopping trip with Mia planned for the week ahead, Bella contemplated some other activities, perhaps a trip to the village farmers' market? A trip or two to the famous and well reputed Sissinghurst Castle and Gardens, created by VitaSackville-West and Harold Nicholson, she felt was most definitely an absolute must as they were reputed to be spectacular.

After another good night's sleep, Bella strolled down to the shop the next morning - the warmth of the day just starting to take the edge off the chill over night - as was becoming her routine to collect a newspaper to read over her leisurely breakfast. The bell pinged as she opened the door. Sharon was chattering at full steam to another woman, pausing briefly to call out, 'Morning Christabel,' before returning to her gossiping. Bella picked up her newspaper and briefly glanced at the magazines, deciding not to purchase one after all. Though she wasn't paying attention to the gossiping, her ears were alerted when she heard Rupert's name.

'Are you sure?' squawked Sharon.

'Absolutely.' replied the short, stout woman dressed in a screamingly loud floral print ensemble in a myriad of mismatched, violently bright colours, which did absolutely nothing for her.

'Dead! I can't believe it!'

Bella paled and felt a wave of dizziness wash over her, steadying herself on the side of the counter.

'You alright Christabel? You've gone as white as a sheet.'

'Fine thanks,' croaked Bella. 'What were you just saying about Rupert? Do you mean Rupert Ireton?'

'Yes. Haven't you heard?' replied Sharon, as though she herself had known for hours and not just been told herself.

Bella shook her head numbly, hoping that she'd heard incorrectly.

'He's dead. Killed himself by driving into a tree apparently.'

'A tree?'

'Yes. Apparently he was way over the legal limit, must have been totally plastered to think that a tree was the road. I always knew the likes of him would meet a sticky end. Serves him right,' she continued spitefully, 'drinking and driving, it's a wonder he didn't kill anyone and he treated that lovely wife of his like dirt. I can't imagine what she saw in him.'

'His bank balance I should think,' muttered the other woman meanly.

'That's awful! What a terrible thing to happen. How's his wife?' snapped Bella.

'Kim? You mean you know them? Tell us then. What're they really like?' Sharon was keen for more information, any snippet of gossip to add to her tale.

'I …' stuttered Bella. 'Can I pay for this? I've got to go.' With that she shoved the correct money haphazardly onto the counter and hurried out of the shop, before she could be plied with further questions. Racing back to the house, her heart pounding furiously, she fumbled with her keys. 'Come on! Open!' she snapped at the door. Eventually the key turned in the lock, Bella flung the paper on the hall table and grabbed the phone, dialling Mia's number quickly. The phone rang and rang at the other end, eventually Mia answered.

'Hello?'

'Mia, it's me.'

'Oh, hi Bella. How are you?'

'I'm fine. Mia I've just heard the most awful thing. I don't know if you know, but I thought I ought to let you know.'

'I know Bella. Rupert,' she sighed heavily.

'It's terrible. When did it happen?'

'Saturday night about 10pm. Seems he was so drunk he just veered off the road and hit a tree. Died instantly.'

'How's Kim? She must be shattered?'

'She's devastated. Anyone would be.'

'Let me know if there's anything I can do to help.'

'Thanks Bella. Everyone seems to be rallying around. We're making sure Kim isn't on her own. She's completely numb with shock, as you can imagine. Something like this always gives people a reality check about what matters in life. But then you know that more than most.'

Bella sighed deeply. 'Yes, I do. You take care. I'll pop up and see you soon okay?'

'Thanks. I'm going over to Kim's in a bit. I'll probably be there for the rest of the day, so maybe tomorrow? Bye.'

'Okay. Bye.' Sadly Bella put the phone down, wandered into the kitchen and gazed trancelike into the garden, painful memories rising to the surface, ones that she had tried so hard to forget. Feeling slightly sick and with her appetite for breakfast having deserted her, she drank a large glass of water and made some fresh coffee in the hope that a shot of caffeine would perk her up, and took it into the garden. She gripped the mug to her and sipped it thoughtfully. Vaguely she became aware of a persistent ringing noise and eventually realised it was her doorbell. She hopped up and went to answer it. Standing on the doorstep were a man and a woman. The man looked familiar but, momentarily, she couldn't place him.

The man looked startled as he realised who she was. 'Bella!' he cried.

'Dave! Nice to see you again!'

The woman next to him looked puzzled. Bella, this is Sergeant Swart. Sergeant Swart this is Bella – Mrs Sparkle. The women smiled politely at each other.

'I'm afraid we're here on official business Bella. May we come in?'

'Of course. Come through.' She led the way as Inspector Dave Ormandy stooped his towering, wiry figure under the top of the door frame. His colleague however was diminutive in height, well-rounded and red-haired, followed her boss in, closing the door quietly behind her.

Bella led them into the sitting room, indicated for them to take a seat and offered them a drink which they duly refused. Puzzled she sat down. It had been a long time since she'd seen Dave. He and her late husband Hugh had trained together, but they had lost touch when she and Hugh moved to Norfolk and Dave moved with his wife to Kent fifteen years ago. Discreetly Sergeant Swart pulled out a notebook and pen, poised, ready for action.

'I'm sorry about Hugh,' said Dave. 'It's just not right that he should have died at such a young age, particularly in those circumstances. He was such a good man and an excellent policeman.'

'Thanks.' Bella tried to keep the tears which were welling up at bay. Rupert's death had brought a renewed wave of the pain she had felt when her husband had died, feelings which had been, overall, starting to soften in their ferocity, but which, from time to time, reared their ugly heads.

His manner changed as he moved into official mode. 'We're here about Rupert Ireton.'

Bella nodded. 'I heard in the shop this morning that he had died. Apparently he crashed his car into a tree because he was drunk?'

'Mr Ireton's car was involved in a road traffic accident on Saturday night, he died instantly from injuries caused by his car hitting a tree. You telephoned the police station late on Saturday afternoon to report Mr Ireton for drink driving. What led you believe he had been drink driving?'

Bella recounted the events of Saturday afternoon, including how Harry and Fred had tried to stop him, but that Rupert had punched Fred and apparently habitually lashed out and hurt anyone who tried to stop him.

Dave paused, conscious of how sensitive he needed to be. He cleared his throat. 'How did it make you feel that he was going to drive whilst heavily under the influence of alcohol?'

Bella blinked. Why the change? 'I felt angry of course. Furious that he was putting other people at risk by his actions, that what happened to Hugh could happen to someone else because of Rupert's blatant disregard for others.'

'Furious enough to do something about it?'

'Of course! I telephoned the station and reported him. Why all the questions? It's not my fault Rupert was so drunk he drove into a tree.'

'At the moment we're keeping an open mind as to the cause of the accident.'

Bella had been married to a police officer for long enough to know what this meant. 'Keeping an open mind? Do you mean to say you think Rupert's death wasn't caused by him being drunk and driving off the road?' She looked expectantly from one to the other.

'Until we can be certain that the cause of death was an accident, or deliberate on his part, as a result of him being too drunk and driving off the road and into a tree, we have to keep an open mind.'

'So you think it may have been deliberate? That he was murdered?' Bella's jaw dropped in shock. 'You can't mean that? I mean, why? Why would anyone want to kill him?'

'Like I say, we're keeping an open mind at the moment. What were your observations of the group you were with on Saturday? Were there any tensions? Any grudges? Arguments? Anyone who could have been pushed too far by Mr Ireton?' He looked expectantly at Bella's kind face, and waited patiently.

After a few moments Bella replied quietly, '*If* it transpires that Rupert's death was not an accident, or deliberate on his part, but was caused by the actions of another person, I will then give you my thoughts and observations of that day. Until such time, I feel it inappropriate to say anything.' She looked determinedly into his pale blue eyes.

Point taken, he thought. 'If you change your mind,' he scribbled down a number, 'you can contact myself or Sergeant Swart on this number.' He rose, terminating the visit. Awkwardly they went to the front door. He hadn't wanted to upset an old friend, but he still had a job to do, he just hoped that she'd realise it. 'Thank you for your time Bella.' It would be an insult too far to be formal and call her Mrs Sparkle. 'Just one thing,' he paused turning on the step, 'did you go out on Saturday night?'

She shook her head. 'No, not at all. Apart from going to the village shop, I've not been out at all since I got back from the lunch party.'

'Sir,' called Sergeant Swart from the direction of Bella's car. They walked over. He immediately saw what she had discovered.

'How on earth did that happen?' yelped Bella. 'My poor car!' She touched the dented bumper and scraped boot.

'How long has it been like that?'

'I don't know. It's the first time I've seen it. I've not been out at all. Looks like a green car's hit it.' As she spoke she had a sinking feeling. Surely it couldn't be?

'We might need to take a sample from this. Don't go getting it fixed just yet,' he said.

Numbly, Bella shook her head. She stood there watching as they drove off, wondering what to do. Should she tell Mia? Did anyone else know that the police were considering that Rupert may not have died as a result of an accident, or that it may have been deliberate on his part? She really didn't want to be involved, but somehow she'd managed to get tangled up in what was probably the biggest incident to hit the village in years. As she turned to go back inside she saw Jennifer hurrying into her cottage up the lane. Decisively she grabbed her house keys from the hall, slammed the door behind her and scurried up the lane. She lifted the wrought iron knocker and knocked loudly on the green front door.

Jennifer opened it, her face pale, eyes red rimmed, and gazed at Bella. She attempted a half smile, 'Hi Bella,' but made no indication to welcome her visitor in.

'Hi Jennifer. How are you? I guess you've heard about Rupert?' Jennifer nodded in acknowledgement. 'Can I come in?' Jennifer politely stood back, closed the door behind Bella and led Bella through to a large kitchen, which ran the whole width of the back of the house. The limestone floor sparkled in the sunlight and reflected off the maple wood units. At one end, to the left, was a large four oven pale blue Aga. The kitchen opened out into a large sitting area, which was constructed in brick with an oak frame, infilled with glass. It was stunning, having a contemporary edge to it, but perfectly blending with the Georgian era house.

'Coffee?' she offered, breaking the silence.

'Please.' Bella watched as Jennifer silently filled the kettle, put it on the hot plate of the Aga to boil and whizzed up some coffee beans in a chrome coffee grinder. She then took up the classic Aga pose – standing with her back to the Aga, leaning into the warmth – and smiled wanly at Bella.

'Gorgeous house and this kitchen is stunning. How long have you lived here?' enquired Bella.

'Thanks. About three years. Did the kitchen and extension last year.'

'Whoever carried out the work has done a great job and you've got fab taste.' Silently Bella wondered how someone so young – for Jennifer could barely be thirty, she estimated – could afford such an expensive house. She hadn't got the impression that Jennifer was a city high flyer who earned vast sums of money and received a massive bonus each year. In fact, she didn't know what Jennifer did to earn a living, not that it was any of her business she reminded herself.

51

'Let's go and sit through here.' Jennifer nodded in the direction of the sitting area as she loaded the cafetière of coffee, jug of milk, cups and saucers onto a wooden tray. Bella wandered through and sat in a deep, comfortable, chocolate brown, designer leather contemporary sofa. The glass doors were folded back on themselves allowing the gentle breeze to float in from the garden and tickle her feet. Jennifer placed the tray down on the large bespoke oak and glass coffee table, which mirrored the construction of the room, and poured a cup out for them both, assuming correctly that Bella did not take sugar. She sank back into another sofa, not identical, but similar to, and complimenting, the one which Bella was sitting in, and sighed heavily. 'I can't believe it, I really can't believe that he's dead. It seems impossible. Rupert was Rupert and he was indestructible.'

'I feel it always seems more shocking when someone you actually know dies,' replied Bella diplomatically, remembering how Rupert had behaved towards Jennifer.

'I know he could be a pain, but he didn't deserve to die. Not like this. Not so young. I know he wasn't really young, but he wasn't old, not like he was in his eighties or nineties and lived a long life and heading towards the natural end of his life.'

'Mmm, no. What was he - fifty? Fifty-five?'

'No. Forty-five. Looked older than he was, but I suspect that was due to the vast quantities of alcohol he consumed.'

Bella waited, hoping that Jennifer would volunteer more information. She sipped her coffee and listened to the peaceful buzz of bees and other insects outside in the garden, the gentle chattering of birds providing a background ambience.

'You know,' said Jennifer, 'I was one of the very few women who had not had an affair with Rupert. There was something about him that made him very alluring. Can't quite put my finger on it, but he never had a problem attracting women. I think that's why he found me so much of a challenge. I resisted him. Part of me was curious, but I would never have an affair with a married man, and certainly not with the husband of a friend.'

'He was obviously very interested in you. How did Kim feel about him playing around? It must have been hard on her and so humiliating.'

'Yup. I don't know why she put up with it. They married after a whirlwind romance. He swept her off her feet and six months later they got married. I think he stayed faithful for the first year, but after that he slowly got up to his old tricks again. I know in her own way she loves... loved... him,' she corrected herself, 'but I got the feeling recently that she wasn't going to put up with it for much longer.'

Bella's ears pricked up. 'Oh? Why do you think that?'

Jennifer screwed up her face as she contemplated Bella's question, her long slim nose wrinkling as she did so. 'I'm not sure. She just seemed brighter, as though she knew the end was coming and her future looked freer.' Her hand flew to her mouth in shock. 'Oh! What have I said? That sounds horrible! As though she were wishing him dead and she wasn't, I meant she was just going to move on with her life.' Jennifer looked horrified.

'It's okay, don't worry I know what you meant.' Bella hastily changed the subject. 'Is the Farmers' Market any good? You know, the one held in the Village Hall?'

'Um. Yes. Pretty good,' she replied distractedly.

Bella drained the remainder of her coffee and decided it was time to go. 'Thanks Jennifer, do pop down anytime you like. You know, if you want to talk or anything. No, don't get up,' she said as Jennifer rose to let her out, 'I can see myself out. You sit, you still look a bit shaken by what's happened.' She patted her in a motherly way on the shoulder and quietly let herself out. Was it possible that Kim had had something to do with Rupert's death? She seemed such a nice person, surely she couldn't have done it? What would be her motive? Bella pondered this as she strolled back down to her cottage. Freedom from him? But if she had killed him it was a big risk to take - if she were found guilty she would be locked up for many years. Did she think it was worth the gamble? Or money? By the looks of things Rupert was pretty wealthy, but I suppose you can't judge someone's wealth just by the way they choose to portray themselves, appearances can be deceptive.

Back at the house, Bella busied herself in the kitchen making herself a sandwich stuffed with cheese and tomato, simple, but her favourite, her appetite now having returned. Her mind was whirring as she chewed. Who else would have had a motive to kill him? After Saturday's performance there were probably quite a few and that was just those who were there, it didn't take into account the many people Rupert must have come into contact with in the course of running his business, or was it businesses? She chided herself for assuming that it was murder rather than the more likely reasons of an accident or suicide, the police were just doing their job and being thorough. Still, it gave her something to focus on and forget the worries of her own life.

Chapter Five

The next morning Bella drove along the Monhurst to Brookhurst Road on the way to Mia's house for coffee. Mia and Fred lived with their sixteen year old daughter Tess in a small, three bedroom barn conversion. It had been a labour of love, ten years in the making, combining Fred working on it at weekends, interspersed with the expertise of a local builder, and hard saving to pay for it. It was prettily situated down a long drive, between the villages of Monhurst and Brookhurst, and set in two acres of garden and a paddock. The bedrooms were complemented by a main family bathroom, and an en-suite to the master bedroom. Downstairs was a large sitting room with wood burner and a study corner tucked off to one side, a cloakroom, a dining room which was used as a music cum family room and a large kitchen/breakfast room with utility off it. Not massive, but beautifully finished, and in a glorious location with views over the fields towards Brookhurst.

'Hi!' called Mia from the oak front door, looking slightly subdued compared to her usual bright, sparkly self.

'Hiya,' replied Bella kissing her on the cheek, 'how are you?'

Mia Shrugged. 'Okay I suppose.'

Mia efficiently made coffee. The house was spotless as usual, the cream kitchen units looking as though they were brand new and the black Aga shined away as though just fitted. She carried the cafetière and milk out onto the terrace, Bella following with the pink spotted mugs. It didn't matter how many times Bella visited, her breath was always taken away by the beauty of the view that the property afforded which stretched as far as the eye could see over fields, gently undulating hills and - on a clear day - even to the coast and adjacent sea; every time was always like the first.

'So, how is Kim coping?' asked Bella.

'She's distraught. But I think it's guilt which is making it worse for her more than the fact that Rupert is dead.'

'Guilt? For what?'

Mia pursed her lips. 'Well,' she said cautiously, 'I know you'll keep this to yourself,' her eyes flicked briefly to Bella's face for confirmation, though she knew her friend well enough. 'Kim was planning on leaving Rupert.'

'Aha! So Jennifer was right.'

'Jennifer? What do you mean?'

'Oh. Um. It was just a passing comment that Jennifer made yesterday when I saw her. She said she had a feeling that Kim had decided to do something about her marriage. Didn't say what, don't even know if she actually knew or was speculating.'

Mia shrugged. 'Kim was being careful, but I suppose it's natural that the others would pick up on something.'

Bella waited expectantly. Eventually she prodded Mia. 'Well? What was she going to do?'

'She didn't go into details. She just said that she'd decided their marriage was no longer a marriage and that it had run its course. She felt that no matter how hard she tried Rupert never reciprocated. He was constantly criticising her and putting her down, nothing she did was right. She tried to change to please him but even that didn't work. I was worried about her. She seemed to be turning into a shadow of her former self, no self confidence, becoming reluctant to go out, even missing tennis sometimes which was unheard of. And I'm not totally convinced that he wasn't hitting her.'

Bella gasped, shocked, but somehow deep down she wasn't surprised. 'How awful! It sounds like a nightmare of a marriage. Abuse doesn't just have to be physical. I don't know which would be worse, mental or physical abuse, each in their own right horrific, but to be, quite possibly, on the receiving end of both – well, I don't know how she coped. Don't know how anyone would cope.'

'I'm not sure what specifically nudged her to evolve back to how she used to be, but it was as though she'd suddenly had her "off" switch flipped. Like she'd hit rock bottom and couldn't take any more. She started turning up to everything again, dressing more like she used to and generally looking happier. When we quizzed her on it she would just smile and say nothing. Finally, we were on our own one day and she blurted out that she was going to leave Rupert. I had the feeling there was more to it but it was as though she suddenly realised she'd said too much. Don't think Rupert knew. I don't think he'd take very kindly to being left, his ego wouldn't be able to cope with the humiliation. He's always been the one who's done the loving and then the leaving.'

'Hmm, interesting. Well she's certainly free of him now.'

'Bella!'

'I didn't mean it in a nasty way, you should know that. I just meant that whilst it is a horrible situation for her to be in, ultimately it will be less complicated and messy. She won't have to put up with his temper, which no doubt would have rocketed when she told him she was leaving him, or put up with him turning up drunk and pleading for her to come back or other such scenarios.'

'I suppose. It just doesn't sound very nice when it's put like that, but you're right.'

For a moment Bella paused, wondering whether she should tell her closest friend about the visit from the police. If she did it would open a can of worms. If she didn't, and Mia found out later that Bella had known more than she'd let on, she'd be cross and hurt. Deciding that the last thing she wanted to do was to cause friction in her friendship with Mia, she told her.

Mia's stunned face said it all. Total and utter shock. The news had hit her as though being slapped in the face. 'You have got to be joking? Please tell me that you are joking?'

Bella shook her head. 'Sorry. It probably was just an accident. You know what the police can be like, don't want to commit themselves to anything until they're sure. They're just being cautious.'

'Do you think Kim knows?'

'I've no idea Mia. I'm sure she would have told you. I think it would be best not to say anything to her. What would be the point of upsetting her further when it's highly unlikely that it was deliberate? It's not going to achieve anything. Best to keep quiet.'

'Yeah. I suppose so,' Mia replied slowly, wondering if she were in Kim's position would she want to know? 'But why would anyone want to kill Rupert?'

'I think we're jumping the gun a bit,' answered Bella, beginning to regret telling Mia. 'There's nothing we can do. It's down to the police - if there's anything to tell they will tell her. All you can do is be there to support her Mia.'

'I guess so. I'll have to tell Fred though.'

'Yes, but no one else. Please promise me. It's speculation as far as I am concerned. There are enough rumours flying around at the moment, there's no need to add fuel to the fire.'

'Okay. Anyway,' continued Mia changing the subject, 'how are you settling in?'

Bella grinned. 'Fine. I thought when I moved here that life was going to be too quiet in the village but it's proving not to be the case! It's an interesting group of friends you've got.'

Mia laughed. 'Eclectic, I think is the word you're looking for. Life is never dull with them. Obviously, I'm more friendly with some than with others but on the whole they're a nice bunch.'

'I look forward to meeting the rest of them. In the meantime, you can fill me in on those I have met. I definitely got the feeling on Saturday that the relationships between everyone are complex and intriguing...'

'You could say that! But right now I've got to get off and see Kim. Said I'd pop in about lunchtime and, as it is about that time, I'd better be going.' She gathered up the coffee paraphernalia and hurried back inside.

'You can't leave me hanging on like that Mia!' chided Bella. 'Tantalising me and then leaving it. That's so cruel,' she laughed.

'You never were good at waiting were you Bella,' smiled Mia with a twinkle in her eye. 'Come on, out you go,' she playfully pushed her friend out of the front door, set the alarm and locked it behind her. 'Catch up with you later in the week,' she said kissing Bella on the cheek.

'Only if you promise to spill the beans,' grinned Bella. 'Thanks for the coffee. Let Kim know I'm thinking of her. If there's anything I can do, give me a call. Take care.' She followed Mia's ancient silver Volvo Estate down the drive, they both turned right towards Monhurst with Mia then turning left into Coppice Lane.

Kim's house was a large Tudor Farmhouse constructed with an oak frame, Flemish bond brickwork and a Kent peg tile roof. Rupert and Kim had completely refurbished the house when they bought it, just before they married five years ago. Within the strict guidelines of being a Grade II Listed house, they obtained consent and were allowed to open up a couple of rooms without affecting the character or disturbing the original structure of the property. The house now had five substantial bedrooms and a family bathroom. The master bedroom had been opened up to access the sixth bedroom, which was now a dressing room and an en-suite bathroom; a large sitting room, a smaller sitting room, both with inglenook fireplaces with wood burning stoves, a study, a cloakroom, a boot room, a dining room, a massive kitchen/breakfast room and a laundry room all surrounded by 10 acres.

Cressa opened the door to Mia, her tall frame - heightened by her spiky high heeled shoes - towering over her. Cressa was looking pale and drawn despite her make-up and hair being perfect as usual.

'How is she?' asked Mia in a muted tone.

'Not good. I've just put a call in for the doctor to visit.'

'That bad? I thought she was getting by, all things considered.'

'She was, until the police came this morning.' Cressa looked grim, her thin lips pursed together tighter than usual.

Mia's heart flip-flopped. Police? Surely it couldn't mean? 'Police?' she stuttered, 'What did they want?'

Cressa ushered her through the relative gloom of the hall, compared with the bright sunshine outside, to the kitchen which was flooded in sunlight due to the extra window and French doors Rupert and Kim had been allowed to put in. 'Drink?' Cressa poured herself a substantial glass of white wine. The bottle was half empty, it looked as though she'd started early.

Mia shook her head. 'Water will do thanks.' Cressa removed a bottle of still water from the fridge and poured the liquid into a simple crystal glass. Mia took it, grateful to have something to do with her hands. 'So, the police?' she prompted quietly, above her she could hear the floorboards creaking as someone moved around. Kim she presumed.

'You'd better sit down.' Cressa pulled a chair out and sat at the large oak table which dominated the centre of the ornate oak kitchen. She fiddled with the stem of her glass, took a long gulp and spoke. 'The police believe that Rupert's death was not an accident.'

'Not an accident?' whispered Mia.

'No. They think the crash was deliberate. That Rupert was killed deliberately. That he was murdered.'

'Murdered?' echoed Mia hoarsely. 'That can't be so? I mean, how can he have been murdered? It was an accident, Rupert was drunk and lost control of the car. It was a dreadful accident.'

'Apparently not. The police believe that he was forced off the road, and that it wasn't an accident, it was deliberate.'

'But how can they possibly know? I mean, what if both cars were going too fast and they had to swerve to avoid one another? How do they know that that didn't happen?'

'They did explain but I was too shocked to take it all in. There's some complicated way they can work things out and all indications are that it was deliberate. You'd have to ask them to explain it to you, if you want to know precisely how they have come to this conclusion.' Cressa was getting paler by the minute.

'You okay? You look unwell.' enquired Mia, concerned by Cressa's appearance.

'I'm fine,' she snapped. 'Do you want me to stay or are you okay to wait with Kim? The doctor should be here soon. Kim's taken herself off to her room and doesn't want me up there. Don't think she wants anyone up there.' Still stunned, Mia nodded without thinking. 'Jen's going to be along later. If you need anything give me a call.' Cressa picked up her keys, patted Mia on the shoulder and hastily exited.

Mia heard the front door close, and then silence. She became aware of the clock ticking in the kitchen, then, despite everything, her stomach rumbled. How could she possibly think of food at a time like this? She stood up and cautiously went upstairs, tapping gently on Kim's door. 'Kim? It's me, Mia. Can I come in?' There was silence. She tapped again. 'Are you okay? Can I get you anything?'

Again silence, then a very quiet 'You can come in,' permeated from behind the door. Mia lifted the latch and braced herself.

Kim was standing staring out of one of the windows. Mia walked quietly across the pristine white, deep pile carpet, which had been laid over the oak floorboards and slipped her arm around her friend's shoulder. Kim looked at her, her eyes red rimmed from crying, her nose and lips swollen and raw from the sobs.

'Cressa told me. I'm so sorry.'

Kim tried to speak, but her throat was so sore it came out as a croak. Mia went to the oak bedside table and poured a glass of water from the glass flaçon. Kim sipped it, allowing the water to soothe her throat. She tried again. 'Thanks. It just seems to be one shock after another. It's bad enough that Rupert is dead, but to think that it was deliberate, that someone killed him,' she shook her head as though trying to get rid of the suggestion. Mia led her over to the capacious oak framed bed and sat her down. She looked so frail, as though she might collapse at any moment. 'Why would anyone want to kill him? I mean, I know that he rubbed a lot of people up the wrong way, but not enough to make someone want to do that. I just don't understand.' She looked beseechingly at Mia who shrugged, at a loss as to know what to say.

'I've no idea either. I think that the police must have got it wrong, that it really was just a dreadful accident.'

'I wish that were so but they seemed pretty convinced. They explained in detail how they'd come to that conclusion, but I can't really remember what they said. I was so stunned.' She sobbed and pulled out a sodden white handkerchief from her jeans.

'So what are the police going to do? If they think he was killed deliberately, how are they going to find out who did it?'

Kim sniffed. 'I don't know. But they'd better find out who did it. I want justice to be done. I know he was impossible to live with and that I was going to leave him, but no one deserves to die like that, no one!' she shouted vehemently.

'Sssh,' soothed Mia, stroking Kim's hair as tears began to stream down Kim's face again. 'I'm sure they'll find out. We'll make sure that they do.' There was a knock at the front door. 'That'll be the doctor. I'll just go and let her in.'

'I don't need a doctor! I need Rupert's murderer to be found! Why did you ask her to come?'

'I didn't. Cressa did. She obviously felt that you might need the doctor.'

'Well, I don't,' she shouted, 'I just need Rupert back.' Mia slipped out of the room and downstairs to let the doctor in.

Chapter Six

The next morning the sky had clouded over, and there was a grey heaviness which replicated the feeling of many in the village. News of the murder had sunk all but the most gossipy into a suspicious malaise. Bella had felt like she was a tasty morsel being fed to a group of particularly ravenous piranhas when she went to collect her paper that morning. Mia had phoned her, to update her late yesterday afternoon once she'd returned from Kim's house. As if sensing this by some telepathic force, Sharon at the shop had gone at Bella like a dog with a bone, desperate to tease every last titbit out of her. Unfortunately for Sharon, Bella was having none of it. Through gritted teeth she smiled politely, and refused to answer any questions from the posse which had secured itself in the corner of the shop.

Having recovered from the ordeal over breakfast Bella decided to risk it, and go to the Farmers' Market in the village hall, hoping sincerely that she wouldn't be pounced upon again for information. She strolled up to the entrance door and was intrigued to see that the plaque on the wall stated that the hall had only been opened in 1998. This surprised her because the hall looked like a very old barn, which had been converted for use by the village. Whoever had designed it and built it had done an excellent job, it blended in perfectly with the surrounding area.

There was a general hubbub of noise coming from within and she was greeted by a large, light, high ceilinged area, crammed full of stalls, laid out around the inner perimeter of the hall with another rectangle of tables in the centre. The goods on offer were produced or sourced locally; there were eggs, cheese, flowers, yoghurts, milk, cakes, jams, chutneys, vegetables, fruit, meat, fish, everything one would ever need to survive on very nicely. Bella chatted to the stall holders as she wandered around, purchasing a variety of produce with which to stock up her cupboards and fridge. All of the stall holders seemed to be local and enthusiastic about selling their produce, in particular they were keen for local residents and visitors to the area to support local businesses, and not rely so heavily on the large supermarket chains. There was an elderly couple who grew their vegetables in their garden and produced just enough to sell at the market. There was the city high-flyer who had made so much money that he'd given it up when he was burnt out at forty-five, and decided to live the good life keeping bees and making his own honey. There were young mums who were trying to juggle the impossible task of fitting in some kind of work to earn money, around looking after their children, and many other fascinating individuals with their own stories to tell and motivation for being there. It was fascinating.

Laden down with bags so full that she had enough food to feed several people for a week, not just herself, she popped her hoard down onto a chair in the area outside the kitchen, which had been set up with tables and chairs for people to sit and enjoy a catch-up and have a drink. Bella queued and ordered a cup of coffee. She eyed the selection of cakes that were on offer, decided that as she'd been useless with her healthy eating and fitness campaign so far she may as well not start the regimen with purpose until tomorrow, and chose a large piece of moist chocolate cake. She took a mouthful, pushing the guilty feeling far away and savoured the sweet, sticky cake – perfect, she concluded.

'Hi,' called a voice, dragging Bella away from her chocolaty reverie.

'Jennifer! Hi, how are you? Please join me,' Bella grabbed the bags from the spare chair and piled them on top of one another on the floor. They promptly all fell over and apples rolled in all directions. 'Typical!' she laughed. Jennifer scurried around helping her to pick them up.

'I'll just get a coffee then I'll join you.'

'That was delicious,' sighed Bella as Jennifer sat down. 'Probably the best chocolate cake I've ever tasted.'

'I know, they're scrummy.' Jennifer looked paler than two days ago. Her hair was lank and unwashed, and the dark circles under her eyes were taking on a purplish hue.

'Tell me,' said Bella, 'I'm slightly mystified. Why are all those people queuing up at an empty table?' She'd been observing them whilst eating her cake, more and more people had joined it, until now there were about 20 standing patiently, one behind another.

Jennifer laughed. 'That, Bella, is known as "The Bread Man Phenomenon".'

'The what? What on earth is that?'

'There's a local baker who bakes the most incredible bread. A huge variety of different breads and suchlike which you can't seem to find anywhere else locally. His prices are reasonable and everything is freshly made every morning. Everyone knows this. If you go to other local Farmers' Markets, you will find that there is always an empty table with a queue of people waiting patiently.'

'But if the table's empty, why are they queuing?'

'Because he's always late. He always turns up. But he's always late. His bread sells out so quickly that quite often, if you don't queue, then you won't be able to get what you want.'

'In that case I'd better buy some, if there's any left by the time I get there! Oh, is that him?' There was a flurry of activity and people parted as though royalty had arrived. Several trips were made to bring in the crates of bread and other baked offerings, all the time the queue waiting patiently. They watched in silence for a minute. Jennifer, used to this weekly scene, allowed Bella to observe it without distraction as she was obviously fascinated by other people's behaviour. 'I wonder if there'll be any left?' Bella murmured.

'Why don't you go and queue. I'll get us another coffee and look after your bags.'

'Oh that's kind, thanks very much. I've got to see what all this fuss is about!' Ten minutes later she returned bearing two loaves of bread, the type of which she'd never heard of before, and a couple of white crusty rolls.

'Get what you wanted?'

'I guess so. There was a bit of a kerfuffle going on. The person in front of me had just bought the last somethingorother and someone else behind me wanted it! Thanks for the coffee.' She picked the cup up and studied Jennifer - she was convinced Jennifer wanted to tell her something. 'I guess you've heard the update about Rupert?'

Jennifer nodded and fiddled with her cup, tears welled up in her eyes. 'I can't believe it. I just can't.' Bella waited quietly. 'It's just …' Jennifer looked furtively around her to ensure no one was listening. She lowered her voice so that Bella had to lean forward to hear her, 'It's just that I think I was the last one to see him alive.'

Bella's eyebrows shot up in surprise. 'Really? How did you work that one out?'

Again Jennifer checked that no one was listening. 'He came to the house. He came to see me. He was pestering me. He'd taken my rejection earlier on badly. He was determined to get me into bed. He was very persistent.'

'And did he?'

She shook her head. 'No, he tried, stuck his tongue down my throat, hand up my skirt that sort of thing, but I managed to fend him off. I gave him a slap round the face and told him that if he didn't leave me alone I'd call the police.'

'And what did he do then?'

'He laughed. Said he'd be back, that sooner or later I'd realise that I wanted him, that I was just playing hard to get and would surrender to him. All sounded a bit like he'd swallowed a ghastly romantic novel the amount of clichés he was reeling off.'

'So then he left?'

'Yes.'

'What time was that?'

'About 9pm.'

'And the crash was at about 10.05pm?'

'I think so.'

'There's quite a time difference between him leaving you and his death. After all, Coppice Lane is only a couple of minutes away, maybe five, from where the car crashed and it's not the most direct route to his house.'

'Have you been there?'

'Where?'

'To their house?'

Bella shook her head.

'So how do you know what the quickest route would be?'

'Mia told me.' Mia had told her, but Bella didn't want to admit that she'd had the maps out to study the local lanes, far more satisfying than looking on the internet she felt, or that she'd driven down the various routes which would take you to Kim and Rupert's house. As soon as she'd found out that it was murder, her mind had whirred into overdrive, sure that somehow she would be able to tease out some useful piece of information and give her some focus and purpose for being in the village.

'Oh, okay,' Jennifer looked suspiciously at her.

'Anyway. What I was saying was that there's quite a time difference between his leaving you and the accident. It's possible that he went on somewhere else. Maybe the pub?'

'No, I don't think so. I got the impression he was on a mission. The funny thing is that though he'd drunk a lot during the afternoon, by the time he came round he didn't seem at all drunk. In fact, for Rupert, I would say he was stone cold sober.'

'Hmm. Have you told the police this?'

'No. Don't think it's relevant really.'

'I think you should. The more information they have, no matter how irrelevant you feel it is, could help them. It's a bit like doing a jigsaw, you need all the pieces in order to fit them together to solve the case; better to have too many pieces than not enough and have great big gaps missing.'

'I suppose…' replied Jennifer reluctantly.

'Give them a call when you get back. After all, you want to find out who did kill him don't you?' She looked questioningly at her.

Jennifer shifted uncomfortably in her seat. 'Of course.'

Wisely, Bella changed the subject and chatted aimlessly about the Farmers' Market until they'd both finished their coffee, then wandered back with her on the way home.

'Take care. Thanks for the coffee. Come down and see me sometime,' suggested Bella as they arrived at the pristine white picket gate to Jennifer's front garden.

'Thanks, I will.'

'And please do phone the police and tell them what you've told me.'

Jennifer sighed heavily. 'Okay,' she replied reluctantly.

'Bye.' Bella carried on towards her cottage, the weight of her over-stuffed bags starting to strain on her hands, she gathered speed the closer she got. She dumped them on the doorstep and stood shaking and rubbing her hands together, there were bright red lines dug into the palms of both her hands and fingers. She was just reaching into her bag for her keys when a voice behind her said.

'Hello Bella. Need a hand?'

She turned to see Dave, Detective Inspector Ormandy, smiling at her, his eyes crinkling as he did so.

'Please. I've definitely bought too much. But there were so many lovely things. It was just too tempting!'

'At the Farmers' Market?'

Bella nodded.

'I've heard it's very good. Never had a chance to go, always working.' He grinned ruefully and bent down to pick up the pile of bags as Bella opened the door.

'Come through to the kitchen. Thanks, just put them on the table and I'll sort them out. Coffee?' She was not entirely sure whether this visit was for official business or not.

'Please. That'd be nice.' He leant against the sink, and watched Bella as she put the kettle on and packed her purchases away into their respective homes. 'Looks like you've bought everything being sold. Did you leave anything for anyone else?' he teased, feeling as though it hadn't been fifteen years since he'd last socialised with her.

'Very funny. I did leave the odd crumb for other people. Shall we sit outside?' she suggested as she unlocked the back door. 'I think we might be in for a storm later, it seems to be getting so muggy.'

'Here, let me.' He lifted the tray and followed her out onto the patio, set it down on the wooden slatted table and settled into one of the matching chairs.

'So, is this an official visit or unofficial visit?'

He smiled. 'I wish it were unofficial but I'm afraid it's not. When I saw you on Monday you said that if it turned out to be murder, you would give me your thoughts on the people you were with at the lunch that Saturday.' He fished out a list from his pocket and put it in front of her; everyone at the party was on it.

Bella shifted uncomfortably. Just because she knew Dave from long ago, didn't mean that what she said wouldn't be off the record and not used as some kind of evidence. She felt unfaithful to those who had befriended her on Saturday and she didn't like it. 'I did, so I suppose

I'll have to, though I want you to know that I really don't like doing this. I hate gossip and that's what it feels like.'

'I know, but any information which may be relevant, or may not even seem to be relevant, will help.' He wished he didn't have to do this as much as she did. He liked her and didn't want her mixed up in police business. 'If you could go through each person on the list and give me your thoughts about them, their relationship with Rupert or anything else which struck you I'd appreciate it.' He waited patiently.

She looked miserably at the list and sighed. 'Okay. Well to start with I think they all know each other through tennis. All the women are members of the local tennis club and play regularly. Some of the men do too I think, Fred, Harry and Seb do but I can't quite remember - one of them will be able to tell you anyway - and I think the other men are members but don't necessarily play - just come along to the social side of things - of which I think there are many. I can't imagine Rupert ever played but I really have no idea.' She sat pondering, Dave nodded encouragingly. 'Fred and Mia are my friends. They're great, really nice people and I know they won't have anything to do with it. Fred tried with Harry to stop Rupert from driving off after the party as he was so drunk, that's when Fred got hit by Rupert. Rupert must have had several bottles of wine to drink. Then there's Sophie and Harry who are delightful and their daughter Jemima, didn't see any tension there between them or anyone else, though obviously they invited everyone and must have known who would or wouldn't get on with one another. Umm …' she pursed her lips as she recalled the afternoon. 'Obviously there was Kim and Rupert. Rupert seemed to treat her like dirt, and didn't take her feelings into consideration when he was busy dribbling all over Jennifer and Ariadne. Kim was quite quiet. Ariadne seemed to know everyone and was so glamorous, a real Hollywood Star, and her agent Kit who was also very attractive,' she blushed as she thought of him, something that did not go unnoticed. 'He was busy flirting with Jennifer and I don't think Rupert liked that. Seb is nice, got the feeling he wasn't impressed by Kit or Ariadne, and there was definitely something going on between him and Rupert.'

'Something? What do you mean?'

'I don't know, but I got the feeling there was some history there. Could be he just didn't like Rupert's arrogance, he seemed quite an unassuming person Seb. He also seemed a bit protective of Kim. But then, I felt protective of her too after the way Rupert treated her. Florence seemed quite pleasant, she was very quiet though and I didn't get much of a chance to talk to her Think she moved to the village a year ago and has been going to the tennis club,' she paused to sip some coffee, glad that it was decaffeinated so she wasn't buzzing from an overdose of caffeine. Her eyes ran down the list. 'Ah, Jack and Cressa, again I didn't get to talk to them that much. Jack was giving Rupert filthy looks but I don't know why and there seemed to be tension between him and Cressa, but that could just be their normal relationship. Oh, and Jennifer, she's lovely, she lives just up the lane, the cottage by the church. She's nice. Rupert was all over her, seems she was a bit of a challenge to him. She refused to have an affair with him…' she hesitated, 'in fact I think she's going to give the police station a call.'

Dave looked questioningly at her. 'Is she? Do you know what about?'

Again Bella hesitated. 'Yes, but I think it's best coming from her, she only told me this morning. It may or may not be relevant but I said that, relevant or not, you would need to know.'

'Is she still at home do you know?'

'I walked with her back from the market, so she was there a little while ago unless she's gone out again.'

'Okay. Thanks. I'll pop in and see her before I head back, and don't worry I'll make it clear that you haven't told me what it is.'

'Thanks. I'd hate for any of them to think I can't be trusted, or that I'm an enemy or spy in the camp. Well I don't think there's anything else to add to what I have told you. I'll let you know if I think of anything.'

'Thanks.'

'So how did he die then?' she was intrigued to know.

'Well, it appears that another car was coming in the opposite direction and forced Rupert off the road. It wasn't helped by the fact that he was over the legal limit. It's a straight piece of road and easily wide enough for two cars to pass, there's no bend or anything. We're also trying to trace all the cars that Rupert appears to have driven into. Seems he bumped quite a few at the party, but there are unmistakable marks, dents and paint from another car on the front wing of the car he was driving, which would be consistent with his car being hit by another.'

'Hmmm,' Bella's mind was digesting the information.

'I'd appreciate it if you kept that to yourself.'

'Don't worry. You can trust me, I won't tell anyone.' And he knew he could trust her. Bella decided to change the subject. 'So, how's Alison?' Bella had known Dave's wife Alison years ago when they all socialised together.

A dark shadow flitted across his face. 'I don't know. She left me two years ago for another man. A younger man. Huh.'

'I'm sorry, I didn't know,' she felt like a fool now, and very embarrassed.

'How would you? It's okay. It's in the past, got to move on and all that. Didn't get the work/life balance right. Can't really blame her, I devoted too much of my time to work and not enough time to her and our relationship, so she found comfort elsewhere. Wasn't helped by the fact that we'd tried for years to have children and couldn't.'

'Oh, I'm sorry.' What else could she say? She knew how painful it was to desperately want children and not have any. She and Hugh had tried for years and eventually she'd finally become pregnant, they were overjoyed. Tragically, three months into the pregnancy Hugh was killed and the stress and strain had caused, or contributed to, a miscarriage. The part of Hugh that had been her sole comfort after his death died too; it had taken a long time for her to recover, to start seeing a point to life again, and even now there were times when life seemed too dark for her.

Dave had heard on the grapevine that Hugh and Bella had not had children. And he could see no evidence in the house of the paraphernalia which normally accompanied children. He knew too well what a sensitive subject it could be and refrained from enquiring.

'I threw myself into work even more when she left. Divorce came through last year. I'm trying to get a better balance, take time off, have holidays etc. I've even started cycling, gets me out of the house. Seems kind of quiet there on my own.'

The big important detective looks like a little lost boy, thought Bella. 'I'm hoping to start cycling. I have got to lose some weight and there's a bike in the shed.'

'You don't need to lose weight! You look great as you are.'

Bella blushed, flattered by the compliment. 'Thanks. I've put on a lot since Hugh died, comfort eating, you know...'

'I did the opposite. Stopped eating. Kind of got used to having my meals all prepared for me, didn't appreciate it at the time. You only realise what you've lost once it's gone.' He sighed wistfully. 'Still,' he tried to brighten up, 'got to go with the flow and all that. I'm quite a dab hand at cooking now. Went on a course, bought Delia Smith's Complete Cookery Course book to start with and progressed from there and there's so much one can access on the internet, it's a revelation! Perhaps,' he hesitated, 'I could show you some of my culinary skills? Maybe dinner or lunch one Sunday?' He looked hopefully at her.

'I'd like that.' She felt all weird, a cross between excitement, being flattered, nervousness and guilt. Was she being asked out on a date? She'd not been on one since Hugh had died and wasn't sure if she ever wanted another relationship. Or was it just old friends catching up?

As if sensing her unease he hastily added, 'It would be good to catch up,' unsure himself whether he wanted simply friendship or more, surprised that he'd asked her. He stood up to go. 'I'll be in touch to arrange a date. And thanks again for all your help.'

'That's okay,' she'd momentarily forgotten that he'd been here on business, it had so easily slipped into pleasure. 'If I remember anything else, I'll give you a call.'

'Thanks I'd appreciate it. I'll go and see if Jennifer Galbraith is in. Bye Bella.' He smiled at her again, the warmth of it radiating from his face.

'Bye.' She closed the door behind her and wondered what had just happened.

Chapter Seven

The next week passed by quickly as Bella started a crash diet, began cycling furiously and caught up with Mia. By the end of the week her muscles ached so much she didn't think she could get out of bed, her stomach rumbled most of the day and she felt permanently grumpy from the lack of food. The upside was that she had lost 4lbs in weight. As she stood on the scales she got a little buzz from seeing 4lbs less on it. The feeling was momentary as she wondered whether it was really worth it. Eating virtually nothing, and exercising hard was not the best way, nor the most effective way, of losing weight. Eating sensibly and building the amount of exercise up slowly would have a longer term benefit she felt sure and questioned why she had not started on that path instead.

The morning of the funeral arrived and, resisting the temptation to go mad and stuff herself with food, Bella opted for a small bowl of muesli, decaffeinated coffee and a glass of orange juice. A pure banquet in comparison to the previous seven breakfasts. As each morsel of food hit her stomach she could feel her blood sugar level rising, along with her normal good nature. Replenished, she got ready for the funeral. Mia had asked if she could attend, and though she'd felt rather awkward as Rupert had been a virtual stranger to her, it did feel like the right thing to do. She'd disposed of her 'funeral outfit' after Hugh's, she couldn't bear to see it in the wardrobe every day as it reminded her so much of one of the worst days of her life. It had therefore been a bit of a challenge to find something suitably sombre, which fitted her and was cool enough to wear in the searing June heat. Eventually she'd found a navy blue linen dress that came down to her calves, had a relatively high neck – up to her collar bones – and sleeves that came to the top of her elbows; with this she was going to wear a navy blue blazer-style jacket. Not a particularly stylishly put together outfit, but one which would suffice.

Mia knocked on the door at 10am. Fred, having parked in Bella's drive, was waiting by the car. The funeral was to be held at the village church along with a burial, followed by a wake in the village hall.

'Ready?'

'As I'll ever be,' replied Bella.

'Looks like the church is going to be crowded,' commented Fred, nodding in the direction of the queue of traffic inching its way up the far side of the green to the church and village hall car parks.

'More likely to be filled out with the local gossips and people gawping. So macabre,' added Mia.

'Hmm, suppose so. I managed to escape the clutches of Sharon at the shop this morning. Think she and her cronies are coming along for a nose. I guess there's bound to be a natural amount of curiosity. After all Rupert was a bit of a character by all accounts and a prominent businessman, and both he and Kim took part in lots of village activities. Until they find out who killed him, it'll rumble on for a while.' Unfortunately Bella knew all too well about the consequences of living in a close knit community, albeit an urban one, and being the focus of local people and local media attention, as Hugh had been a well respected policeman in the town where they had lived. The pressure had really been on his colleagues to find out who was responsible for his death. Fortunately, there had been several witnesses and it didn't take long for them to track the culprit down. Justice had been done when the case was successful, and the drink driver was sent to prison for his deadly misdemeanour.

'You okay?' asked Mia softly, squeezing Bella's arm.

She nodded. 'I'm fine.' She cleared her throat. 'It'll be quite interesting to see who's there. I imagine the police will be lurking in the background - doesn't the person who committed the crime usually have a compulsion to be there at the funeral, or have I been watching too many detective programmes on television?'

Mia and Fred laughed. 'Haven't got a clue.'

They walked in silence the rest of the way. When they arrived inside the church they found it was packed, with people even standing at the back of the church and down the sides. Fred craned his neck and saw Cressa waving at him. They weaved their way down the aisle towards her and slipped into the pew next to her. Bella smiled and politely said hello. She noticed that two pews were taken up with those who had been at the lunch party, all except Sophie and Harry.

'Where are Sophie and Harry?' she whispered to Mia.

'Coming with Kim and her parents.'

'Oh. Has she not got any other family?'

'No. She is an only child, as are her parents, and her grandparents are dead.'

'What about Rupert's family?' she scanned around looking at who was there.

'Not invited.'

'What?!' squeaked Bella, hastily lowering her voice as people turned to stare at her. 'Why not?'

'Apparently they had a big falling out - about thirty years ago. He's not been in touch with them since, and they haven't with him.'

'But he would have been only fifteen years old, thirty years ago. Surely it can't have been just teenage angst which caused the falling out?' Bella's curiosity was piqued.

'Don't know,' whispered Mia, 'don't think he has ever really talked about it. Kim doesn't really know much. She tried to persuade him to ask them to their wedding, but he went ballistic. I don't think she dared mention it again.'

'How very peculiar. I know families fall out and all that, but he was still a child.' Her brain ticked away as she ran through numerous scenarios as to why the fall-out could have occurred, but couldn't come up with anything which sounded vaguely realistic. The organ started playing and everyone fell silent, turning round to see the coffin being carried slowly up the aisle, Kim and her parents clutching on to one another for support with Harry and Sophie bringing up the rear.

Throughout the service Kim sat up ram rod straight. It seemed to Bella that she was doing the comforting to her parents, not the other way round. Fred read the lesson and Harry gave a carefully worded eulogy. Bella found that the service wasn't as excruciatingly painful as she had feared it would be; she'd been worried that it would rip open old wounds and she would become a weeping wreck again.

The sky had clouded over and there were heavy dark clouds and an oppressive air by the time the service moved outside. It was as she was standing beside the open grave that she noticed Ariadne and Kit. It would have been impossible not to have. Ariadne was dressed completely in black in a tight-fitting, knee length skirt, tight-fitted jacket, which was buttoned low and no blouse, her breasts appearing desperate to burst out – Rupert would have loved it - and on her head she had a clutch of black feathers with a net veil which just covered her eyes and stopped at the top of her nose. She looked like a 1930s movie star. Kit next to her was sharply dressed in a hand-tailored black suit, black shirt and black tie. There was a lot of whispering and pointing from the outer echelons of the mourners as they recognised the globally known movie star. Trust her to steel the limelight and detract from the true reason for the gathering, thought Bella.

Bella vaguely heard the Vicar going through the motions of the final stages of Rupert's burial as he was committed to his grave. Kim gripped her weeping parents to her and stood as though a stone statue, her face blank and as pale as alabaster. Bella saw Seb hovering slightly behind her with a pained expression on his face, and couldn't work out whether it was over Rupert's death or Kim's pain. Cressa and Jack stood just along from Kim on the other side of Mia and Fred. The apparent emotional distance that was between them may as well have been as wide as the Grand Canyon. Strange couple - she couldn't work them out.

As the mourners started to disperse and those invited headed off to the wake, Bella noticed the waif-like figure of Florence standing under a tree slightly apart from where the rest of them had been.

'You okay?' asked Bella gently as she looked into her ghost-like face.

'Fine. Thanks,' she replied tightly.

'Would you like to walk over to the village hall with me?'

Florence shook her head. 'No. Thanks. I've got to go.' And with that she fled like a startled rabbit in the direction of the church car park.

Weird, thought Bella shrugging. Suppose grief shows itself in different ways. I wonder if Rupert had had an affair with her?

'Hi Bella.'

Bella spun round, startled.

'Sorry to make you jump.' It was Dave.

'That's okay, I was deep in thought. Seen anything interesting?'

He smiled. 'Have you?' he bounced back to her.

'I find watching people fascinating,' she replied, deliberately avoiding his question.

He looked intently at her and decided not to push the subject. 'Sorry I haven't phoned. Been a bit busy at work,' he smiled guiltily.

'I guessed as much. What's happened to your new resolution to achieve a good work/life balance?' she joked.

He laughed. 'I know, I know. Bit difficult when you're investigating a murder though.'

'I suppose. Forgiven then.' She became aware that Sharon and a few of her fellow gossips were edging closer, having ascertained who Dave was. Bella gave Dave a beady look and raised her eyebrows trying to indicate that they were being listened too.

He understood and without turning round swiftly turned on his official voice and said, 'Well if you do think of anything, please contact myself or one of the officers working on the case.' He gave her a wink and walked off without even bothering to see who was behind him.

Seizing their moment, Sharon and her posse surrounded Bella. 'What did he have to say then? Any breakthrough? Go on, you can tell us. We're as discreet as anything. Won't tell a soul.'

Bella tried hard not to laugh. As if they could ever be discreet! 'Nothing to tell I'm afraid ladies.'

Fred, having observed the scene, called out to Bella and wandered over. 'Sorry to interrupt. Bella, I think Mia needs you.' He took her by the elbow and led her purposefully across the churchyard.

'Thanks,' giggled Bella, 'it was like being surrounded by vultures.'

'My pleasure,' he grinned back, releasing her elbow.

'Quick, let's get out of here before they follow us. Hope they're not coming to the wake.'

He shook his head. 'Nope. Don't think so. I believe that so many people were expected to turn up that it's by invite only, otherwise they wouldn't all fit in.'

'Good idea having it here at the village hall, right by the church and no mess to tidy up at the house afterwards, and more importantly no intrusion by a lot of people you don't know or barely know but felt obliged to invite.'

'Yeah. It's been organised by the tennis club committee. They got the caterers in they use for their events.

Kim's still paying but everything has been organised for her. One less thing to worry about. There's always so much to think about when a loved-one dies, even worse when it's not been from natural causes or an accident.' He gave her arm a comforting squeeze, appreciating that the whole affair would be reminding Bella of Hugh's death.

'Mmm, I know.'

A queue of people was edging slowly into the village hall when they arrived. They stood chatting easily together as they inched their way forward. Eventually they made it inside and squeezed their way over to Kim to offer their support, then jostled their way back across the room to make way for the many other people who wished to speak to her. Jammed up against a wall, Fred was sent off on a mission to acquire drinks and food for the three of them. Bella scanned the room - if you didn't know it was a wake you would think it were some kind of fun social gathering. It was as though as soon as the service was over everyone felt that was that, all done and dusted, and they could get on with having a jolly good time. Were they there cele-brating Rupert's life or had he been forgotten the moment they walked out of the churchyard? The person who caught her attention was Seb who was still hovering behind Kim in an attentive, almost husbandly, way.

'Mia.' she poked her friend in the side to get her atten-tion, for the noise in the room was rising at an incredible rate. She flapped her hand indicating that she wanted to speak into Mia's ear. 'What's the story with Seb?' she asked.

'What do you mean?' replied Mia warily.

'I don't know, it's just that he's so attentive, like a hus-band or lover might be.'

Mia looked round furtively and, not recognising anyone close to her, she bent her head to whisper to Bella. 'It's common knowledge, but old news now, best not to be resurrected.' Bella looked expectantly. 'Before Rupert came on the scene Seb and Kim had been together for several years; they were engaged and were due to get married. Rupert came along, swept her off her feet and before we knew it they were getting married. Seb was devastated - Kim was, and I suspect still is, the love of his life - he's not had a relationship since. He was also furious - he was convinced that Rupert was doing it to spite him or seeing it as some sort of challenge. Most of us agreed with Seb, because as soon as Kim and Rupert were married it seemed as though Rupert was bored and ready for a new challenge. Obviously none of us knew what went on behind closed doors. Kim kept painting a rosy view of their marriage for a long time and maybe it had been good in the beginning - it's not for me, or anyone else, to say otherwise. Personally, I think Kim and Seb were a perfect match.'

Bella's eyes were virtually out on stalks at this nugget of information. What if Seb had finally decided to get his revenge? What if he were so obsessed with Kim that he'd do anything to get her back? Surely this was a motive for murder?

'Now don't go bringing this all up,' warned Mia knowing full well the look on Bella's face, 'It's ancient history.'

'But it could be relevant?'

'Bella, I don't want to fall out with you over this. Seb would never in a million years hurt anyone. So just leave it, okay?'

Before Bella could reply, Fred turned up balancing three drinks and three plates of food on a tray, it was a miracle that he'd been able to get through the sea of people. Following closely behind him was Jennifer.

'Hi. Bit of a squeeze isn't it?' she said.

Bella noticed her white pinched face was covered in red blotches, and her nose was red and swollen from crying. She was clutching a glass of champagne for support.

'You seen the others?' bellowed Mia over the noise.

'Yeah, Jack and Cressa are busy having an argument in the lobby. Ariadne and Kit are holding court on the other side of the room. Seb's over with Kim. Harry and Sophie were following me but it looks like they've got caught up with someone, and I've not seen Florence since the service.'

'I think she's gone home. I asked her if she wanted to walk over with me but she ran off like a frightened rabbit.'

'Strange. Oh well, perhaps she felt intimidated, she's quite shy and I guess she doesn't really know anyone here apart from us. I'll give her a call later.'

They chatted for a while, eventually the hall began to thin out. Walking as though she were doing the red carpet, Ariadne, followed by Kit, ambled towards them and arrived with a flourish and the heavy scent of exotic, oriental perfume. She kissed everyone, including Bella, called them all "darling" and acted as though this were a reunion after many years apart. Taking centre stage as usual, Bella observed, wondering how much of it was an act and how much of it was who she really was. Watching Bella watching Ariadne, was Kit, who slid over to be beside her and whispered a lazy "hi" in a slightly dubious American accent. Bella smiled politely.

'It's good to see you again,' he murmured. Bella's heart fluttered, and she told herself not to be so ridiculous.

'You too,' she replied in a slightly strangled voice. 'So sad about Rupert.' She was sure she saw a flicker of something in his eyes.

'It's always sad when someone dies,' he replied in a hard voice.

'Yes, but to be murdered. Not nice at all.'

Kit shifted from one foot to another, seeming uncomfortable with the direction of the conversation.

'Did you know him well?' asked Bella feigning forgetfulness, as Kit had supposedly been introduced to them all as an unknown quantity.

He stared hard at her, his dark brown, almost coal black eyes piercing into her, making her shiver, but not from lust. 'No,' he replied curtly. He turned and went back to Ariadne, slipping his arm around her microscopic waist and switching his lazy smile back on. Bella was left standing slightly bewildered. Why so hostile? If he hadn't known Rupert, what was the problem? Her gut instinct was telling her that he wasn't telling the truth - somehow, somewhere, he and Rupert had met before and it was blatantly obvious that he didn't want anyone to know.

Unbeknown to Bella, Harry had caught the conversation. He smiled at her and raised his eyebrows, she felt slightly better and moved over to chat to him. A little while later she became aware that Kim, her parents and Seb were hovering near the door, everyone else had gone. Bella murmured a few more words of condolence and decided to slip away, leaving the cohort of friends together with Kim

Chapter Eight

Bella changed out of her funereal outfit and into a pair of beige linen trousers with an elasticated waist along with a loose-fitting linen top in a slightly darker shade of beige. She poured herself a glass of chilled sparkling mineral water, straight from the fridge, and wandered out into the garden, strolling round, contemplating the flowers in full bloom, a gorgeous splash of colour, her mind still whirring in the background, mulling over and over earlier conversations. Should she tell the police? Was it all speculation and gossip? Did her suspicions about Kit have any foundation?

Like a light bulb going on, she realised she could find out more about him on the internet. Surely a well known agent, with exceedingly famous clients, would come up in a search? It would be hard to believe that in this day and age of 2006 with the internet booming, that he would not have a media presence of some kind. She hurried inside, grabbed her laptop - yet another technological growth area, Bella had read, and being one of the lucky 67% to own a laptop - from the kitchen table and took it outside. She drummed her fingers impatiently, as the computer started itself up, irritated that it seemed to take so long. Finally she typed in her password, logged on and started the search.

First hit was his agency website, which had the usual self-appreciating guff meant to fool everyone into thinking what an amazing agency he owned and ran. She then spent the next two hours typing in his name in different configurations, then trawling through whatever came up, which ranged from glowing reports from appreciative starlets, to backstabbing and bitching from those who had either been dumped, or never been taken on in the first place by his agency, or rivals. She was beginning to get frustrated that nothing distinctly personal about him was coming up. There seemed to be nothing about his past prior to becoming an agent, other than the rosy picture which was painted in interviews or press releases. There was no real information about his family, childhood, adolescence, what he did before becoming an agent, nothing that could indicate a link between him and Rupert. She'd managed to ascertain that he was two years younger than Rupert, but that was it.

Sighing heavily, she decided to make a sandwich as it was now mid afternoon and she'd barely eaten anything since breakfast, a few nibbles at the wake and that was all. She took the butter out of the fridge, and just as she was about to sink the knife into it- thought better of it - a few calories she could do without. Instead she chopped up some cucumber and tomato, ground some pepper over it and looked at the calorie-light sandwich unenthusiastically. But at least it was food. She took it outside and munched on it thoughtfully. The sun was trying hard to break through the dark gloomy sky, rather like someone constantly switching a light on and off.

One last go, she decided as the food gave her a bit more energy with which to concentrate. Her hands hovered over the keyboard as she waited for inspiration to come, as to what to type into the search engine. Eventually she typed in "Kit Kerr gap year work". Bingo, she thought, as new information popped up. Quickly she clicked on the link and waited to see what would appear. A flashy website for a well respected vineyard in Australia popped up. Hmm, wonder what the connection is, she mused, clicking on link after link, in the hope that it would bring some morsel of information up. Maybe he'd just bought some wine from there and because he was well known it came up? She felt a twinge of disappointment, but clicked on the "Our Beginnings" section. Up popped a blurb about how the vineyard had been started thirty years ago. The owners had scraped together enough money to buy the vineyard and replanted and nurtured it for ten years, before it had started to flourish and make money. These days the grapes were picked by machine or by hand, depending upon the grape variety and which wine it was to be made into, but twenty years ago all the grapes were picked by hand. People backpacking around Australia contacted them for work and would spend the harvest season crammed into basic accommodation, with meals and a small amount of money paid, in exchange for long days spent toiling in the vineyards. Along with the information were ancient photographs of the backpackers and the owners, from the first year they'd introduced the scheme. Bella peered intently at the photographs, one by one, excitement rising in her, convinced that she would find what she was looking for. She stopped at one. Could that be him? She peered closer - she was sure it was him. Twenty years younger, but those eyes looked distinctly familiar. She saved it to a file and hurried inside to print it off, enlarging it before she did so.

The sun was now fully out, making the light perfect for looking at the rather grainy picture. Yes, she was convinced it was him. She buzzed with excitement, then very carefully studied each and every person in the picture again, peering at them closely, trying to take into account the fact that it was taken twenty years ago. There at the opposite end of the row to Kit, was a young man she was convinced was Rupert. It had to be. That had to be the connection. But if they knew each other twenty years ago, why would they deny knowing one another?

A memory flashed into her mind as she suddenly remembered the look on Rupert's face when Kit had arrived. He'd gone deathly pale, not the face of someone seeing a long lost friend from the past. What had gone on? And who would know now? She could tackle Kit, but had a feeling he would stonewall her. Kim? Not the right time to be asking questions about Rupert's past. Mia? Maybe she would know but Bella was doubtful. If something had gone on, which neither Rupert nor Kit wanted anyone to know about, then it was doubtful they had told anyone.

Jennifer? Maybe in his scheme to bed her, he had told her things he'd told no one else in order to get her to trust him? A possibility, but a dubious one. Bella resisted every urge within her to go straight round to Jennifer's house, now was not the time. Jennifer was upset from the funeral, and asking probing questions about Rupert's past would not result in any answers. Tomorrow would have to do.

Restraining herself until 10am the next day, Bella hurried up the lane to Jennifer's house, printed out copy of the photograph tucked safely in her pocket. She rapped loudly on the door and waited. Silence. She rapped again. Just when she was about to give up, the door opened and a miserable looking Jennifer stared back at her.

'Oh, hi,' she said unenthusiastically.

'Hi Jennifer, how are you?'

She shrugged. 'Okay I suppose. Do you want to come in?'

Bella could tell from the way she asked that it was politeness, rather than desire, which had prompted the question. Still she was keen for answers, and responded with an affirmative. Jennifer led the way through to the kitchen which was looking unkempt; unwashed crockery and detritus piled up in the sink waiting to be cleaned, dirty work surfaces covered in crumbs and debris.

'S'pose I ought to tidy up,' she commented lethargically. 'Can't seem to muster up the enthusiasm.'

'Well, it's understandable, you're still upset about Rupert's death, and with his funeral only being yesterday, it's hardly surprising,' soothed Bella.

'Guess so. Silly really, but somehow I feel guilty.'

'Guilty?'

'Yeah. As though I denied Rupert his dying wish. Ridiculous I know, and completely illogical, but that's how I feel, and maybe if I had slept with him he wouldn't have been driving down that road and he'd still be alive.' She poked a few dishes in the sink and turned away from them, there were still a couple of clean mugs, they'd do.

'Unlikely. Would it have made any difference if you'd known he was going to die?'

'Probably not,' she sighed, 'just one of those irrational things. I'll get over it.'

Eager to keep the subject on Rupert, Bella tried to subtly turn the conversation to his past. 'How well did you know Rupert?'

'About as well as anyone I suppose. Why?'

'Oh, er, just curious really. I noticed his family wasn't there yesterday? Mia said they'd had a falling out about thirty years ago, didn't know why. Do you?' she asked hopefully.

'No idea. Not something he talked about. Don't even know if Kim knows. She tried to persuade him to ask them to their wedding but he went ballistic apparently. Why the interest?'

She hesitated. Be honest or not, she dithered. 'Curiosity, I suppose. I got the impression that Kit knew Rupert.'

'Don't think so. I believe that Saturday was the first time any of us had met Kit.'

'Hmm. It's strange that's all. When I chatted to Kit about Rupert at the funeral, he went all peculiar on me, clammed up and walked off to speak to someone else. Like there was something to hide. Also, I noticed, though it may have been a coincidence, that Rupert paled dramatically when Kit arrived on that Saturday.'

'I think you're probably reading too much into it. I'm sure if Rupert knew Kit, then Kim would know about it, and would have said so.' She looked at Bella, her interest roused. 'Was there anything else that made you think that?'

Bella didn't want Jennifer to think that she was a snoop, and shifted uncomfortably, but she felt that Jennifer might at least be able to give an opinion as to whether, or not, it was Kit and Rupert in the picture. She took the picture out of her pocket. 'I don't want you to think that I always go nosing around in other people's business, but there was something about Kit yesterday, something almost sinister it sent a chill through me, so I did a bit of research on the internet. I found this picture, I'm sure that it's Kit. Here, have a look. What do you think?'

Jennifer peered at the photo. 'Well,' she paused, 'I suppose it could be him, but it could be anyone. I've only met him twice, and if this was taken twenty years ago when you suspect Kit and Rupert first met, he will have changed a lot.'

'Hmm. Have a look at the others. Is there anyone else there that looks familiar?'

Jennifer studied it closely. One by one, she looked at each person. Suddenly she frowned and pursed her lips. 'I…' she hesitated. 'It …' she looked up at Bella, who was holding her breath in anticipation. Could she really have found the connection?

'What is it?' Bella didn't want to put words in to Jennifer's mouth.

'This person,' she pointed, 'looks a bit like Rupert. I mean, again I didn't know him twenty years ago but this person seems to have his features; thinner, yes, but I'm sure it's him.'

'I thought so too, but I only met him once,' Bella replied excitedly.

'So if they did know each other why the big secret?' Jennifer echoed Bella's very thoughts.

'What happened so long ago that made them both be economical with the truth? And if they could be deceitful about that, could Kit lie about where he was when Rupert died?'

Jennifer gasped and clutched her throat. 'You don't think…'

Bella shrugged. 'I don't know, but why be so shifty? Do you know where he says he was, when Rupert died?'

'Um. I think Sophie said something about him having gone out for cigarettes.'

'So it's possible. Did he get any?'

'Cigarettes? I don't know. Sophie might. I'll give her a call.' She picked up the phone and asked Sophie, who must have been wondering why she was being asked such a peculiar question. Jennifer put the phone down, her eyes sparkling. 'Sophie says that she remembers he didn't get any because Ariadne had a bit of a strop about it as she'd run out and was desperate. She remembers that he was a bit distracted when he returned, snapped at Ariadne, telling her she could go and get them herself if she were that desperate, and stomped off to his room, from where he did not reappear until the next morning. Ariadne had to go out and buy some. She was in a foul mood and livid with Kit. Ariadne went out at about 10.20pm, about ten minutes after Kit got back, and she returned at 10.35pm. Sophie's sure about the time, because she was shattered after the party and just wanted to go to bed but felt obligated to stay up until Ariadne got back.'

'So, he could have done it. The timings fit,' said Bella excitedly.

'Yes. But I think we might be rather getting ahead of ourselves and jumping to conclusions, don't you?' She asked rhetorically.

'True, but you have to agree that it's a bit suss.'

Jennifer nodded, and they lapsed into a thoughtful silence. Bella's mind was whirring as she tried to decide what to do next. It was Jennifer who broke the silence. 'I can't really see any way of finding out more. I mean, I suppose we could ask Kim, but I'm sure she would have said she knew him if they'd met before, or if Rupert had told her about him.'

'Yeah. I couldn't find anything else particularly relevant about Kit on the internet, so I guess there's no point searching again. Do you think I should tell the police?'

'Tell them what though? It's pretty circumstantial, don't think they'd take you seriously.'

'Maybe not.' she paused. 'Only thing is that the Inspector who is heading up the case, trained with my late husband. I hadn't seen him since he moved to Kent fifteen years ago, but we knew each other quite well before then. I think he'd listen to me, and maybe look into it, even if he thinks it's not relevant.'

'I suppose you could tell him, though I'm reluctant to have the police digging around in something which may be irrelevant, and might just resurrect things from the past which should be left well alone.'

'Suppose…'

Jennifer sighed deeply. 'But if it were my husband who'd been killed, I'd do anything to try and find out who did it but I really don't want Kim upset any more than she already has been.'

'I can see that, but it's a bit late for that. Rupert's dead.'

'Mmm. I think perhaps I, or we, should speak to Kim first, tell her what we think we've discovered. She might look at the photo and say it's absolutely not Rupert, and produce a picture of him when he was that age to disprove our theory.'

'Okay. Sounds like a plan. At least then she will be aware of what's going on, and not think that we're sneaking around behind her back. Even though I barely know her I would hate to upset her, or anyone for that matter. I'm not doing this because I enjoy digging around in other people's lives and being nosey. I guess with what I experienced with my husband it has struck a chord and I know how desperately I wanted the culprit found and brought to justice and would like the same for Kim.'

'I didn't think you were. If you're a really good friend of Mia's, then I couldn't imagine her having a friend who was a meddling busybody. And I am really sorry about your husband.'

'Thanks. Kit acting so strangely seems to have triggered something in me,' she paused, still reticent about divulging too much about her past. 'So you know that my husband died two years ago. He was killed by a drink driver. It helped me a great deal to know who was driving that car, and that justice was done. It would have been so much worse for me if that person had never been caught. I would have looked at everyone as though they were the one responsible, and would have wondered if he or she had done it before - done it again - made other people suffer the way I had suffered. I feel I can empathise in some way with Kim given the way Rupert died.'

'It must have been so painful for you,' replied Jennifer softly. Bella nodded and tried to hold back the tears which were pricking at her eyes. 'I think I can understand why you want to find out what Kit is hiding. It may be perfectly innocent but, combined with the fact that he came back without cigarettes, it does seem a little suspicious.'

'Shall we go to Kim's now?'

'Not sure. Bit soon after the funeral.'

'Hmm, true.'

'Still, if we're barking up the wrong tree, I'm sure she'll understand, and if we're not then the police can look into it and tell us that we've got over-active imaginations when they find nothing. I'll give her a call first, see how she is.'

Kim was apparently holding up well and, intrigued by Jennifer's mysterious phone call, invited her and Bella to pop round.

Fifteen minutes later, having driven together in Jennifer's VW Beetle, they pulled up in front of the magnificent house. Bella was bowled over by its beauty, she was always rather in awe of anyone who lived in such a huge house. She tried not to gawp as Kim ushered them through to the sitting room, where she had already prepared a pot of coffee for the three of them. Considering she had buried her husband the previous day, she looked remarkably well. Her skin seemed to glow more than it had done at the lunch party, and there was a slight air of confidence about her which Bella had not noticed before.

Jennifer explained, to an intrigued Kim, what Bella had discovered, and handed her the photograph. She and Bella held their breath as the minutes ticked by, Kim studying it intently. Silently she rose and walked to a bureau at the back of the sitting room. She rustled around for a moment or two and fished something out. She sat back down and studied the photograph again.

'I'm sure it's Rupert. Not so sure about Kit, as the first time I'd met him was at the party, but it does kind of look like him. Here, have a look at this.' She offered them an old photograph of Rupert. 'That was taken about fifteen years ago I think, you can see the similarities.'

Sure enough there was Rupert looking remarkably similar to the man in the photograph Bella had printed off. She felt a frisson of excitement.

'He must have recognised Kit,' said Kim. 'If they were working on a vineyard together for several weeks, I find it hard to believe that he wouldn't have. But I have no idea who Kit really is. I mean I know who he is now, Ariadne's agent/friend/lover, whatever he is, but nothing about his past. Tell you what, I'll give Ariadne a call and ask a few subtle questions, maybe she knows if there is a connection.' Kim disappeared off in the direction of the study, Bella and Jennifer could hear the muted tones of her voice drifting through the open door.

'Does Kim know that Rupert came round to your house shortly before he died?' asked Bella.

Jennifer shook her head and chewed on her bottom lip.

'Do you think you should tell her? You've told the police and it may well come up at some point when they're talking to Kim.'

'I was kind of hoping that if I buried my head in the sand it might go away and I wouldn't have to tell her. After all, it's not going to achieve anything, it'll probably just upset her further.'

'Tricky. But would it be better coming from you or the police?'

'Since you put it like that, I suppose I have no choice,' she replied reluctantly.

At that moment Kim hurried back into the room. 'No luck I'm afraid, she doesn't know anything. She was starting to get suspicious so I changed the subject.'

'What would you like us to do then Kim?' asked Bella.

'It's a bit of a mystery, but I can't believe that it has any bearing on Rupert's death,' she paused as her mind ticked through the options. 'I suppose, as long as the police are discreet in their enquiries, then it would do no harm. I don't want to go upsetting Ariadne, but if Kit has nothing to hide then even if he found out it shouldn't be a problem.

'You sure?'

Kim nodded.

'Okay, I'll give Inspector Ormandy a call when I get home. He's a good man, he'll be tactful.'

They spent a while chatting, Kim seeming quite animated, though rather overwhelmed by the amount of paperwork there was to sort out. There were Rupert's businesses to decide what to do with and his personal finances. She was seeing Rupert's solicitor that afternoon about the will, and was hopeful that he would give her some guidance as to how to proceed. Surprisingly, Kim was keen to arrange a game of tennis as she was eager to get some "fresh air and exercise" as she put it. A date for Friday of that week was arranged, Jennifer offering to contact Cressa, Mia, Sophie and Florence, the venue being Kim's own tennis court, rather than up at the club where she would have to deal with other people's sympathy towards her. Jennifer couldn't bring herself to tell Kim about seeing Rupert before he died, justifying not doing so by reassuring herself that it was too soon after the funeral to break such news to her.

The next day Bella picked Mia up and they went off for the morning to the small town of Cranbrook. Mia berated Bella all the way about digging around in other people's business, but eventually conceded that actually Bella had done the right thing. She was concerned that this crusade to find Rupert's killer had too much to do with Hugh's death, that Bella was having trouble re-building her life. Despite Bella's reassurances that this was not the case, she decided to reserve judgement and keep a closer eye on her friend.

They parked the car in the free-of-charge car park and walked down the hill into the pretty little town which, though small, had everything you could possibly need. Several banks/building societies, post office, supermarket, book shop, hardware store, hairdressers, grocer and health food shop, optician, dentists, charity shops, clothes shops, restaurants, travel agents, the list was endless but the beauty of them all was that they seemed to complement one another and that there was a real sense of community, something that was disappearing in the country as each year went by.

Bella had to go to the bank so left Mia basking in the sunshine whilst she popped inside. Bella busied herself at the cash point, obtaining a balance and withdrawing some cash. As she moved to the side in order to place everything into her purse and allow the next person to use the cash-point, she heard a vaguely familiar voice at the counter behind her. She glanced round, it was Cressa, who hadn't seen Bella.

'Look,' she was saying in a fierce, patronising voice to the remarkably patient cashier, 'all I want to do is get a statement from my husband's account. We've banked here for the past twenty years, you know who I am, you know who my husband is, we have our joint account and all I am asking for is a statement from his own account. It's quite simple.'

The cashier patiently reiterated that she would not be able to do that as the account was in Cressa's husbands name, and only his name. Cressa became more and more agitated. Bella tried to slip out through the door unnoticed, feeling awkward, unfortunately Cressa saw her. Bella smiled, blushed deeply and scurried out before Cressa drew her in to her campaign.

'What's up? Machine eat your card?' laughed Mia as she saw a flustered Bella come hurrying out.

'No, thank goodness. It's a bit embarrassing,' she went on to explain what had happened.

'I despair with those two. They have always seemed like such a solid couple, but all they do is bicker now. I don't know what's going on but Cressa hasn't been a happy bunny for a while.'

'Should we wait for her?'

'No. She could be a while. If Cressa wants something she will do virtually anything to get it, so that poor cashier might be there for a while, in fact, Cressa has probably asked to see the manager by now. Come on let's go and get a cup of coffee.'

They wandered down the High Street and round into Stone Street, reaching a small Italian delicatessen situated in a very old, beamed building. They walked in past the delectable range of fresh pasta, meats and cheeses and up the steps to the few small tables, which were partially occupied, the ones outside being fully occupied, and sat down at the remaining available table by the window, affording Bella a good view up and down the street.

It was while they were sipping their drinks, Bella a cappuccino and Mia a latte – and very good it was too – that Mia saw Cressa stride by. Catching sight of them out of the corner of her eye, Cressa diverted briskly into the deli and marched up to them.

'Cressa! How are you?' ventured Mia as Cressa pulled up a chair to join them. She barked her order for a cappuccino and sat down heavily on the chair.

'Furious! That's how I am! Absolutely furious!'

'Oh dear. Why's that?' Mia had a sinking feeling, once Cressa was in a foul mood and ranting there was no stopping her.

'That bloody bank! I've banked there for twenty years and they won't even do me a simple favour!' She ranted and raved for five minutes with both Bella and Mia doing their utmost to make soothing noises.

'Surely Jack can get his own statement can't he? Or he can look at it online?' asked Mia bravely.

'Pah! It's not for him. It's for me.'

Mia frowned. 'But why do you need to see his bank account?'

Suddenly to their dismay Cressa's face crumpled and big fat tears rolled down her face.

'Cressa! What's wrong?' asked Mia. Cressa continued to sob. Bella ordered more coffee for the three of them, not sure what else to do as she was not well acquainted with Cressa.

'It's Jack,' she sniffed, 'he's gone all secretive on me. I used to do all our banking, I could access everything online, Jack left everything to me. Then one day he changed his password and I've not been able to access his account since.'

'Have you talked to him about this?'

Cressa nodded. 'Yes, but all he does is get tetchy. Ever since then we've been arguing. I think,' she blew her nose loudly, 'I think he's having an affair.' She looked beseechingly at them.

'An affair? Jack?' Mia looked incredulous. Of all the people she knew he was one of the least likely candidates to have an affair she felt. 'No, I don't believe it. He wouldn't do that. Just because he wants a bit of privacy over his account doesn't mean he's having an affair.'

She sniffed some more. 'I think he's paying me back.'

'Paying you back? What on earth for?' Mia was completely confused by now.

Cressa looked miserably at them. 'For what I did,' she replied in a hoarse whisper. Bella and Mia waited silently. 'I ...' she gulped, 'I had a brief affair, in fact not even an affair, a stupid, stupid fling.'

Mia's jaw dropped in astonishment. Cressa? An affair? Surely not?

'You're disgusted by me aren't you? I can't say I blame you, I hate myself.'

Bella was wishing she were anywhere else but there. This was way too personal for her to be hearing. It was absolutely none of her business.

'When? Who? Why?' stuttered Mia.

'Eight years ago.'

'Eight years ago? That was such a long time ago. I can't believe Jack would wait until now to get his revenge, he's just not like that.'

'I thought we'd got over it, we were having a rough patch, as any marriage does, and Jack was away on business a lot and not talking to me, not really, not about what mattered - our marriage. I made a stupid mistake, had a fling for two weeks when he was away. Realised as soon as I saw him what an idiot I had been, regretted it ever since. I had to tell him, we'd never had any secrets, nor have we since until now. He went mad, he was so angry and hurt it was awful.' she shook her head in shame at the memories. 'I've always loved him, never stopped, I was so, so stupid.'

'But you've moved on since then. He forgave you didn't he?'

'Yes. It took a long time but he did, and I thought our marriage was stronger than ever, that's why I'm so confused and normally we talk about everything. I don't know what to do.'

'Who was it?'

'Who was what?'

'Who did you have a fling with?'

'It doesn't matter now.'

'I suppose not. Did you tell Jack who it was?'

She nodded, then blurted out. 'It was Rupert.'

'Rupert!' exclaimed Mia and Bella in unison.

'Oh Cressa! How could you? Of all the people!'

Of all the people, what, thought Bella. I'm definitely missing something here.

'I know, I know, you don't have to reprimand me.'

'I'm surprised he didn't go and thump Rupert.'

'I think he went round and had a good old shout at him. Thank goodness Rupert, for once, had some sense and didn't laugh at him, otherwise I think Jack would've killed him. Oh, no, I didn't mean that!' she flustered realising what she'd just said. 'He wouldn't, he didn't.'

He wouldn't wait eight years, thought Bella, he would have done it there and then, unless he was the type of man who brooded on something and preferred his revenge "served cold". But what was Cressa scared of?

'Of course not,' soothed Mia.

'It's just…' she broke down sobbing again. Bella and Mia looked at one another, mystified.

'Just what?' whispered Mia.

'It's just … Just … I'm so scared,' she whispered.

'Scared?'

'The night Rupert died Jack went out just before 10pm and came back about five minutes later. The accident happened just down the road from us. What if…' she looked at them, terrified.

'He wouldn't have, trust him Cressa, you know him.'

'I know, but he's been acting so weird.'

'Have you told the police?' asked Bella.

She shook her head. 'No, I said he was at home all night,' she replied fiercely.

'Um,' Bella was trying to think of a sensitive way of phrasing it, 'he might have seen something which could be relevant. Could be important? You can't not tell them. It could be the difference between finding Rupert's killer and not.'

Mia shot Bella a fierce look to shut her up. Now was definitely not the time.

'Maybe. But I'd do anything to protect Jack.'

Mia suddenly had an idea. 'Did Jack's car have a dent, a scrape, or anything on it? I'm sure that whoever ran Rupert off the road must have some sort of damage to their car.'

'No!' relief flooded over Cressa's face. 'Not a scratch, neither of us has on either of our cars. The police came and checked them over when they came to talk to us. Mia, you're brilliant. I've been worrying all this time Thank you. Thank you!'

'My pleasure.' Phew, thank goodness that disaster has been averted, thought Mia.

Meanwhile Bella was mentally crossing Jack and Cressa off her suspect list.

A little later, after Cressa had fully cheered up, they waved her off and ambled back up the High Street to Bella's car, popping into a variety of shops on the way.

'So,' started Bella, 'what did you mean by "of all people"?'

'Hmm? Don't know what you're talking about?' replied Mia distractedly, as she glanced in the window of the well equipped cook shop.

'You know. About Rupert? About Cressa having a fling with him?'

'Oh, don't start Bella, it's not relevant.' She was becoming exasperated by all Bella's questions and her current obsession with behaving like a sleuth in an Agatha Christie novel.

'Don't be so tetchy! It's obvious that, whatever "it" is, it's public knowledge, it's just that I don't know!'

'Oh all right, but don't go blabbing about it, it'll just drag up unpleasant memories for some people. I don't know the full details, I never asked, but basically about ten years ago Jack and Rupert went into some kind of business deal together. Now, I don't know what happened, but Jack

110

later pulled out, and a few months after that Rupert made a killing from the deal. Only problem was that none of the profits went to Jack. Jack claimed he was ripped off by Rupert, but there was no hard evidence so he couldn't take him to court. Rupert had stuck to the law – only just – but there was no doubt he knew that the deal, which was turning sour, had the potential to more than reverse itself. Trouble is he didn't tell Jack, and Jack needed to make sure he got his money back as he was committed to paying school fees.'

'Somehow that doesn't surprise me, Rupert doing something like that. I wonder how many other people he treated like that?'

'Yeah well, best keep those thoughts to yourself eh Bella?'

'Don't worry, I shan't say a word.'

Chapter Nine

The thunderstorms during the night had cleared the mugginess from the air and the day felt fresh and bright with a warm sun and beautiful blue sky. Bella picked through her resolutely dull and dowdy selection of clothes, which definitely needed a transformation, attempting to find something suitable to wear for tennis. It had been several years since she'd last played – she and Hugh had played tennis a lot together – and though she'd tried to squeeze into her old size 8 tennis dress she hadn't even managed to get it down over her arms. Feeling gloomy, she reluctantly settled on a pair of navy Bermuda shorts and a pale pink polo shirt. Not, she felt, particularly appropriate for a game of tennis, she was sure the rest of them would be kitted out in their perfect white tennis apparel. On the upside, at least her feet hadn't swelled like the rest of her, and she could get them into her trainers.

In the kitchen she carefully wiped down her rather dusty tennis racket and munched on a banana to give her an energy boost. Whilst she was looking forward to an afternoon of exercise and fun with a group of nice people, she was worried that her rusty tennis skills and lack of fitness would spoil it for the others.

Bella shut the house up, and saw Jennifer drive past in her blue VW Beetle as she was locking the front door. She waved, but Jennifer didn't see her. Climbing into her own VW Golf, she followed in Jennifer's wake. Unlike the lunch party when everyone arrived in dribs and drabs, all the girls turned up virtually simultaneously. A bright cheery, chattery group was assembled in Kim's drive.

Kim greeted them from the front door and they wandered over having retrieved rackets and balls out of their respective cars. She ushered them through to the kitchen, where a copious quantity of cold drinks awaited them.

'We'll go out onto the terrace,' said Kim. She touched Bella on the arm and indicated for her to wait back. When they were alone Kim spoke. 'Have you heard anything?'

'No, sorry. I haven't spoken to Dave, I mean Inspector Ormandy, since I told him what we'd found out. I'm sure as soon as there is anything to tell he'll let you know, and don't worry, I did emphasise how sensitive this was.'

'Thanks.'

To Bella, Kim didn't seem as bright as she had the other day. The dark circles had returned under her eyes and these were accompanied by hefty bags. Still, it was only to be expected she reasoned. 'You okay?' she offered.

Kim smiled tightly. 'Fine. Thanks. Let's join the others shall we?'

'Florence not coming?' asked Cressa as they rejoined the group.

'No. She had to go into work or something, which is a shame. She doesn't normally work on a Friday, which is why I arranged it for today.'

'What does she do?' asked Bella.

'She's a nurse at a local doctor's surgery. Only works four days a week though, which is why she's been able to play so much tennis with us,' replied Jennifer.

Cressa was busy planning the rota of play, so that all six of them would have a good game on the single court. She organised everyone into pairs, and the tennis started. Those not playing were quite happy to sit back and bask in the sunshine, chat and watch the others running around exerting themselves on the court. Bella was paired with Mia, which was a relief as she'd played with her before. After three hours all of them were hot, sweaty and tired, but the endorphins seemed to have kicked into all of them, so it was an even happier group who sat in the shade of two large cream canvas umbrellas and sipped on Kim's home-made lemonade.

'That was great, thanks for asking me, hope I didn't slow you down too much?' said Bella. She was surprised at how quickly she'd got back into the swing of things, helped by the fact that there was only one court and time was therefore limited for each game.

'Not at all! In fact, I think it's just as well we stopped or you might have wiped the floor with us!' replied Sophie who was thoroughly enjoying an afternoon without having to worry about Jemima, much as she loved her, as Harry was at home looking after her.

'D'you manage to get everything sorted out that you wanted to at Rupert's solicitors the other day?' enquired Jennifer.

Kim looked miserable. 'I don't know.'

'Don't know? Did you not get to see him?'

'I did, but …' her voice trailed off. The others stopped chatting.

'What's wrong Kim?' pressed Sophie.

'It's just weird. I still can't believe it.' The others glanced nervously at one other, wondering what on earth Rupert had done this time?

'He hasn't gone and done something stupid has he Kim?' continued Sophie, 'I mean, he has left you every- thing hasn't he? He hasn't left it all to a cats home or something?'

'No. Nothing like that. There's more than enough money. More than I thought actually, and the house is 100% mine, but I don't know what's going to happen to the business.'

'The business? What do you mean?' Rupert had spent the last ten years building up a reputable wine business. He had converted an oast house into offices and a shop, which was situated midway between the house and the vil- lage, in addition he'd had many fingers in many pies, with different subsidiary companies dealing with different as- pects of his mini empire.

'The will states that 50% of his business assets i.e. ex- cluding his personal effects, share of our house and savings etc, be bequeathed to a Charlotte Willingham.'

'Who?' they chorused.

'I don't know. That's the weird thing, I have no idea who she is, or what she meant to Rupert. His solicitor doesn't know, or is not allowed to tell me. The only thing he would say, was that she was a beneficiary of his will before he married me, and obviously remained in it after our marriage even though we both re-did our wills.'

'And you have absolutely no idea who this Charlotte person is?' asked Cressa.

Kim shook her head. 'No idea at all. It's confusing. I mean, why didn't he tell me about her? I wouldn't have objected if there was a good reason. I'm more than well provided for. I don't truly know about all the ins and outs of his business dealings, and am not that interested in any of them, other than the wine business. I really don't want to lose that, so until Rupert's accountant and solicitor can work out the value of the companies, I won't know if, after any taxation implications, the value of my share of the other companies will provide me with enough to buy out her share of the wine business - assuming she is willing to agree to that. I've got no idea if she would be happy to settle for cash, or want to sell any of the businesses or want to be involved or anything. If Rupert had left me 51% then I would have had the majority share and therefore have more control and say over how, and in what form, the business assets are distributed.'

'She isn't a member of his family is she? A long-lost sister, or cousin or anything?' suggested Mia.

'Nope. I know the names of all his family. I might never have met them, but at least he told me their names, as far as I know, though now I am beginning to have doubts.'

'Perhaps it would be worth contacting them? Maybe they might be able to shed some light?' offered Sophie.

'It's possible, but they don't even know who I am. Rupert and his family had not had contact for thirty years.'

'So they don't know he's dead?'

Kim shook her head. 'I have asked his solicitor to track them down and inform them. I thought about doing it myself, but I have no idea why they've not had any contact, and I could be getting involved in some sort of horrific situation, and I've got enough to deal with at the moment anyway. It'll be a shock for them, but maybe they think he's been dead for years, I don't know? I can't get my head round the fact that they've had absolutely no contact with their son since he was fifteen. I did manage to prise out of Rupert that he hadn't run away from home and therefore they've not spent the past thirty years wondering where their little boy is. I don't suppose I'll ever know why this situation arose, and perhaps it's best this way.'

'Have you thought of hiring a private detective?' suggested Cressa.

'For what? To find his family, or find out who this Charlotte person is?'

'I was thinking about Charlotte Willingham, but I guess you could do the same for his family too if you wanted to?'

'Hmm, all sounds a bit over the top and I am hoping my solicitor will be able to come up with something and deal with the matter and leave me well out of it. What do the rest of you think?' Kim looked around at them.

'Difficult really. I suppose you could,' replied Mia.

'Or you may get to meet this Charlotte person when the solicitor has tracked her down?' added Sophie.

'Not sure if there's any point finding more out about his family. It's not going to change anything now, unless there's something you're desperate to find out about Rupert, and will always wonder about?' said Jennifer.

Kim gave a big sigh. 'I don't know. Sometimes I think my head is going to explode there is so much to think about and sort out.' she rubbed her temples, trying to tease away the tension which was building up. 'What do you think Bella?'

Bella was surprised to be asked. As a newcomer to the group she felt hesitant about giving an opinion as she felt sure she had already over-stepped the mark with her ferreting around for information. 'I'm not sure,' she replied diplomatically, 'why don't you go with your gut feeling? That's usually a pretty good sign of what one should do.'

'Right,' said Kim decisively getting up, 'on that basis I've decided that today I've spent enough time thinking about it. I'm going to make a large jug of Pimms. You up for it?' There was a slight hesitation, as they knew how easy it was to down glasses of Pimms, which tasted so innocently like a soft drink, and not realise how imbibed you were becoming. 'Don't worry, I'll make it exceedingly weak, and bring an extra bottle of lemonade out and some nibbles to snack on. Besides, you can't abandon me just yet, it's only 5 o'clock!'

'I'll give you a hand.' offered Sophie, getting up and following her across the terrace to the back door.

The rest of the group lapsed into silence for a little while as they luxuriated in the late afternoon sun. A gentle breeze started to stir in the trees, making their leaves rustle like the grass skirt of a hula dancer.

'Do you think she's okay?' questioned Jennifer. 'She seems so upbeat, all things considered, despite the circumstances.'

'I was thinking the same thing,' added Cressa.

'Should we, or one or two of us, stay d'you think?' suggested Mia.

'Might be an idea. I can't - Henry and Emma are coming home for the weekend. Jack's picking them up from the station at 7 p.m. so I can't stay late,' replied Cressa, referring to her two children who were away at university.

118

'I can, I've got nothing planned.' volunteered Jennifer.

'Bit tricky for me too,' added Mia. 'Tess is coming to the end of her GCSEs, she's got her last one on Monday. Fred and I are taking her out for dinner and a movie, to try and get her to relax a bit. I've never known a child to work so hard for exams. Usually it seems to be more a case of dragging your child to the desk to revise - from what the other parents are saying - but Tess has been the total opposite.' she spoke proudly of her only child.

'Bella? Don't suppose you could help us out? Why don't you and I offer to take Kim out to dinner? There's a pub in the next village which serves excellent food. We won't get a table in the restaurant it'll be fully booked by now, but we could sit in the garden. Might be chilly later on, but it'll be glorious for a while.'

Bella felt flattered to be asked. 'Sure. I've got nothing on, it'd be nice and a good opportunity to start to discovering some of the local pubs.'

'Right, that's settled then.'

'What's settled?' asked Kim carrying a tray laden down with glasses, and a massive jug of Pimms stuffed full of cucumber, strawberries, mint and an assortment of other fruit.

'That you are coming out to dinner with me and Bella. Time we showed her what the local pubs are made of.'

'Tonight?'

'Yup. You haven't got anything on have you?' It hadn't crossed Jennifer's mind that Kim might have already made arrangements for the evening.

'Oh, er no, it'd be nice to get out of the house. What time?'

'Whenever we're ready. Half an hour will be enough for me to jump into the shower and change. I'll pick up Bella, and then come and collect you. At least you two can then have a drink.'

Sophie had been busy playing at being a waitress, pouring glasses of the sweet amber coloured liquid, and handing around the assortment of nibbles, which Kim had produced - baby crostini with an olive tapenade, strips of smoked salmon filled with cream cheese and chives, home-made honey roasted nuts.

Two hours later Bella was hopping out of the shower, frantically trying to get ready within half an hour - she had fifteen minutes left until Jennifer picked her up - and she still needed to dry her hair, do her make-up and get dressed. With the former and the latter completed she gave up on the idea of make up as Jennifer knocked on the door. But as a half hearted attempt she whisked a pale rose-pink lipstick across her lips and opened the door.

'Ready?'

'Just about,' she laughed, grabbing her bag and locking up. She still felt an all-over glow from all the exercise, and was convinced that her beige linen shift dress felt looser than it had done the previous week when she'd worn it. 'You look nice,' she commented to Jennifer, admiring the pastel coloured patterned dress, which accentuated every curve in her body. Bella felt a twinge of envy, and berated herself for it. Soon enough she would be back in shape she convinced herself, and she would treat herself to a brand new - non dowdy - wardrobe. She slipped into Jennifer's car beside her, and chatted lightly about nothing in particular on the way to Kim's house.

'Shall I hop out and get her?' she suggested as Jennifer pulled the car into the drive.

'Thanks.'

Bella hopped out and rang the bell. 'You ready?' she enquired as the door opened.

'Absolutely.' Kim seemed now to be radiating happiness, and Bella was puzzled as to how Kim's mood could change so quickly.

'You seem happier.'

Kim blushed scarlet. 'Oh. Well it's lovely to be going out. Gets a bit lonely, a bit maudlin, sitting in this big house all on my own.'

'I can imagine. So, what's the pub like that we're going to?'

'The Cow and Cart? The food's great, really good. Nothing fancy, but good, home-cooked food. Proper food, none of this haute cuisine stuff. I always think that if you want that kind of food you'll go to a high end restaurant rather than a pub. A pub is for pub food as far as I'm concerned.'

Bella clambered inelegantly into the backseat, feeling a tiny bit claustrophobic sitting in the back, with no direct access to a door. She distracted herself by gazing out at the countryside, as they whizzed down the winding lanes to the pub, which was quite literally in the middle of nowhere. Despite this the car park was packed, and it took some careful negotiating to squeeze the car into a tight spot by a hedge. So tight that Kim had to climb over the driver's seat to get out and Bella exited just as inelegantly as she had entered - she was relieved that there was no one else around to see.

'I'll go and get some drinks while you two go and prowl for a table,' said Kim. With their orders, she hurried off through the low door, which was the main entrance to the 16th century ancient brick, detached building. Bella could see through the low windows that it was packed inside, and most of whom she could see were tucking in to large plate-fuls of food, each table squeezed or manoeuvred round the quirkiness of the wonky shaped rooms, higgledy piggledy walls, low beams and ceilings and large fireplaces, which she could imagine would roar with flames from log fires in the winter.

'It's heaving!' commented Bella, as they walked around the side of the building into the beautifully kept gardens with expansive lawns, borders and trees providing much needed shade during hot, heady, summer days.

'Usually is. They must make an absolute fortune. In winter, when it's too cold to sit outside - though some brave souls do - you have to book a table about two weeks in advance if you want to eat. The bar is always crammed full with drinkers squeezed in like sardines. It's so nice that there is a smoking ban inside, years ago I'd never go into the bar because I'd choke as soon as I entered, but now it's heaven as far as I'm concerned.'

'I'm with you on that, it's made such a difference. Don't mind if people want to smoke, that's their choice, but as a non-smoker I don't want to inhale their smoke.'

All the time she was talking, Jennifer was scanning the packed tables in the garden, like a lion waiting to pounce, she was waiting for her prey to move. She tugged on Bella's arm and whispered surreptitiously. 'Over there,

122

they're getting ready to go, let's sidle over.' Jennifer was aware that more people had arrived after them, and that if they didn't move quickly the table would be nabbed from right under their nose, unfortunately, the latest arrivals had seen the opportunity to nab a table too. Jennifer's subtle amble turned into a race to get there first. She weaved through the other tables as elegantly as she could, and got there moments before the others. She smiled politely at the rather startled current occupants. 'I don't want to chase you away, but I thought you looked as though you were about to leave?' she politely enquired.

The rotund, red-faced man laughed a deep booming laugh. 'Don't worry, we are going, it's always a challenge to get a table, looks like you made it in the nick of time!'

By this time, Bella had caught her up and gave what she hoped was a winning smile and thanked them profusely for the table, quickly sitting down as they were getting up so that there could be absolutely no doubt as to the new ownership of the table. Jennifer meanwhile, was smiling politely at the tall lanky male who had rather impolitely pushed past people in order to try to get to the table first. He scowled at her, and his girlfriend laid into him in a high pitched whining voice, complaining at his ineptitude for not getting there first.

Kim arrived with their drinks and the chalk board with that night's menu written on it. 'Fun getting the table, eh?' she whispered, for all in close proximity were now in no doubt as to who had not got the table.

'I feel almost sorry for him having to put up with that,' smirked Jennifer, 'but we were here first, there's no disputing that. Cheers!' she said picking up her glass of beautifully chilled Sauvignon Blanc – her only alcoholic drink of the evening - and chinked glasses with Kim and Bella who had opted to share a large jug of Pimms.

Life seemed good to Bella, basking in the evening sunshine, enjoying the company of new friends, in a beautiful rural setting, which - apart from the general hum of talk radiating from the other tables - was peaceful, no road noise, just the chattering of birds as they prepared to settle down for the evening, and the occasional bee who was out for the last drop of evening nectar. She virtually salivated at the menu, everything on it sounded delicious and the plates which were being brought out to surrounding tables made her tummy rumble in anticipation. She settled on cold poached salmon with salad – apparently the salads would be like none she'd ever come across before – along with baby new potatoes, opting to have a pudding instead of a starter as she knew she would not have room for three courses. Kim also chose the Salmon, and Jennifer chose the homemade haddock fish cakes.

They chatted whilst they waited for their order to arrive, which took some time as it was so busy and the food was all made to order. Kim seemed animated and happy and kept furtively glancing to the side of the building from around which Bella and Jennifer had walked earlier. Suddenly she jumped up.

'Oh look!' she cried. 'There's Seb! What a lovely surprise!' She waved at him and he strolled over.

Bella turned to look. A surprise? She was not so sure. He looked clean and fresh, and his face was bright and shining as he greeted Kim, they cautiously kissed each other on the cheek. He greeted Jennifer and Bella, kissing them both on the cheek too.

'What a lovely surprise!' reiterated Kim. 'Are you meeting someone?'

'No. I just thought I'd pop in for a drink. I saw Jen's car in the car park and thought I'd drop by and say hello.'

'Why don't you join us? We'd love it if you did, wouldn't we?' Kim looked expectantly at the other two, who smiled in agreement.

'Before I do, I'll get a drink. What can I get you?' He hurried off to get the drinks, a mineral water for Jennifer, and another large jug of Pimms for Bella and Kim. Bella couldn't remember the last time she'd drunk so much, and was beginning to feel light headed, particularly as her empty stomach was protesting ferociously for its food. As luck would have it, the food turned up and Bella tucked in as though she'd not eaten for a week. True to what she had been told, the food was excellent and the salads unusual and varied, not the run of the mill lettuce and tomato which was the standard offering in pubs.

Feeling slightly more sober as a result of the food hitting her stomach, Bella observed with interest the interaction between Seb and Kim - they were so easy together, as though they were two pieces of a jigsaw which fitted together perfectly - made for each other. She remembered what Mia had told her about their history together, and wondered how Kim could ever have chosen Rupert over Seb. Still, we all make mistakes, and it was apparent to Bella that Rupert had been Kim's. Bella wondered whether Kim regretted marrying Rupert? Did she regret breaking off her engagement to Seb? Sporadically Bella joined in the conversation, but felt sure that Jennifer was watching Kim and Seb as closely as she was. They seemed so wrapped up in one another and lapsed into periods of appearing not to notice that Jennifer and Bella were still present, only to remember with a jolt and then act cooley towards one another, as though hoping that neither Bella nor Jennifer had noticed how they were interacting. Having polished off a large bowl of creamy, homemade, strawberry ice cream, Bella felt replete, but slightly guilty that she'd eaten so much - so much for her diet!

Eventually at 11.30pm, she and Jennifer managed to get Kim into the car, who was on such a high that if Bella had not seen her with Seb she would have been convinced that Kim was popping mode enhancing pills or on the edge of some dreadful breakdown - the high before the plummeting low. They dropped Kim off, and she cheerily waved to them as she went inside. For a few minutes Bella and Jennifer sat in silence as they drove towards the village.

'Did you notice?' asked Jennifer.

'What?' Bella answered cautiously.

'Seb and Kim.'

'Yeah. You couldn't help but notice. Do you think Kim arranged to meet him at the pub? When we first suggested going out, she looked slightly disappointed. Do you think she had already arranged to see Seb?'

'Hmm, I wondered that. Bit quick after Rupert though.'

Bella remained tight lipped about what Mia had told her regarding Kim preparing to leave Rupert, sure that it was not generally known within the group, and she was not going to be the one to break a confidence. Instead she said 'Maybe they're just friends? They've known each other for years, he could be comforting her through this very difficult time.'

'Possibly. Not convinced though.'

Fortunately, they had just pulled up outside Bella's cottage and she felt relieved that she wouldn't feel obliged to be drawn into further discussions on the subject of Kim and Seb any further. 'Thanks ever so much for tonight. I've really enjoyed myself. See you soon.'

'Pleasure. We should do it again.'

'Absolutely! Bye.'

Bella snuggled down for the night, leaving her mind to assimilate the information whilst she slept peacefully.

Chapter Ten

Bella's head throbbed when she woke up, and gradually she recalled how much she'd drunk. Although she hadn't been drunk, a steady stream of alcohol had processed its way through her system. - something it was unaccustomed to. Worst of all, she'd forgotten to drink water before bed, so she felt dehydrated and her mouth felt dry and disgusting. She struggled out of bed and into the bathroom and winced at her reflection, hair wild and knotted and skin looking sallow. Repeatedly she splashed handfuls of ice cold water onto her face, and patted it dry, waking her up enough to pull on her dressing gown and go downstairs to make, what she hoped would be, a restorative cup of coffee. Whilst waiting for the kettle to boil she glugged down a large glass of water, and prepared a couple of pieces of toast and marmalade. As the terrace at the back of the house was not overlooked, she went out in her dressing gown to eat her breakfast, the warm sunshine making her have to fight the soporific effect it was having on her. Reluctantly, at ten o'clock, she went upstairs and put on a pair of beige Bermuda shorts and a pale blue polo shirt. As she was dragging the brush through her hair for the final time, there was a knock on the door. Hurriedly she scooped her hair into a loose ponytail, and trotted downstairs to see who it was.

She smiled with pleasure when she saw it was Dave. 'Hi! Come in,' she welcomed. 'Coffee?'

'Love some please. Hope I'm not disturbing you?' He stooped under the doorway and followed her out to the kitchen, where she hurriedly tidied up her breakfast things, which she had left littered across the surfaces.

'Beautiful day,' he commented as she whizzed about tidying up and making the coffee.

'Certainly is.' She glanced up into his pale blue eyes and was once again struck by the kindness she saw reflected in them. 'Is this business or pleasure?' She didn't want to be presumptuous assuming that the visit wasn't for business, but she wanted to be sure, very much hoping that it was for pleasure.

'A mix really.' He saw a flutter of disappointment flick across her face, and was inwardly pleased. 'Mainly pleasure though.' He was even more delighted by the smile which came back to him. 'On the business front, we're still looking into the connection between Rupert and Kit. Once I can tell you anything, I will.'

She looked at him curiously, convinced that he had more information, but for whatever reason could not, or would not, tell her.

'That's the business over with. I know it's short notice, but I wondered if you're free for lunch tomorrow? Give me the opportunity to dazzle you with my culinary expertise?' he joked, but smiled hopefully.

'I'd love to! Nothing planned for tomorrow. What time?'

129

'Come whenever you like, come for coffee first, whatever suits you.'

'Okay. How far away do you live?'

'Not far, about ten minutes, in the village of Brookhurst.'

'How about 11.30 then? Church will be finished by 11 a.m., I'll come after that.'

'Perfect. Let me scribble down some directions and my address.'

She passed him a pad and pencil and watched the concentration on his face as he deftly drew a little map, wrote directions, address and telephone number. He could feel her gaze on him and glanced up; she blushed as though caught in the middle of something she shouldn't be doing.

'Here you are,' he said handing her the details.

'Thanks,' she tucked it safely under the fruit bowl so that it wouldn't blow away in the breeze. 'Let's have the coffee outside, it's glorious out there.'

They chatted about old times, happy times, when they were both still happily married, not dwelling on their very different reasons as to why it was no longer the case. Eventually Dave got up and bade Bella farewell until the next day. She closed the door behind him, and felt a rosy glow about her. Dreamily she munched her way through a salad sandwich, then went for a cycle ride - yet again determined to get fit and lose some more weight. She huffed and puffed her way through the country lanes and returned red-faced, and sweating profusely, her hair plastered to her head underneath her helmet. Thank goodness there's no one to see me in this state, she mused, as she pushed the bike into the garage and hurried inside to have a shower before someone did. The cool water splashed down onto her overheated body, gradually chilling her down. The endorphins had kicked in, and she felt on a high as she washed her hair, scrubbed her body, shaved her legs and primed herself in readiness for the lunch tomorrow. As she stepped out of the shower, she caught a glimpse of her body in the mirror, convincing herself that she had lost weight since this morning.

Wanting to get a little gift of some kind to take the next day, she gulped down yet another glass of water, picked up her purse and keys and strolled across the village green to the delicatessen, which was further along from the post office. The post office and delicatessen acted like the bread to the terrace of houses in between, which were like the jam. Despite having lived in the village for a few weeks, for one reason or another Bella had never made it in to the delicatessen. The windows looked enticing, and there was an old fashioned, dark green awning shadowing them, keeping the bright sun away from the delectable goodies on display.

Bella walked through the already open door onto oak floorboards - the store had a traditional feel but with a slight contemporary edge to it. She browsed through the unusual products which lined the walls and then inspected the glass fronted, chilled display cabinets. The woman behind the counter gave her a cheery hello and left her to it, something Bella appreciated - she was obviously not related to or of the same ilk as Sharon at the post office - and for which Bella felt relief. Having gone in just to buy a gift for Dave – a bottle of champagne, not original, but she felt it would suit the occasion, a celebration of friendship – she ended up buying several small pots of delicious looking salads, a few slices of Parma ham, a small portion of cooked lobster, and a small raspberry tart.

Whilst she was waiting for her purchases to be wrapped, she noticed that in the other half of the shop, behind a multitude of products, was a small coffee shop area where you could have a drink and order some of the offerings from the shop to eat. As she paid, she became aware of someone standing beside her and glanced to politely smile at whoever it was. Bella was surprised to see Florence, whom she'd not seen since Rupert's funeral.

'Hello! How are you?' she smiled, noting that, in her opinion, Florence didn't look well at all. She looked even thinner than before, her skin was grey and dull and her long, straight, golden blonde hair was lank and unkempt.

'I'm fine,' she replied quietly.

Bella rustled with her bags whilst Florence bought some ham and a pot of salad, curious to know why such a beautiful English rose - albeit currently obscured - should now look like one which had finished blossoming and needed dead-heading.

'I don't suppose,' Bella said, suddenly having an idea, 'you'd like to have a coffee with me? Here, or you could come up to the house?'

A haunted and panicked look flitted across Florence's face.

'Just a quick cup. If you've got time. I've not been in here before, I'm sure their coffee must be great, everything else looks it.' ploughed on Bella. The woman who had been serving them hovered discreetly in the background.

Reluctantly, realising that it would be tricky to get out of given Bella's persistence, Florence politely agreed and followed Bella over to a small, round, wooden table with two chairs. There were a few other people enjoying a drink, and the young girl serving appeared almost immediately to take their order. Must be a weekend job, thought Bella, as the girl could barely be sixteen or seventeen.

Bella chatted away whilst their coffees were being made. It was only when their cappuccinos were in front of them that she looked steadily at Florence, who was doing her utmost to avoid eye contact. 'So, how are you, really?'

Florence smiled feebly, her green eyes looked sad, and the gold in them had lost their shine. 'I'm fine.'

'You look, um…' Bella sought for the right word, 'distracted, a little stressed, compared to when I met you at Sophie and Harry's party?' I must sound really impudent, she thought, I hardly know the woman yet I'm quizzing her.

Florence stared at her for a moment, and then with an almost imperceptible shake of the head, she forced a smile onto her face. 'Oh, just busy, you know, work and that sort of thing. How are you? Are you settling in to the village alright? Sorry I couldn't make it to the tennis yesterday, had to work, would have been such fun. How is everyone?'

Hmm, thought Bella, odd that she's asking me, they're her friends. Hasn't she been in contact with them? 'They're fine, everyone seemed on good form yesterday, even Kim, considering what she's going through.' Did Florence just wince when I mentioned Kim's name? She felt something go ping in her head. Of course, how could she be so stupid? Florence must have been one of the many who had had, or was having, an affair with Rupert! That would explain why she looked so awful, because she's mourning him herself.

'Good. It must be difficult,' she stuttered, tears welling up in her eyes.

Bella patted her hand. 'Difficult for a lot of people,' she replied with meaning.

Florence looked startled. 'I guess so,' she replied in a whisper.

Bella sipped her coffee and felt it wise to change the subject. 'So, how do you enjoy living here? You've been here about a year right?' Florence nodded. 'Where did you move from?'

She shrugged. 'It seems a long time ago now,' she replied wistfully.

Bella frowned. 'Really? Did you move away from family?'

Florence shook her head sadly. 'My parents died within six months of each other, two years ago. I have no family.'

'I'm sorry. I didn't mean to pry.' Bella felt guilty, she'd tried to move the conversation onto innoxious ground, and failed. Wracking her brains for something more light-hearted to discuss, she changed the subject again. 'What's the village fête like? Were you here for the last one?' The fête was a much talked about event, particularly in the post office, and would be taking place next month.

'It was fun last year. It was rather a traditional fête, seemed very popular.' She gulped down the remainder of her coffee and stood. 'Thanks for that. I'm sorry, but I really do have to go. Perhaps another time?'

'Sure. Thanks. Bye, take care.' Bella watched the waif-like figure disappear as fast as it could through the door. She felt unsettled by the meeting: was I too inquisitive, did I over-step the mark? Bella wasn't sure. She picked up her bags, paid for the coffee, and wandered thoughtfully through the late afternoon sunshine back to her cottage. Bella couldn't put her finger on it but there was something bugging her, she just couldn't work out what it was.

The next morning Bella spent an inordinately long period of time preparing herself before church, far longer than she normally would for a lunch with a friend. The previous evening had been spent rummaging through her wardrobe, in an attempt to find the perfect outfit for the lunch. She found it difficult to find the right balance – not too casual, not too formal – and finally settled on a cornflower blue cotton dress which was loose but with a touch of shape to it. She fiddled with the buttons which ran from top to bottom, should she leave one or two undone at the top? At the bottom? She pursed her lips and peered into the mirror, studying herself. Sighing, finally she decided she was being ridiculous and did all the buttons up - as it was a shirt-type dress the shape of the neckline came down in a V shape, she decided that if she exposed too much flesh Dave might get the wrong idea. Or was that what she wanted?

Carefully checking her make-up again, she slipped out of the house, and hurried up to the church, all her deliberations having made her later than usual. She slid into a pew just as the service was starting and, try as hard as she might, found she couldn't focus or concentrate properly, surreptitiously checking her watch every few minutes, eager to get away. With relief, and guilt, that the service was over she made polite conversation with a few of the congregation and made her getaway without staying for coffee. She hurried back to the house, trying not to run and make herself all hot and sweaty in the humid sultry morning.

Bella raced upstairs, went to the loo, swept her long, brown/blonde hair into a knot at the back, and secured it into place. Carefully she checked her make-up and reapplied her rose pink lipstick. Giving herself a final once-over in the full length mirror in the bedroom, and, satisfied with what she saw, she trotted downstairs, retrieved the perfectly chilled bottle of champagne out of the fridge along with the directions from underneath the fruit bowl. Though she'd read them a dozen times since yesterday, she still read them again to ensure she wouldn't get lost.

Slipping behind the wheel of her blue Golf, she eased the car out into the lane and turned left at the bottom, in the direction of Brookhurst. Cruising along the country lane with the windows open just a crack - so her hair wouldn't get spoilt - she glanced up in the direction of Fred and Mia's house as she whisked by the end of their drive. What would they think of her having lunch with Dave? They'd met him a few times at various parties she and Hugh had thrown, before Dave and Alison moved away. She wondered whether they would remember them both?

Brookhurst, like Monhurst, was a pretty little Kent village. It had the church, the pub, the post office cum shop and a tiny little bakers, but no green. She drove past the post office on the left and took the second left, into a small cul-de-sac of about six modestly sized, detached houses. She pulled up outside Number 4, and admired the pristine, postage-stamp sized piece of lawn in front of the house. There was no car on the drive, her heart sank, but hoped it was in the garage and he'd not been called out, realising that she'd forgotten to check her answer phone in her rush to get to his house.

The modest, modern, red brick house, built in the 1970s or 1980s she estimated, looked very neat and well cared for from the outside. The front door was central in the façade, and on either side was a window along with three windows on the first floor. As she walked up the path, the front door opened, and her fears that he'd been called out were allayed. He beamed at her and gave her a soft kiss on each cheek.

'You found it alright then?' She nodded, beaming back at him, feeling slightly off-kilter that she found him so attractive in his pale beige chinos and short sleeved pale blue shirt. 'Come in, let me show you around.' Still grasping the bottle of champagne, Bella followed him into a small sitting room, that - whilst tidy and neat - looked worn and tired; the small dining room looked unused, and the downstairs loo had an avocado suite which had gone out of fashion a long time ago. She followed him into the kitchen, which was bright and airy; there was a small table with room for two, and a dated, wooden, fitted kitchen, all spotlessly clean and tidy.

'Oh, here,' she said, suddenly remembering the champagne, 'I brought you this.'

He took it appreciatively. 'Thanks. It's been a while since I've had champagne! I'll put it into the fridge to keep cool and open it shortly.'

'Great,' she replied, feeling tongue-tied, like a schoolgirl on a first date.

'Let me show you the garden. Shall we have coffee out there or would you actually like to go straight to champagne?' he grinned.

'Coffee'd be lovely. I think one glass of champagne will be my limit as I'm driving.'

'Not that I want to encourage you to drink, but I think you could have a couple, along with lots of water, after all you're going to be here for a while?' he said hopefully.

She grinned back, and followed him into the garden, expecting it to be the usual microscopic size - of which modern houses tended to be allotted. Instead she was taken aback to see a large, colourful garden which disappeared off into the distance towards a little wooded area. 'Wow! I wasn't expecting this.' she cried.

He laughed. 'You mean, because of the size of the house?'

She blushed and stuttered. 'Oh, I didn't mean that, I just meant it's huge, it's beautiful.'

'Don't worry. Everyone has the same reaction. I did too when I first saw the house - it's what made me fall in love with it. The previous owner negotiated with the landowner who owns all the land at the back of these houses and purchased an acre from him. Half a dozen of the trees at the bottom belong to me then there's a fence. Apparently, he refused to sell any land to the other householders, just to the previous owner of this house. Needless to say all the neighbours are jealous.

She laughed. 'I'm not surprised. It's stunning. The lack of land is the only issue I have with modern houses, the gardens are normally so small that you can barely fit in a garden table and chairs.'

'I agree. Gardening has become one of my passions since Alison left. We used to just keep it as grass. Alison wanted a patio, grass and nothing else. It was hideously bland. Guess there's got to be some pluses to one's wife leaving!'

She smiled, not knowing whether he was joking or feeling wistful. 'It's certainly not bland, it's beautiful. You must spend hours weeding the borders.' They strolled slowly down the paths, which weaved in and around the borders and round the lawn.

'Oh, it's not too bad. If you keep on top of it, it doesn't take long at all. I usually pop out and potter around for half an hour each night or morning, and spend more time at the weekend, or whenever I have a day off. My next grand plan is to create a vegetable plot.' They arrived at the grassy area towards the end of the garden. 'I thought I'd create it here. The shed's nearby and the tap. It gets plenty of sunshine, and it's far enough away from the wooded bit to not be affected by it, in terms of shade and leaves fluttering down onto it in the autumn.'

'Sounds good. When are you going to start?'

'Later this summer. Missed my chance to grow things for this summer, but I might still have the opportunity to grow some vegetables over the winter if I get it done before summer ends, though I'm not sure, I'll try and get it ready before the autumn anyway.'

They chatted easily together, coffee turned into champagne, champagne into lunch and before Bella knew it 5pm had arrived. She was reluctant to leave, but keen not to outstay her welcome.

'I'd better be going,' she said, getting up out of the comfortable chair she'd been ensconced in for the afternoon.

'If you think so?' he replied, hopeful that she'd stay longer.

Bella hesitated, tempted to stay, but decided she'd best leave whilst the going was good. 'Thanks. It's been a lovely afternoon. I've really enjoyed myself and your cooking is great, those classes have certainly paid off!'

He grinned back at her. 'Glad you approve. Perhaps you'd let me dazzle you again sometime?'

'I'd like that, but maybe you should sample my cooking first - though don't go getting your hopes up!'

'But you're a super cook. I remember all the delicious dishes you'd cook for your parties. I always thought how lucky Hugh was to come home and have a tasty meal waiting for him every day, he often mentioned what you'd cooked him - being the food-lover that he was.'

Bella blushed deeply and muttered "thanks" as she hurried to the door.

'Thanks for coming Bella. I can't remember the last time I enjoyed myself so much.' He kissed her gently on the cheek, lingering for a moment longer than necessary.

Bella didn't think it was possible for her to blush much more, but she did. 'Thank you too. I've really enjoyed myself. See you soon.'

'I hope so,' he called as she got into her car, waiting by the door and waving until she was out of sight.

Once on the main road, she put the windows down to cool herself down. She was buzzing, on a total high, and not due to the champagne which had long gone through her system. It had been years since she'd felt like this, could it really be possible that she, Bella Sparkle, might find love again? Hugh had always been the love of her life, and no one could ever replace him, but she missed the companionship which came with a good, solid, loving relationship. She'd thought so many times that she would never be able to feel anything for another man, how could she possibly after loving Hugh so much? She'd never been able to understand how widowed wives or husbands could go on to have relationships and marry again, but now she had an inkling. However, balanced with the excitement was also the guilt - the sense that she was betraying Hugh, that somehow she was diluting her love for him and their relationship, that she might forget her love for him. In the space of a few minutes she went from high to low and back again. On impulse, as she approached Fred and Mia's house, she indicated right and drove up their drive, pleased to see that their cars were there.

She hopped out and knocked on the door. No reply. She trotted round the side of the house, calling out. She could hear the faint thump of rock music coming from upstairs, no doubt from Tess's room.

'Hello!' cried Mia who was sitting on the terrace. She put the pile of Sunday newspapers down and got up to greet her. 'It's good to see you. Fancy a drink?'

'Please. Cup of tea would be nice,' she whispered, having noticed that Fred was tilted back in his chair fast asleep, jaw drooping, mouth open. She waited until they were in the kitchen, before speaking again. 'Hope you don't mind, I was just passing and thought I'd pop in.'

'Don't be an idiot, of course I don't mind! You ought to know you can pop in anytime.' She looked suspiciously at her friend. 'Been out somewhere nice?'

Bella blushed the colour of a particularly ripe tomato. 'Oh, er, just out.'

'Come on Bella, you're as red as anything. What have you been up to? You've not been snooping have you?'

'No I have not!' she responded hotly, then giggling nervously.

'Come on, spill the beans, there's obviously something.'

141

'Well, I just had lunch with a friend.'

'Really?' Mia stared hard at her.

There was a prolonged silence as Bella decided what, or if, or how much, to tell Mia.

'I'm waiting.'

'Just lunch with Dave. You know. Inspector Ormandy, he trained with Hugh.'

'Of course! I knew I'd seen him somewhere before how on earth could I have forgotten! My brain must be going to mush, didn't you even mention something in the last few days about him training with Hugh? And?'

'I might have. And what?'

'You're determined to make this as painful as possible aren't you? Lunch, what about it?'

'He just invited me to lunch, to, you know - to catch up.' She glanced away, not wanting to look Mia directly in the eyes.

'Isn't he married? Didn't he have some ghastly wife, as I seem to recall.'

'Mia! She wasn't ghastly. Anyway she left him. They're divorced now.'

'Ah,' replied Mia with feeling.

I'm not getting into this, thought Bella, regretting having said anything to Mia. 'Have you had a nice weekend?'

'Yes, and you're not getting off that easily,' she retorted.

Bella ignored her comment. 'I saw Florence yesterday.'

'How is she? I called her last week and left a message but she's not phoned back, I really must try again.'

'Bumped into her in the deli in the village. She looked awful, I thought. Really thin and run down, depressed even, like something was weighing her down, worrying her.'

'Oh? I hope she's okay. I'll track her down this week.'

'I don't suppose…' Bella hesitated, 'she wasn't one of Rupert's women was she? I mean she looks like she's in mourning.'

'Florence? I don't think so. Not his type, not glamorous enough. I don't think they'd met before Sophie and Harry's party.'

'Mmm. She is pretty - I know she doesn't seem to dress very stylishly - not that I can talk! - and certainly doesn't do anything to show off her features, but she's got that English Rose look about her, and she's not likely to tell anyone if she's had, or was having, an affair with him.'

'I suppose. I guess anything is possible.'

At that moment a sleepy looking Fred appeared in the doorway. 'Hi Bella. Thought I heard voices.'

'Sorry Fred, hope I didn't wake you?'

'No, just resting my eyes for a bit,' he grinned.

'Do you know if Florence was having an affair with Rupert,' asked Mia bluntly whilst busily making a pot of tea.

Fred looked puzzled. 'Where did that come from?'

'Bella saw Florence yesterday, and said she was looking awful. Just wondered if you'd heard anything.'

He shook his head. 'Nope. Tried to steer well clear of Rupert's private life. He was playing with fire messing around the way he did. I'm surprised Kim put up with it for so long. Rupert was a great guy in many respects, but I think he was a total idiot when it came to women, and he seemed to be getting more reckless, more careless as the months went by.'

Bella pondered on this. So it could quite easily have been possible for Florence and Rupert to have been having an affair? Did anyone else know? Did Kim know?

'Perhaps she's got other worries on her mind. Just because she's looking depressed doesn't mean to say she was having an affair with Rupert,' commented Mia, flapping at Fred to come over and take the tray outside. 'Maybe she's having problems at work.'

Bella grabbed another chair and seat cushion, and pulled it over to where her friends had been sitting, and settled back with her cup of tea. 'Suppose.' she murmured thoughtfully.

'Enjoying village life Bella?' enquired Fred amiably.

'Well… it's not as quiet as I thought it would be!'

The conversation flowed easily and, despite Mia's attempts at trying to extricate further information about the lunch Bella had had with Dave, Bella managed to extract herself after an hour, without having revealed anything else.

Chapter Eleven

In a frantic attempt to keeping improving her fitness levels, Bella spent the early part of the week cycling - a lot - and eagerly checking her answer phone and mobile for a message from Dave. The former was successful, but the latter was not so. She'd left a message on his mobile on Sunday night to thank him for a delightful day, and had heard nothing from him since, not even a text. It niggled away at her, worried that she'd scared him off in some way, and cross with herself for get carried away and allowing herself to start feeling emotions for another man.

By Wednesday there had still been no call from him. Every time the landline or her mobile rang she raced to pick it up in the hope that it would be him, and each time was disappointed. However, that afternoon she was off to Cressa's house. Cressa had phoned the previous day: the girls were going round for a catch up she'd said, and she wondered if Bella would like to join them? This at least perked her up. It was nice to be included, be welcomed and given the opportunity to develop new friendships. And to keep her occupied that morning, and in an attempt to get her mind off Dave again, she'd been for an early cycle, had breakfast and was now ready to go to the Farmers' Market.

This time Bella went prepared, armed with several bags stuffed into her shoulder bag which would make it easier for her to carry her goodies home. As usual it was crowded and Bella weaved her way in and out of people, making purchases at the stalls which took her fancy. In fact, she was again tempted to make a purchase from every stall but restrained herself, after her previous over-purchasing during her last visit she didn't want any food left over which might go to waste. She glanced at the clock, it was 10.20am, then looked at the queue which was again forming by the empty table, and smiled to herself. They knew he was coming and that their patience would pay off: Bread Man would make his entrance soon, though obviously he was late as usual as the Market started at 10am, but many stall holders were ready well before then.

Bella decided to have a cup of coffee, and somehow managed to balance the cup and saucer whilst carrying her bags and shoulder bag. She didn't recognise anyone sitting at the other tables, and felt a twinge of loneliness as she sat sipping her coffee. Bella observed the, what she assumed was, regular group of elderly people, who had pushed several tables together and marked their territory, as they had done previously. They were busy sharing out cakes which one of them had made, not, Bella noticed, purchased from the market which she felt was a little bit cheeky, but at least they were purchasing cups of coffee and tea and it looked as though a few of them had bought some produce from stall holders. They very much gave the impression that they were holding court, and Bella felt woe betide anyone who tried to mess with them - elderly they may be, but I bet they're not wallflowers, she thought. She mischievously imagined various scenarios of what would happen if someone sat at "their" table before they had arrived.

She was interrupted from her musings by a pleasant-faced, well-rounded woman in her fifties, who enquired whether it would be alright for her to join Bella at the table as the others were fully occupied. Bella smiled, happy to oblige and made polite but friendly conversation with her. It gave Bella a warm, fuzzy feeling, so many strangers being so friendly. Realizing that Bread Man had not only arrived but almost sold out, she made her excuses and hurried over to purchase a fresh loaf and a large white floury bap. Trotting happily back to the house, it was only as she opened the door and saw the phone that she thought about Dave. Determined not to check the answerphone - situated bizarrely in the unused dining room and of which she didn't feel was her place to move - nor her mobile, she hurried though to the kitchen, put away her purchases and made herself an early lunch of fresh smoked salmon pate inside the white flour bap with vibrant green rocket. She sunk her teeth into it and sighed with contentment at the delectable combination. Replete from this delight, she picked up the - as yet untouched - newspaper and did her best to concentrate on reading it, determined that she would not check the answerphone. She was not going to become emotionally reliant on any man again, she told herself fiercely, she'd coped somehow since Hugh had died, and that was not going to change.

Having managed to restrain herself from the temptation and get to 2pm, she briskly walked upstairs and changed into her pale blue dress. Bit of a mistake she thought as she did it up, as memories of lunch the previous Sunday came flooding back. Still, I am not going to let him, or

147

anyone else, dominate my life. So with resolute determination she left the dress on, swept her hair up into a twirl, smoothed on some lip gloss and left the house for Cressa's.

In her car, Bella turned left at the green, and first right after a short distance into Coppice Lane, where the trees lined the road and branched over high above, creating the appearance of a leafy arch through which to drive. A short distance further on she turned left into their drive, noticing that, not too much farther down the lane, was where Rupert had died.

The house itself was beautiful, and Bella wondered if all of Fred and Mia's friends lived in such large, fabulous houses, which were most definitely not a true representation of the average property. She knew it had four bedrooms from earlier conversations, and that it was constructed of brick and tile hung under a Kent peg tile roof. There was a faded - slightly neglected air about the house - the sort of impression you get when you visit a stately home where there isn't enough money to maintain it properly. It looked neat, and the drive - and what she could see of the garden - was well manicured, but she supposed that it didn't cost much to maintain a garden if one did it oneself.

She rapped on the door using the cast iron door knocker and waited. Mia's car was already in the drive, as was Kim's ice blue Mercedes SLK. It was only then that Bella realised she could have given Jennifer a lift, annoyed she didn't think of it earlier.

'Hi Bella, come in,' welcomed Cressa upon opening the door, her tall willowy frame filling it.

She followed Cressa down a long dark corridor, past the staircase, surreptitiously glancing in through the door to the sitting room as they passed by. It, like the exterior of the house, looked as though it needed a bit of money spending on it, small bits of plaster had fallen off the wall and the sofa was frayed around the edges. Despite this, the house had a very warm, homely feel about it, one which suggested it was a happy home. They arrived in the dated kitchen, similar to the one that Dave had. There he was again popping into her head when she didn't want him to - she scowled inwardly to herself but outwardly smiled at Mia and Kim. The kitchen was spacious, with the requisite AGA - this time in a traditional green colour - located in the fireplace at one end of the room, making the room stiflingly hot on this warm summer's day, but there appeared to be no other form of cooking facility, so Bella assumed there was no alternative but to leave it on and swelter.

Cressa pulled the large jug of Pimms she had prepared earlier out of the fridge and placed it on a tray with some glasses.

'Come on, let's get out of here, it's too hot,' she grimaced, leading the way through an open doorway into the back garden. They sat on some wooden garden chairs which had seen better days, but were still usable, and the matching table wobbled slightly as Cressa placed the tray down onto it. 'Anyone want water?' she asked pouring four glasses of the amber liquid.

'Yes please,' replied Bella all too aware, from the other night, of the effect Pimms now had on her.

Cressa returned a few moments later with a jug of water and several glasses, followed by Jennifer, Sophie and baby Jemima. Bella wondered whether the baby ever stopped smiling, every time she saw her she had a big grin on her face.

149

'How's Jack?' enquired Mia.

Mmm, how is he, mused Bella. Wonder if she's tackled him about his behaviour?

'He's fine,' Cressa replied, sitting back and taking a big gulp of Pimms.

'Really?' added Sophie.

It was obvious to Bella that Cressa had vented to the others about Jack, and not just to her and Mia.

'Yes. I asked him out-right whether he was having an affair.'

'And?' urged Mia.

'At first he looked shocked, then he looked cross, and then he looked as though he was trying hard not to laugh. He said he'd absolutely not been having an affair, but when I asked him why he was being so secretive he refused to tell me. Said I'd just have to be patient, and all would become clear in the fullness of time. I mean, what's that all about?'

Sophie, Kim, Jennifer and Mia all glanced at one another as though they now knew something, Bella was convinced of it. Cressa hadn't picked up on this, but Bella was intrigued to find out what was going on.

'I'm sure if he says he's not having an affair then he's not. He's never lied to you before has he? No. So just trust him Cressa.' advised Kim and she of all people knew what it was like to be lied to and cheated on.

'I do believe him. I think if he were having an affair he would tell me if I asked him directly. I just want to know what he's up to! I've wracked my brains and I can't come up with anything.'

Sophie laughed. 'You're too much of a control freak Cressa. Just let him get on with things for a change.' If

150

that had come from someone who didn't know her quite so well Cressa would have had reason to be furious at such a personal jibe, but she just laughed.

'I know, I know! I like everything to be perfect. Guess that's why the house irritates me so much. I want it to be all pristine and perfect. I want to spend some money on the house, do it up a bit, get some new furniture but Jack says no. I don't know why not, we've got a little bit saved now. It is really irritating.'

'Maybe he's just being cautious? After all, it wasn't so long ago that it looked as though you might lose this house.'

'Don't remind me. Thank goodness we managed to scratch around and find enough to hold onto it.'

Jack and Cressa's financial life had been full of ups and downs, more downs since the failed business deal with Rupert.

Jemima's cute baby giggle broke the contemplative silence the group had slipped in to. How could anyone be gloomy with that gorgeous girl grinning away?

'Any news yet?' asked Cressa, changing the subject.

'No.' Kim gave a long sigh. 'I've had the police poking around, they've wanted access to Rupert's bank accounts, business accounts and all that.

'Why?'

'Dunno. If it helps them find out who killed Rupert then they can snoop as much as they like. I just wish it would all be over. But that's me being rather naïve in hoping that the case will be solved instantly, done and dusted in a flash, so I can push it into the past.'

'Haven't they got any suspects in mind?' enquired Mia. 'I mean, surely they must have some kind of idea?'

Kim shrugged. 'If they have, they're not telling me.'

'Can't you ask your Inspector friend?' asked Jennifer, looking at Bella.

Bella shifted uncomfortably in her chair. 'I don't think that's really appropriate, he must be so busy with the case. Kim would have more chance of getting hold of him as she's the victim in all this - apart from Rupert obviously.' She could feel Mia's questioning gaze burning on the side of her face, and resolutely refused to look in her direction.

'Yeah. But as you've known him for so long he might push it along a bit more as a favour to you?'

'I don't think so. He's far too professional for that, and I'm sure he's doing everything he possibly can. I think he'd be insulted if I suggested otherwise.'

'Oh well, perhaps if you see him you could let us know if he tells you anything?' Jennifer gave her a beady look as she was keen to find out if there was a connection between Rupert and Kit.

'Sure. Anybody taking part in the village fête?' Bella not so subtly changed the subject.

'I've donated a couple of cases of Rupert's wine,' replied Kim.

'Think I've been roped in to help out on a stall,' added Jennifer.

'Gotta make some cakes,' said Cressa.

'Me too,' declared Mia.

'I hear from Florence that it's a good afternoon.'

'You've seen Florence?' asked Cressa, 'I've been trying to track her down for ages, she's not returning any of my calls.'

'Nor mine,' echoed Jennifer, Mia, Sophie and Kim.

'But why? Is there something wrong? How did she seem to you?' asked Kim.

Bella glanced at Mia who shook her head slightly. 'Perhaps a little tired? Not quite as bright and chirpy as she was at the party,' replied Bella diplomatically.

'Hmm. I think I might pop along and see her one evening. Once Harry's back from work he can look after Jemima,' said Sophie.

'Good idea. We don't all want to pounce on her though. Can you go tonight?' asked Jennifer.

'I'll try to.'

Out of habit, and not because she was thinking of Dave, Bella automatically checked her answer phone when she returned late afternoon. Still no messages and still no communication of any kind on her mobile. She sighed miserably and went to change into a pair of shorts and a t-shirt. She flung open the French doors in the sitting room and switched the television on, deciding to lose herself in an evening of rubbishy television after the 6 o'clock news. The sky had clouded over, and there was a heavy greyness in the air which matched her mood. The air was stifling and needed to be cleared and she felt sure that they would be in for a big storm that evening. After an hour she restlessly made herself a salad and rejected the open bottle of wine that was in the fridge, opting for a glass of water instead.

The thunder started to rumble in the distance, followed a little while later by the splosh, splosh, splosh of large drops of rain building up into a downpour. Reluctantly she closed the doors and turned the television up a bit louder in order to hear it over the rumbles and crashes crescendoing outside. She didn't hear the knocking on the door and let out a scream when there was a rap on the front window. It was Dave.

'You almost gave me a heart attack!' Bella cried, letting the bedraggled looking man in. She took his dripping coat and hung it over the banister.

'Sorry. I did knock several times but I suppose there's rather a lot of noise outside.'

'Come through,' she led him into the sitting room, 'would you like a drink?'

He hesitated. 'A cup of tea would be nice, thanks.'

Bella trotted off to make a pot of tea and returned a few minutes later with a couple of mugs of steaming liquid. She passed his to him then sat on a chair across from him, and waited for him to speak.

He looked sheepishly at her. 'I'm sorry I didn't return your call. I meant to, it's just that work has got in the way, and every time I thought I had a few minutes in which to phone you something came up, and I've been getting back really late.'

She felt slightly mollified by this explanation, but still miffed that he hadn't phoned or at least sent a text.

'I'm meant to be getting better at this work/life balance thing but not doing a very good job at the moment. Could we meet up this weekend?' he asked hopefully.

'What did you have in mind?' she replied noncommittally.

'If the weather is fine I thought maybe we could take the bikes up to Bedgebury Pinetum and have a cycle and a picnic?'

She couldn't stay irritated with him for long and smiled. 'That sounds like fun. There aren't too many steep hills are there?'

He laughed. 'No. Don't worry, there are a few slopes but nothing I'm sure you couldn't handle. Is Saturday okay?'

'That'd be lovely.'

'Okay. I'll pick you up about 10 o'clock. I've got a bike rack for the car and it'll easily take two bikes.'

She settled back into the armchair feeling more relaxed, and felt the warmth seeping through from her tea. She sipped it slowly and watched him. The slightly bedraggled look suited him, made him look vulnerable.

He smiled back at her. 'Anyway, as I said, I've been busy at work. I think you'll want to hear this.'

Her ears pricked up and she sat up alert. 'Really? What?'

'You were right. There's a definite link between Rupert and Kit. Unfortunately we haven't been able to find out precisely what it is, as Kit is in America at the moment and is not returning my calls. I've tried tracking him down to every place his office says he's going to be at, but mysteriously he never seems to be there when I phone at the precise time I've been told he is going to be there, and whenever I phone his mobile it either goes straight to voicemail or it rings and is then diverted.'

'Mmm, intriguing. So what have you got to go on?'

'This is confidential, but I trust you not to say anything to anyone. Not yet, not until I am ready.' He looked into her clear blue, beautiful eyes and awaited some kind of acknowledgement.

'Of course,' she murmured looking directly back at him.

155

'We've gone through Rupert's bank accounts and have discovered that regular payments have been made from one of his accounts into an account which is registered in Kit's name. Now, there could be a simple explanation for this but we can find no paperwork to clarify what, or why, this money has been transferred.'

Bella felt a frisson of excitement. Had she found out something relevant? Something which would assist the police in discovering Rupert's killer? 'How much are you talking about and how often?'

He hesitated again. 'Two or three times a year for the past two years. The latest one having been made six months ago, which would mean that, in theory, going on the previous pattern, another payment would have been due about a month ago.'

'And the amounts?' She held her breath in excitement, her heart beating furiously in her chest.

'That's the interesting part. About £50,000 each time.'

Bella let out a whistle. 'That's a lot. So how much has he paid in total? About £250,000?'

'Yes.'

'Wow! That's a huge sum of money. Could he afford that? And what on earth was it for?'

'That's what I need to speak to Kit about. And I think he knows it, but he can't avoid me for ever.'

'Does Kim know? Maybe she knows?'

He shook his head. 'I think if she were aware of these payments she would have confided in someone and it would have got round her close group of friends, but more than likely she would have told me as she is exceedingly keen to find out who is responsible for Rupert's death. Besides which she wouldn't have asked us to find out what the connection was between Rupert and Kit because she would already have known. Now, you are sure that at the party they were, on the face of it, introduced for the first time?'

'Absolutely. No doubt about it. Rupert had this strange look on his face but the impression I got from Kit was that these were first-time introductions, and I'm sure Mia would have told me if they'd met him before.'

'Okay. Until I've tracked Kit down and have more information, I'm not going to discuss this with Rupert's wife. With such large sums involved, it might just cause her more distress.'

'Sure. They have already asked me to ask you to hurry up with the case.'

He frowned at her.

'I told them that you are a professional and that you would be doing your utmost to solve this case.'

'Thanks. For a minute I thought you were implying I wasn't doing my job!'

'Of course not!'

'Good.' He took a long swallow of tea from his mug and felt himself finally starting to thaw out.

'Do you think it's blackmail?'

'I'm keeping an open mind, but it certainly is an option. It's unusual - and annoying - for there not to be any kind of paperwork or hint of a paper trail of some kind, no matter how minimal. The rest of his accounts, both business and personal, have all been meticulously kept. All the paperwork matches up, there is nothing missing, even down to the smallest of receipts. So, yes, it is definitely a possibility.'

Bella's mind tore through the numerous reasons why, she thought, Rupert could have been blackmailed. 'It must have been some pretty massive secret if it was blackmail. What on earth could it be?'

Not prepared to get into speculation, he rose reluctantly from the comfort of his chair. 'Thanks for the tea, I'd best be getting home.' He glanced at the clock - it was 9.30pm already. How quickly the time went when he was in her company. 'But please remember, not a word, not a hint, okay?'

'My lips are sealed. I promise.'

'Good,' he slipped on his still sodden coat and peered out of the door at the rain which was still rushing down in torrents. 'It's supposed to clear by Friday so it should be good for Saturday. I'll see you then.'

She smiled broadly at him. 'Looking forward to it. Take care.'

Chapter Twelve

Bella awoke at 7 a.m. feeling lethargic and unrested. Her mind had been working overtime since Dave had left the previous evening. Curiosity was gnawing away at her and she was becoming illogically desperate to discover why Kit had been blackmailing Rupert. She had concluded that it had to be blackmail, what other possible explanation could there be? She lay there, too weary to get up but annoyingly unable to get back to sleep. With great effort she dragged herself out of bed half an hour later and, having soaked her face in an ice cold flannel, staggered downstairs to make an extra strong cup of coffee.

Rustling in the cupboards, she found an unopened packet of ground caffeinated coffee, and put a couple of scoops into her cafetière. She felt in need of all the help she could to get her body going this morning. Outside the sky was still grey, but the torrential rain had merged into a fine, misty drizzle which gently tickled the window panes. Bella sat at the kitchen table sipping her coffee, waiting for the buzz of caffeine to kick in. After a few minutes of flicking through the day before's paper, she could feel the surge as the potent liquid lit up her veins, as though somebody had suddenly flicked the 'on' switch and energised her whole being.

I wonder, mused Bella, making a start on her second cup: Sharon at the shop seems to know everything - fact or fiction - about so many people, and goings on, in the area, perhaps there's a tiny nugget of information she's forgotten about Rupert which could be teased out?   Though the thought of being ensnared by Sharon was not one Bella relished, if it were a means to an end it would probably be worth it.

An hour later, and with the caffeine still working its magic on her, she hurried down to the post office underneath her blue spotty umbrella, and braced herself for what was to come. As someone who, in general, drank little caffeine - preferring decaffeinated - it had an incredible, mood-enhancing effect on her when she did finally succumb, so it was with relatively high spirits that she entered the shop. Relieved, she found that Sharon was on her own and that they would not be interrupted or overheard by inquisitive busybodies eager to spread more gossip.

'Good Morning Christabel,' smiled Sharon, 'how are you today? Bit wet still out there isn't it, but we need it - my tomatoes are suffering dreadfully, keep forgetting to water them and with not enough rain...'

Bella smiled politely and listened to Sharon witter on whilst she pretended to be looking at the magazines. Feeling that it would be mollifying to make a purchase, she picked up a copy of Kent Life and The Times and took them across to the counter to pay. Sharon continued on with her monologue, whilst Bella fished around in her purse for the correct change and gave, what she hoped was, a winning, friendly smile as she handed it over. As Sharon paused to catch her breath Bella swooped in, having rehearsed a way to bring Rupert into the conversation in a not too conspicuous way.

'I'm hoping to buy some wine, Sharon, and thought I might go up to Rupert's wine place in Stream Lane. Do you know anything about it?'

'You should know, you mix with that lot,' retorted Sharon enviously.

'Well, yes, I'm newly acquainted with them, but I only met Rupert the once. As you seem to know everyone, and everything, about the area...' she trailed off, hoping flattery might get her somewhere, '...I thought you would be the most knowledgeable person to ask. You know, for an unbiased opinion,' she smiled conspiratorially at her. Sharon took the bait.

'Well, since you're asking, I wouldn't normally say, you know I don't like to gossip, too many of those in the village do.' Bella tried hard not to laugh at the irony of it. 'It's a bit pricey. He buys, or rather bought,' she corrected herself, 'fancy wines. Don't know why people want to spend twenty quid on a bottle of wine when you can get a very nice box of wine which lasts longer and costs a lot less.'

'Mmm,' murmured Bella. She thought boxes of wine were hideous but had to admit they'd come a long way in the past few years and were proving to be quite popular. Psychologically she couldn't get her head round drinking wine from a box, it made her think of packets of juice.

Perceiving this as approval and agreement, Sharon continued, fluffing up with self importance. 'If you don't mind pricey though, it's supposed to be quite nice. Never set foot in there myself, wouldn't give him the satisfaction.

161

He was always a jumped-up, snobby, condescending man and that wife of his used to be lovely, why she married him I have no idea! Could only be for the money, why else? She was supposed to marry that lovely Seb, dumped him to go off and marry Rupert. It's beyond me.'

'Really?' Bella tried to act surprised and inwardly gritted her teeth. She loathed gossip - having been the subject of a lot of it when Hugh died - and was beginning to think that she'd made a mistake, that it had been an ill-considered idea to try to tease information out of Sharon.

'Oh yes. If there was a dodgy deal to be done, it would be done by Rupert, ripping people off left right and centre, just look at the prices of his wine! Says it all.' She stood there with her arms folded across her ample chest, with a self-righteous, smug look on her face.

Bella did her best to force a smile and felt it was futile to continue, she wasn't hearing anything of significance, and couldn't stand to listen to the gossipy, spiteful (whether Sharon meant to be or not), drivel spouting out of her mouth any more. 'Well, thanks for that. I might pop along and have a look at the wine, at least you have forewarned me that the wine is not going to be the cheapest. Bye.' She exited hastily and fumbled hurriedly with her umbrella, anxious to get it up and get away from the shop.

Without bothering to take off her coat, she slapped the magazine and paper onto the kitchen table and picked up her car keys. No time like the present, she thought. May as well visit the place now. She hopped into her car and took a right turn onto the village road off the green, shortly after she turned left and half a mile later right into Stream Lane. Another quarter of a mile further along, in the middle of nowhere, she came upon Rupert's wine shop. Aptly named Oast Wines, as the building itself turned out to be a beautifully converted triple kiln oast house. The cowls swung gently in the breeze which had sprung up, misting the drizzle into Bella as she got out of the car.

It was apparent that he had spent a fortune on the place. Everything about it screamed "money". The car park was pristine and there were beautifully filled terracotta pots, filled with a variety of fresh white blooms, welcomingly set by the entrance. I wonder how much local and/or passing trade it gets, mused Bella, after all it's not exactly on a busy through route. There surely could be no significant passing trade to talk of? You'd need to know where it was, and make a special trip. She noticed a couple of smart and relatively new vans parked to one side with "Oast Wines" imprinted in the logo each side. Perhaps a lot of its trade was done on the internet or by phone and then delivered?

Bella pushed the door open and heard a gentle ping from somewhere towards the back of the shop. She stood there in awe at what she saw. The area was enormous - two of the roundels and the adjoining barn sections were opened up to full height, running around at first floor level on each roundel was a galleried area with metal balustrade. On ground floor level Bella could see a huge quantity of stock, but whilst there was obviously a massive range of wines, it was not crammed to the rafters making it impossible to see the wine, nor was it overwhelming or intimidating. In fact it had a comforting, relaxed, welcoming air about it. Something that Bella had not expected.

'Hello. Can I help you at all?' asked a pleasant-looking woman in her thirties, who was dressed in jeans a white shirt and a dark green apron emblazoned with "Oast Wines" on it in gold.

'Oh, er, I think I'd just like to browse at the moment,' replied Bella.

'Of course, please do. If you need any help or advice, just let me know.' She gave Bella a friendly smile and went back to whatever she was working on at the computer.

Bella took a tentative step forward on the mellow oak stripped floor, there were discreet notices indicating which country and which area the wines came from, by far the largest section was dedicated to French wine, but as the whole shop was so huge there was an impressively enormous range from many different countries and regions - almost overwhelmingly so for someone such as Bella who was relatively ignorant about wine - and she was particularly pleased to see a decent sized section dedicated to English wine, which was a rapidly expanding market with a growth in award-winning wines.

Despite what Sharon had said, there was a broad variation in prices, the cheapest she could see was at £4.99 and the most expensive was £70. However, as she weaved her way around she saw a glass door with a sign that indicated that the more expensive wines were on the other side of it in a strictly managed, temperature-controlled environment. How much more expensive? £70 seemed like an awful lot for a bottle of wine to her. Intrigued, she turned the handle and walked through into the cool room, which was rather more dimly lit, presumably an attempt to create the perfect conditions in which to store the wine. She wandered around looking at the prices and whistled to herself. £70 turned out to be rather "cheap" compared to the prices in here, there were plenty of bottles at £1,000 and locked away behind a wrought iron gate were some selling for upwards of £2,500 - for a single bottle. These must be the wines that top London restaurants charged thousands and thousands of pounds for, often triple or more of the price they purchased them at, assumed Bella.

How on earth can anyone possibly pay so much for a bottle of wine? It cost more than the average monthly wage! If Rupert sold plenty of these, with a substantial mark-up, then it was no wonder he had been a multi-millionaire.

Despite their price, there was something very alluring about the wine; it reeked of luxury and extravagance, the likes of which she - and most of the general population - would never experience. As Bella finished looking round, she noticed a discreet security camera tucked up in the corner, inevitable, she concluded, as they would undoubtedly be a prime target for thieves.

She strolled out of the room and continued to wander around, selecting half a dozen bottles of wine, three red, three white. She was intrigued as to what taste difference there could possibly be in the wines. Did the price really match the quality? She therefore chose, in both red and white, a bottle at £4.99, one at £9.99 and one at £20.00.

Bella took her opportunity to - subtly she hoped - probe for information from the sales assistant behind the till, while the bottles were wrapped individually in tissue paper and then placed into a six bottle box with "Oast Wines" emblazoned on the side. Very slick, she thought. At most places you had to make do with a charged-for plastic bag or a redundant old box.

'Lovely place this. I've not been here before.'

'Thank you. I hope we will see you again. We regularly hold wine information evenings and tastings; if you are interested I could take a note of your details and contact you when we next hold an event?' She smiled encouragingly at Bella.

Oh, very smooth, thought Bella, get your details without you even realising it, and be on their mailing list for ever. In an attempt to keep the woman chatting, and to tease information out of her, she agreed. 'Thank you. That would be nice.' She peered at her name badge which was pinned to the top of her apron. It said "Libby".

'I'll just finish packing these for you, and then I'll take your details.'

'Thanks.' She watched as Libby taped up the box then deftly tapped into the computer and produced the bill. 'Have you any events coming up?'

A hint of sadness flickered across Libby's face, and her eyes welled up with tears behind her bright red-rimmed glasses. 'Er, no,' she croaked, then tried to clear her throat. 'Sorry.'

Bingo! Thought Bella. 'That's okay,' she paused hoping that Libby would expand on her response.

'I'm afraid the owner died recently, he was the expert and the owner of the business. We anticipate having some new events lined up for the autumn though.'

'Oh dear!' replied Bella feeling a fraud, 'how awful. That's very sad, was it unexpected?'

'Oh, it was,' Libby sniffed, doing her utmost to remain as professional as possible.

Guessing that Libby had been instructed not to go into any details, Bella tried a different tack. 'It would appear from the set-up here that he knew a lot about wine. I don't think I've ever seen such a huge variety of wines under one roof.'

Libby gave her a watery smile. 'Rupert definitely was an expert, he knew everything there was to know about wine, he was just so knowledgeable and a fantastic person to work for. He was so kind and caring.'

Bella tried to hide her surprise. Kind? Caring? From what she'd seen, though she admitted it wasn't that much, he'd been a horrible person, particularly to his wife. Unless of course Libby had benefited from a few extra 'perks' with the boss. A few after-hours sessions perhaps? 'Sounds like he was a good boss.'

'Oh he was. He was the best.' She looked dreamily into the distance.

'Do many people work here?'

'Oh, quite a few. Some in the office, others like me who work in the shop, the delivery drivers - quite a little family really. And Rupert always made sure that we were trained up properly. He didn't want anyone selling the wine who was ignorant of the products being sold, he took a lot of time and trouble over that. He was so kind, giving me extra tuition if I needed it.'

Yeah right, I know what sort of extra tuition that was. Bella immediately berated herself for such a thought. She smiled encouragingly at Libby.

'That's £69.96 please. I'll pop one of our wine lists on top of the box for you to read at your leisure, you can also see the stock online, the website address is at the bottom. And if you want any information about a specific wine - or the wines you have purchased - or have any queries, please do not hesitate to phone or email us, we're always happy to help.'

'Thanks,' replied Bella handing over her bank card. 'Rupert must have achieved a lot of qualifications to be so knowledgeable about wine?'

She shook her head. 'Oh, no, it was all self-taught. He spent several years travelling the world, picking grapes, working on vineyards and gaining first-hand experience.'

'Really?' she was surprised that Kim hadn't mentioned this when she'd seen the photo.

'Yes, he started off in France, went to Australia, New Zealand, California, Chile, Argentina and South Africa and probably more I imagine.'

'Wow! He did travel. I bet he had some tales to tell!'

'No. He was quite a private man, didn't like people asking questions about his past, he was very much a "living in the moment" sort of person. Shame, I'm sure he would have had some fascinating tales to tell.'

'I'm sure.' Well, there's further confirmation that he was in Australia, noted Bella.

'Let me take your details and I'll contact you when we next have an event coming up.'

Bella dutifully gave Libby her details, though by the time the autumn arrived, she'd be thinking of where to live next. The cottage was only rented for 6 months, but as the owners were away for a year there was possibly potential for a further 6 months, something Bella had initially discounted, not wanting to commit herself for such a long period of time, but her mind was slowly changing in that regard. Libby summoned a young man in his late teens, also wearing an Oast Wines apron, to carry the box out to her car, and Bella thanked her for her help.

When she got back home, she opened the front door, then returned to the car to carry the box in. The white wine she put straight into the fridge and the red she left on the side.

Intrigued by the fact that Libby knew that Rupert had travelled the world picking grapes and developing his knowledge of the wine business, but that Kim appeared not to have known, nor Jennifer either, she popped out to chat it over with Mia in the afternoon, as Mia knew about the photograph.

Bella recounted what Libby had said, and waited for Mia's response. She looked puzzled.

'Rupert never talked about his past. I'm surprised that Kim didn't know though, particularly if a member of Rupert's staff knew.'

'That's what I thought.'

'I guess she could have forgotten, grief can do funny things to the mind.'

'I suppose, but I'm not convinced.'

'But I don't think it's worth mentioning to Kim, she's still emotionally all over the place not surprisingly.'

Bella was impatient to tackle Kim, her sleuthing antennae on red alert. Perhaps, without realising it, Kim knew more than she thought she did?

'I'm sure it must be the stress that's made her forget. I mean, if she'd driven past a few minutes later she would have seen Rupert's accident,' muttered Mia absent mindedly.

Bella gave a start. 'What? What do you mean?'

Mia blushed. 'Bother. Fred made me promise not to tell anyone.'

'Mia! I can't believe it! Are you saying that you saw Kim drive past on the night of Rupert's death?'

Mia fiddled with a fold in her skirt.

169

'Mia?' said Bella sharply.

'I didn't. Fred did. We'd been out to dinner and come back quite early. I opened up the house and Fred walked back down to close the gate as he always does at night. He saw Kim drive past.'

'What time?'

'About 9.50 p.m.'

'And have you told the police?

She shook her head.

'Mia! I can't believe you'd hold information back.'

'Well, neither Fred nor I can possibly believe that Kim had anything to do with Rupert's death, she just wouldn't. I know she wouldn't.'

'Are you sure? Didn't you say she was planning on leaving Rupert?'

'Well, yes. But why would she bother to kill him if she were leaving him? And if she had wanted him dead, I'm sure she would have done it months ago.'

'You're going to have to tell the police. You know you are. Maybe she didn't kill Rupert, but alternatively, she may have seen something - or someone - and that titbit of information could help the police, even if it is to discount a person who may be under suspicion.'

Mia looked cross and upset. 'Just because your friend is leading the investigation, it doesn't mean you can tell me what to do, and don't you dare go sneaking to him!'

'Mia!' sometimes her friend exasperated her. 'It's got nothing to do with Dave being a friend. You know in your heart that you should have told the police, otherwise you wouldn't be reacting like this. You're cross with yourself and you're trying to deflect it onto me. I know it's hard, because Kim is a friend of yours, but don't you think it's important to catch the person who killed Rupert?'

Mia nodded miserably.

'I can't believe you and Fred kept this secret you are probably the most honest people I know.' A thought struck her as she looked at Mia, who was looking decidedly deflated. 'Which direction was she driving in?'

Mia looked furtively away.

'Well?'

'Towards Monhurst.'

So she could have done it, thought Bella. She was going in the right direction close to the time of the accident.

'Shall I call the police, or will you?'

Mia sighed. 'I will. But not until I have spoken to Fred, and then to Kim. See what she has to say for herself.'

'Mia, you know you can't do that, you'll be warning her, giving her a chance to work out her alibi.'

'I don't care. She's my friend and I know she didn't do it.'

'Okay. But I'm coming with you. I like Kim, she's a nice person, but I'm not as emotionally attached to her as you are. I can impartially observe her body language and listen to what she says and I WILL give my opinion to the police.'

Mia glowered at Bella even though she knew her friend was right.

'Let me phone Fred now, and then - but only then - we can go and see Kim.' Mia took herself off to another room and closed the door, precluding Bella from hearing their conversation. After a few minutes she reappeared, scowled at Bella, and tersely said, 'come on then if we're going.'

171

They took Bella's car and Mia sat sulkily throughout the journey. Bella deliberately drove down Coppice Lane and past where Rupert had died, slowing as they passed the exact spot, trying to make a point. When they arrived at the house Bella was relieved to see that Kim's blue Mercedes convertible was in the drive.

Mia stood and continued to glower at Bella as they waited on the doorstep for Kim to answer the door.

'Hi!' she said, looking surprised to see them. 'Come in, it's lovely to see you.'

I doubt you'll think that in a minute, thought Bella.

'Drink?' Out of politeness they suggested a cup of tea. Kim ushered them both out of the kitchen and into the sitting room while the kettle was boiling. It seemed gloomy and dark, matching the weather outside. She switched on a couple of lamps then returned to the kitchen to make the tea. Several minutes later she entered the sitting room, balancing three boiling mugs between her hands. 'Ow!' she yelped, putting them down quickly, 'knew I should have used a tray.' She settled herself down in a big comfy chair and tucked her bare feet under her, then frowned as she looked at Mia who, in return, was looking incredibly miserable.

'What's up? You don't look very happy.' Concern was etched over Kim's face.

Mia sighed, and scowled again at Bella who was waiting expectantly, eager to hear what Kim had to say for herself. She studiously ignored Mia and observed Kim who had a radiant glow about her. Interesting, mused Bella.

'Well, um…' Mia's voice trailed off.

'What is it Mia? You look awfully pale.' Mia was looking decidedly grey.

172

'It's a bit awkward really,' she paused and smiled feebly at Kim who smiled back and nodded encouragingly. 'It's, well,' she sighed, 'um, on the night that Rupert died, you told me, and I guess the police, that you were at home all evening,' she looked at Kim for confirmation.

Kim's smile wavered slightly, she leaned forward, picked her mug up and fiddled with it as a distraction. Bella noted every move, every change in her demeanour. Kim nodded and waited.

'It's just that Fred saw you drive past on the Monhurst Road at about 9.50 p.m. going in the direction of Monhurst.'

Fear flicked across Kim's face, but she held it together as she waited for Mia to continue.

'Why did you lie?'

There was an oppressive silence. Keenly Bella watched as Kim, obviously torn between sticking to her lie and telling the truth, wrestled with what to say. Could she really have done it? Was she actually responsible for Rupert's death? Bella held her breath in anticipation. Was she going to confess? She felt a bit like Miss Marple, maybe she was going to crack the case before the police.

Mia also sat waiting, miserable and fearing the real reason why Kim had lied to her - and to the police.

Eventually Kim spoke in a small, thin, defeated voice. 'It was the first thing that came to my head. I was in shock.'

'Okay. So what's the truth?'

Kim looked beseechingly at the two of them. 'I didn't want people to know,' she whispered.

Bella's body tensed in anticipation.

'Mia, you know what I was planning to do. To leave Rupert, I was leaving him for Seb.' She looked at Mia, then at Bella, expecting her to look shocked, and was surprised when she didn't.

'I told her that you were leaving Rupert,' offered Mia in reply to the unspoken question, 'the one thing you can usually do is trust Bella to keep a secret.' This confirmed what Bella had suspected, that Kim was leaving Rupert for Seb.

'So what was it that you didn't want people to know?' prompted Bella, eager to get the truth.

Kim sighed again. 'I didn't want anyone to know that I had been with Seb that night. I mean, how would it look if they knew that I had been having sex with my ex-fiancée on the night that my husband died?'

Put like that, Bella could see her point of view. Or was this just a clever ruse?

'No one would have believed that I didn't have anything to do with his death, and even if they did, they would have thought that I was some kind of dirty little slapper, someone who was as bad as - if not worse than - Rupert. And it wasn't like that. I love Seb, I always have done - I was a fool to be blinded by Rupert, to be swept off my feet. I've regretted it for so long. I thought I'd lost Seb forever. I never thought he could forgive me for what I did, for betraying him like that. I mean, how could he after what I'd done to him? But he did, and not only that, he still loves me and wants me, and it wasn't some kind of competition to get me away from Rupert, score one over on him. He loves me, truly, and for who I am, the real me.'

It all sounded so romantic to Bella, the sort of thing you'd read about in a magazine or trashy romance novel. But surely this could be even more of a motive for murder?

Now Kim gets all Rupert's money, whereas if she'd left him and divorced him she'd possibly only get a fraction of it.

'Did Rupert have any cause to suspect that you were planning on leaving him?' she asked.

Kim shook her head. 'No. I was very careful. Seb and I were meticulous in planning our meetings to ensure that no one would find out. The only person I had told was Mia.'

'And the only person I told was Bella. I've not even told Fred.'

'And I've not told anyone. Did you sign a prenup?' Bella inquired impertinently.

'Yes,' replied Kim not seeming offended. 'Rupert wanted to protect his businesses. I know what you're thinking. You're thinking I killed Rupert so that I could get all his money?'

Bella blushed. Mia rolled her eyes at her.

'I might have signed a prenup, but it was a very generous prenup. I'd get the house, which hasn't got a mortgage on it, and £50,000 a year for life whether I remarried or not.'

Bella whistled. Wow! That was generous. Rupert went up in her estimation.

Mia's mouth gaped open in shock too

'And even if the prenup had left me nothing, I wouldn't have cared. I love Seb for who he is, he may not be rich but he's an incredible person, completely amazing. Having money doesn't make you happy, I should know, I've had shed loads of the stuff to spend, courtesy of Rupert, but I've never been so unhappy in all my life. Sure, it means you never have to worry about where your next meal is coming from I don't deny that, and that is a huge privilege and one I have never ever taken foregranted. But a life with Seb means a life of love, a life of fulfilment, we'd have a small roof over our heads and enough food to eat. What more could we need?'

True, I guess, though Bella wasn't entirely convinced. It would not be easy moving from such a large house with copious amounts of money on tap, to a small place where careful budgeting would be inevitable. But she had no idea what sort of house Seb had and was being presumptuous in her assumptions. If the prenup held up they'd be set for life anyway.

Mia got up and went over to Kim and gave her a big hug. 'I'm sorry,' Mia whispered 'I had to ask. You understand why?' She pulled back to look into Kim's sad blue eyes.

'Yeah,' she replied hoarsely.

Bella shifted uncomfortably. Disquieted because she couldn't believe she'd got so carried away with her imagination that she could believe that Kim had killed her husband. Guilt crept all over her.

'I'm sorry too.'

Kim shrugged. 'I suppose I have to tell the police don't I?' She looked from Mia to Bella.

'I think so. What you tell them, no matter how small or irrelevant you feel the detail is, could help the investigation. Seb will also need to talk to them.'

'I feel so ashamed. So guilty.'

'Why?'

'There was I, full of the joys of life, having spent the most glorious evening with Seb, planning our future, and while I was doing that Rupert was dying, all alone in a country lane. I feel terrible, I must be such a bad person.'

'But you mustn't,' comforted Mia, 'how were you to know that this would happen? That he was going to die?'

Bella was tempted to tell Kim that Rupert had been trying to get Jennifer into bed that evening anyway, to make her feel better but Bella had promised Jennifer that she wouldn't tell anyone. It was up to the police, or Jennifer, to tell Kim.

'Do you think they'll believe me?' Kim looked beseechingly at them.

'Tell them exactly what you told us.' advised Mia.

Bella nodded. 'They're not idiots, somehow they'll discover whether you're telling the truth or not and it's better coming from you than them finding out some other way. I certainly believe you,' she added hastily in case Kim took umbrage at what she'd just said.

'I'll go and phone them now.' She went out of the room in search of the telephone number she'd been given. Shortly afterwards Mia and Bella could hear her talking on the telephone.

When Kim returned she said. 'They'll be round in a little while. I spoke to Sergeant Swart, she's going to come round along with Inspector Ormandy.'

Bella's heart fluttered when she heard his name and she tried not to blush.

'Would you like us to stay with you?' asked Mia. 'We don't mind, if it'll make it easier?'

'No. Thanks. I'd rather do it on my own. Don't worry, I'll tell them everything I've told you.' She twisted her fingers nervously on her lap.

'You sure?'

'Yup. Absolutely.'

'You do know you're doing the right thing don't you?'

'I guess so. Do you think they'll be able to keep this quiet?'

Bella shrugged. 'I don't know. I wouldn't have thought there'd be any need to tell anyone, unless it turns out to be a key piece of evidence in the case.'

Mia got up. 'We'd better leave you to it then. Call if you need anything. See you at tennis tomorrow?'

'Okay. See you tomorrow.' Kim returned Mia's huge hug of support, absorbing comfort from her friend.

'Bye,' said Bella meekly, feeling mean at having dragged all this up, even though, deep down, she knew it was the right thing to do.

'Bye Bella. See you tomorrow.'

The awkward silence dragged out between them as they got into the car. Bella pulled out into the lane and cleared her throat. 'Are you going to forgive me?'

'I suppose so. I know you're right, but why did it feel so horrible, so sneaky, so mean?'

'Because you wanted to protect your friend, you didn't want to contemplate that she might have had something to do with Rupert's death. I understand why you kept it quiet.'

'Sorry if I was horrible to you.'

'S'okay. I felt mean and guilty myself. You do know I wasn't doing it to impress Dave don't you? I was following my gut instinct.'

'Yes. Guess I'd better phone the police myself when we get back. They'll need a statement from both Fred and myself. Hope we won't be in trouble.'

'You'll be fine. Don't worry.' Secretly Bella was horrified. She hadn't thought about the ramifications for Mia and Fred, and prayed fervently that they wouldn't be in trouble for withholding information.

Chapter Thirteen

Bella fretted and tossed and turned all night worrying about Mia, Fred and Kim. Had she done the right thing in forcing them into a corner so that there was no option for them but to tell the police? She could have just kept quiet, kept their secret, but would that have helped? Deep down Bella knew the answer, but it didn't make her feel any better. She spent the morning pottering around the house, half heartedly pushing the vacuum cleaner around, dusting, washing, ironing, keeping herself occupied in an attempt to keep her mind off the three of them. She had been looking forward to going to tennis that afternoon, but was now a tad apprehensive about the sort of reception she might receive from Kim, given that she should have spoken to the police by now.

With reluctance she changed into a pair of shorts and a t-shirt, smothered herself in sun cream as the sun was now beating down with a vengeance, as if wishing to make up for the previous couple of days of gloomy weather. At least the forecast was good for tomorrow, she smiled to herself at the prospect of the planned cycle and picnic.

As the tennis club was situated on the edge of the village in the direction of Sophie and Harry's house, and therefore not too far, Bella decided to get her bike out and cycle. Popping on her cycle helmet, Bella stuck her racquet into the rear side bag, with the handle protruding out of the top, and set off down the road. With the breeze in her face, the sun on her body and endorphins starting to kick in, Bella felt her spirits rise. There was definitely nothing better than an English summer when the sun was shining and the sky was clear and a vibrant blue she felt. There was a toot, toot of a horn as Jennifer drove past waving. Bella waved back, wobbling on her bike as she did so. She upped her speed and before too long she was bumping along the stony track to the cricket pitch and tennis club.

Red-faced with her exertion, she removed her helmet to cool down and took a long swig of water from the large bottle she'd remembered to top up at the last minute and slip into her bike bag.

Mia waved at her from a distance. 'Hi!' she called strolling over to her.

'Hi! How are you?' Bella peered anxiously at her friend.

'Fine.'

'How did it go?' she lowered her voice.

'It was okay.'

'And Fred?'

'Not impressed at first, more embarrassed that he'd suggested we omit say anything in the first place. The police were fine. In fact it was your friend Inspector Ormandy who called in, must have been about 8 o'clock, I suppose he was on his way home. Anyway, he was very understanding and he remembered who we were! I must say, he's got a jolly good memory.'

'Oh, great,' her heart fluttered again.

Mia grinned at her.

'What?' bleated Bella.

'Nothing. Just enjoying the look on your face when I mentioned him.'

Bella gave her friend a playful poke on the arm and turned to busy herself with locking her bike to the bike rack. 'Kim here yet?' she enquired whilst doing so, scanning the group that was gathering.

'Not yet.'

'Do you know how it went for her?' Bella's face darkened, her ridiculously over-active imagination again going into overdrive as she envisaged Kim locked up in a cell somewhere.

'No.' Mia looked equally concerned.

They were interrupted by Florence driving up in her old blue Honda CRV. There was a collective murmuring of pleasure at seeing her from the girls as they hurried over to Florence. They crowded round, eager to find out how she was. It must be nice to be missed so much, felt Bella standing slightly back from them. Florence looked as pale and thin as she had at the end of last week, but was putting on a brave face.

'Hi Florence,' greeted Bella, once Florence had extracted herself from her friends.

'Hi Bella. How are you?'

'I'm fine thanks,' she replied politely, 'how are you? Work still as manic?'

She nodded. 'Yeah.'

'Anyone know where Kim is?' called Sophie, who was trying to organise the matches.

Bella looked furtively at Mia. A general murmur of "no" responded to Sophie's enquiry.

'Oh well, sure she'll be here soon. I'll slot her in when she arrives.'

Mia, Sophie, Florence and Cressa were lined up to play their games first. Bella and Jennifer warmed up on the neighbouring court awaiting their turn in a doubles match. Half an hour later Jennifer called for a break.

'Phew! It's so hot!' she gasped, flopping down onto a bench in the shade and wiping the sweat from her fore-head.

'Certainly is,' gasped Bella, offering her some of her water. Jennifer took it and eagerly gulped down some of the cool liquid.

'Any news on the photo yet?'

'Inspector Ormandy said he'd let Kim know when there was something to tell,' replied Bella guiltily, omitting - as promised - what else he'd told her.

'Fair enough. I'll be interested to see what they come up with. Oh! Here's Kim now. Hi! Thought you'd got lost,' she called out.

'Sorry I'm late. Had things to do.' She sat next to Bella who smiled at her, fervently hoping that Kim wasn't furious with her. Kim smiled back.

'I'll get some more water,' said Jennifer getting up and disappearing into the smartly-painted white club house.

'How did it go?' whispered Bella.

'Okay. Embarrassing, but I think they understood. Gave me a bit of a telling off about not being completely honest in the first place and how it could have had a detrimental effect on the investigation, but other than that they were fine. At least I wasn't dragged off to the police station and thrown into a cell!'

Relief flooded through Bella from head to toe. 'It was the right thing telling them. I'm sorry if I put you in an awkward position…'

Kim looked surprised. 'But you didn't! You didn't know.'

'No. But it was me who told Mia that the police ought to be informed.'

'It would have come out eventually, these things usually do,' replied Kim philosophically. 'Oh, there's Florence! It's good to see her out and about. Sophie didn't have any luck catching up with her the other night, and I think we've all left messages for her. I'm so glad she's been able to come.' She waved at her, Florence hesitated then gave a small wave back.

Jennifer returned with some more water and they chatted amiably until it was their turn to play. The afternoon passed swiftly and easily and, before she knew it, Bella was back home having supper and looking forward - with eager anticipation - to her day out the next day.

Bella awoke early and leapt enthusiastically out of bed, whipping the curtains back eagerly to see what the weather was doing. It matched her mood – the sun was bright, the sky was blue and there was not a cloud to be seen in the sky. Quickly she showered and got dressed, putting on the clothes that she had picked out the previous night. She couldn't wear anything glamorous - or particularly feminine - as they were cycling, so had opted for a freshly laundered pair of navy Bermuda-type shorts and a pale, sky blue, polo shirt. Her hair was swept back into a low pony-tail, low enough to enable her to put the helmet on, and her make-up was simple, just a fresh a touch of concealer, mascara and a slick of lipstick.

She trotted downstairs to prepare breakfast, something more substantial than just a piece of toast, and glanced at the clock. It was only 7.30 a.m. - hours to go until he arrived. Flicking the kettle off, she decided to stroll down to the post office - which was open from 7 a.m. for newspapers - to pick one up to peruse over her breakfast.

She sat in the garden basking in the warmth of the early morning sunshine, and took her time munching through her large bowl of muesli with a chopped banana and yoghurt on top, followed by a slightly warmed croissant and a large cup of tea. Meticulously she read every page of the paper. When she finally allowed herself to glance at her watch she was surprised - and then panicked - to see that it was 9.30 a.m. already. Hurriedly she scooped up her breakfast things, along with the newspaper, and took them into the kitchen. All of a fluster, she raced upstairs, brushed her teeth, checked her hair, re-did her lipstick and put some cash, lipstick, handkerchief and keys into a small handbag about the size of a paperback book, small enough to comfortably fit inside her cycle bag. With the windows checked and closed, she quickly washed up her breakfast dishes and tweaked things impatiently in the kitchen as she waited for Dave to arrive. Spot on 10 a.m. there was a knock at the door.

Bella took a breath to calm herself and opened it with a broad smile on her face. 'Good morning!'

'And a very good morning it is too,' replied Dave beaming back at her, 'shall I get your bike onto the rack?'

'Thanks. I'm all ready. I'll just get the bike out and then I'll lock up.'

With her bike tightly secured next to his bike on his silver VW Passat Estate she sank down into the passenger seat next to him, and tried to contain the over-excited, hormonal-teenager-type feelings. They chatted easily as they sped along the leafy country lanes on the twenty five minute journey. When they pulled up into the stony car park there were few cars, but from what she had heard it would be rammed full of them later in the day. Dave got out, paid the parking charge and then set about unloading the bikes. Meanwhile Bella trotted off to find a loo as all the excitement was playing havoc with her bladder.

Hurrying back, she could see Dave in the distance, standing tall and looking rather gorgeous, she felt, in his khaki, knee-length, fitted shorts and moss green polo shirt. She watched as he clipped his helmet on and checked the bikes once again.

'I'll just put my helmet on and I'll be ready,' she said as she slipped her handbag into the bike bag. 'You won't go speeding off without me will you?! I've only just started cycling again and I'm not terribly fit.'

He smiled kindly at her. 'Of course I won't, we'll take it as slowly as you like. There's no rush we've got the whole day ahead of us and the picnic is all ready and waiting for us,' he patted the bulging bike bags attached to the back of his bike.

Unfortunately for Bella the start of the cycle route was uphill, it felt like it went on for ever, but she was determined not to whinge even though every part of her body felt as though it was going to explode in agony. When they got to the top she stopped.

'Sorry,' she gasped, trying to catch her breath, 'just gotta stop for a few minutes. I thought you said there weren't any hills.'

Dave grinned. 'Well I suppose it depends what you call a hill. We can always walk up any more, we don't have to cycle at all if you don't want to, it's not meant to be tortuous!' He passed her a fresh bottle of water, then took a swig from his own.

Bella wiped away the sweat, which was trickling down from under her helmet, and gulped down the water greedily. She passed the half-empty bottle back to Dave.

'Come on, you'd better catch me!' she called mischievously as she cycled off, whilst he was still putting the bottles away.

'Oy! Wait for me!' It didn't take him long to catch her up and they cycled in silence for a while, enjoying the peace, beauty and tranquility of the forest. The diverse range of trees and foliage synthesising together in harmony, the birds singing happily in their beautiful environment, far away from any road. After half an hour they stopped by a small lake and, though it was only 11.30 a.m, Dave suggested that they picnic.

'Fine by me. It's a charming spot.' She laid her bike on the ground and gazed at the still, calm water.

'We should be alone for a while - give it another hour or so and there'll be hoards of people stopping for their picnics.'

'I'm not surprised. It's so beautiful here.' She turned back to see that he had laid out a large picnic rug and was busy unpacking plates, glasses, food and drink. She settled herself on the rug and watched as he worked, startled and unsettled at the feelings stirring within her.

'It looks like a banquet,' she murmured to him.

'I aim to please!' he smiled. 'Drink?' She nodded and he poured her a glass of chilled elderflower cordial. The sweet, aromatic, sparkling drink slipped down easily - it was like being in a dreamy tableau from another era, she felt.

Hungrily Bella ate the smoked salmon sandwiches, the mini quiches, the cherry tomatoes, the mixed salad, the French bread, and still had plenty of room for the fresh strawberries, raspberries and cream that he produced. Leaning back on her elbows, replete, she felt contented and happy. Conversation continued to flow easily and enjoyably between them. With the sun dancing on the lake, and a breeze gently brushing over them, everything seemed idyllic. They lapsed into a contented silence and Bella, now lying flat on her back gazing up at the sky, could feel herself drifting off. It was only when the excited screams of children racing past on their bicycles, competing with their parents to see who could go the fastest, which prevented her from falling into a deep sleep. Reluctantly she opened her eyes and saw Dave propped up on his side gazing down at her.

'You looked so peaceful.'

She smiled and sat up, pushing her desire to kiss him away at the same time. 'I felt it. This is just perfect.'

'Good,' he sat up too. 'Feel like anything else to eat? I've got chocolate brownies in here,' he patted the cool bag.

'Oh, I'd love to, but I think I'd pop if I had another morsel to eat at the moment! I'll definitely have one later though!'

'You ready to continue then?'

She nodded, pushed herself up and stretched, her body was definitely going to complain at having to get back onto the bike. Between them they quickly and efficiently packed the picnic things away.

'Just in time,' said Dave, nodding towards a group of about fifteen friends who were descending upon the area with their picnics.

Despite protestations from her body, the remainder of the cycle didn't seem nearly as hard for some reason. They'd spent so long by the lake that by the time they reached the end of the trail it was half past three.

'Fancy a cup of tea here?' he asked, nodding in the direction of the small café.

'What about a cup of tea and one of those brownies back at my house?' she replied.

'Perfect.' He deftly stowed everything away and put the bikes back up onto the rack. She settled herself into the car whilst Dave finished securing the bikes and a few minutes later they were on their way back to her house.

'I think you chose the right time for us to come,' she commented as they drove out. The car park was jam packed with cars and there were still more arriving. Some people were here to cycle, others were families going off to the spectacular wooden play area, and older children and adults going off to use the aerial walkway.

'Saturdays are always busy, but when the weather's as gorgeous as this it brings even more people out.'

They drove in a companionable silence until they got to the cottage. Dave got Bella's bike off the rack whilst she went and unlocked the house, putting the kettle on first before she opened up the back door and windows in the house to let the breeze flow through.

Dave settled himself in a comfy chair under the shade of the big, white umbrella and watched as Bella poured them each a cup of tea to accompany their chocolate brownies.

'Thank you. That was a lovely day,' she said passing him a mug.

'My absolute pleasure. I had a great time too. See, I'm not so bad at getting the work/life balance right!' he joked.

She laughed. 'Maybe. We'll see.' She hesitated, not sure how he'd react if she asked him a work related question, but her concern for Fred, Mia and Kim won out.

'You look worried.' he commented, having noticed the change in her demeanour.

She shrugged. 'I'm not. It's just…'

He nodded encouragingly.

'I hope you don't mind, but I just wanted to ask you about Fred, Mia and Kim.' She glanced nervously at him and noticed an almost imperceptible change as he sat more upright in his chair.

'Go on.'

'It's your day off and I feel awful about asking.'

'That's okay,' he replied gently.

'Fred, Mia and Kim aren't going to get into any trouble are they? You know, for withholding information and for Kim not being, well, entirely honest about her whereabouts on the night Rupert died.'

'Fred and Mia will be ok, although they should have been upfront at the beginning. As for Kim, well, she shouldn't have lied and it remains to be seen what will happen.'

'Oh, okay. It's just, I feel a little guilty as I was the one who pushed them into telling you.'

He looked surprised. 'Really? How long had you known?'

'Earlier that afternoon. As soon as Mia accidentally let it slip, I insisted she tell the police. She, in turn, was adamant that she see Kim first, though I advised her not to, but I did accompany her to Kim's.'

'And what did you observe when you were at Kim's house?'

'Well, I'm pretty sure she was telling the truth. I really don't think she was lying. She seemed genuinely shocked that she'd been found out and had no time to make up an alibi as good as the one she gave, and I can totally see why, with the shock and all that, she wasn't thinking straight and wanted to protect Seb too. As far as I could see there was nothing about her body language that made me in the least bit suspicious.'

He looked thoughtfully at her.

'You're not cross are you?'

He smiled. 'No. If it hadn't been for you we'd be none the wiser about it at the moment, and the more information we can gather about that night the better.'

'While we're on the subject of work, have you had any luck speaking to Kit?'

'Yes. I managed to finally get hold of him yesterday. According to him, he lent Rupert some money years ago and Rupert was just paying it back.'

'Yeah right. You don't believe that do you?'

'It is possible. But no, I don't believe him. At the moment we cannot prove otherwise. There's no paperwork, nothing, and nothing to suggest that there was anything improper going on either.'

'Did he provide any evidence at all regarding the loan? Anything to back it up?'

He shook his head. 'Nope. Nothing.'

'My gut feeling is that he was blackmailing Rupert over something, but over what I don't know.'

'I think you might be right, but I have no way of proving it. As Rupert is not here, unless we come across some documentation or other evidence to suggest that he was being blackmailed, then there is nothing we can do.'

Bella's curiosity had been nudged again. 'Did you find out whether it was him in the picture? Was he in Australia with Kit and if so, why the big pretence about not knowing one another? Did they know each other before Australia? Did they grow up together?'

'You should be a detective the amount of questions you ask!' he joked, 'and to answer your questions, no, they apparently didn't know each other before Australia, and no they didn't grow up together, though not too far apart: Rupert in Salisbury, Kit in Winchester. Yes he was in Australia and the reason for the big pretence was apparently because Rupert liked to keep the past in the past and didn't want questions being asked.'

She raised her eyebrows. 'Really? Why was that?'

'He wouldn't say, just said he was doing what Rupert had asked him to do.'

'Sounds dodgy to me. But what would be his motive for murder?' she pursed her lips together as her brain ticked away. 'Perhaps he wanted more money and Rupert refused to give it to him?'

'Maybe. But if he killed Rupert he was killing his golden goose and would definitely not get any more money from him nor from his estate when dead, as there was nothing to corroborate the fact that he was owed money by him.'

'Hmm. But perhaps in a fit of anger he drove off somewhere - maybe to calm down, I don't know - and, seeing Rupert, ran him off the road?'

'Anything is possible, but let's not leap to conclusions.'

'Did you find out anything else about him? What about his past?'

'Who? Kit's?' Bella nodded. 'Nothing really to tell, seems like he's kept his nose clean, hasn't got a record or anything. Parents are still alive, as is his sister, only traumatic event was his twin brother dying when they were younger. Apart from that nothing.'

'Oh, how sad! Poor Kit. Hang on, you just asked me if I meant Kit. Who else did you think I meant? Rupert?' Her eyes glistened with excitement. 'Have you found something out about him? What?'

'I think we've discussed quite enough work for today. I've told you all I can, but please remember to keep this to yourself. I'll be speaking to Kim about the picture in due course.'

Dave's mouth was firmly set. Bella knew there was something else, something about Rupert that he hadn't told her, or rather couldn't tell her, in which case it must be something really relevant to the case, she thought excitedly. But how am I going to find out?

193

'Here, how about a chocolate brownie?' He offered her the plate and, though frustrated that he wouldn't tell her anything else, she took one and bit into the soft, rich, chocolate brownie. It was melt-in-the-mouth divine.

'Where did you get these from?' she moaned in delight and took another mouthful, 'they are heavenly. So delicious.'

He finished his mouthful and had to admit they were rather good. 'I made them myself,' he replied proudly.

Her eyes opened wide. 'No! Really?'

'No need to look so shocked!' he laughed, 'they're not that difficult to make.'

'Don't be so modest. Anyone can make them, but not everyone can make them as divinely delicious as you have. A man of many talents,' she smiled coquettishly.

He blushed which made her smile as she didn't think anything would make him blush. 'You're too kind.'

'Mind if I have another one?' She couldn't resist. Forget the diet! She'd been cycling for what felt like all day, surely she deserved to have another one of these?

'Be my guest, think I'll join you, he couldn't remember the last time he had had such a pleasurable day. Secretly, he'd always been attracted to Bella, but had never made a move on her because she'd been married to one of his best friends, and certainly not whilst he himself had still been married. Maybe that was why he'd lost touch with Hugh? Maybe deep down, on another level, he'd realised what a temptation Bella was to him, and kept his distance to avoid such temptation. Had it really been such a good idea to lose touch with a good friend? He and Hugh had been so close, but the high hopes he'd had when he'd married Alison had soon diminished as he realised what a demanding, selfish female she was. Nothing was ever good enough for her, and all she did was nag. When the two of them moved away he thought a fresh start would do them both good, and he wouldn't be constantly reminded of how lucky Hugh was. How naïve - or stupid -he'd been, he reflected.

'You look lost in your thoughts? Penny for them?'

He looked lovingly at Bella's bright, open face. 'Just thinking about the past. About Hugh.' He searched her face for her reaction, not wanting to upset her, but eager to see her response. Her face clouded and he felt cross with himself for his stupidity (again) and tactlessness.

'Yeah. I often think about him.'

'Naturally, you were together so long.'

'Of course. He was such a big part of my life, he always was and always will be. It's been so difficult,' her eyes welled up with tears. Where was this coming from? She still missed him desperately, but it had been a while since the tears had sprung up quite so quickly. Was this guilt? Guilt at feeling so attracted to Dave even though she wasn't even sure if they were dating? Could she really move on or was she fooling herself?

'I can only imagine. It must have been,' he corrected himself, 'must be awful.' He was desperately sorry he'd brought Hugh's name up and could kick himself for spoiling what had been an otherwise perfect day. 'He was an incredible person. A really honourable man. You knew where you stood with him, and his total honesty and compassion were traits which appear not to be so prevalent these days.'

Just like you, reflected Bella, startled that the comparison had popped into her head. Companionably they sat in contemplative silence for a while. Eventually Dave made his excuses to leave - as far as he was concerned, he'd ruined the day. But if he had been able to read Bella's mind he would have known that that was the opposite to what she felt

'Thank you so much for a lovely day. I really hope we can do it again soon,' she said, feeling unusually shy.

'Really?' he replied hopefully, 'I'd like that. I'll phone you.'

She laughed. 'That's if you're not too busy at work!'

'Point taken.' He smiled back - perhaps he hadn't totally ruined the day after all. 'See you soon and I WILL phone.' He wanted to kiss her but didn't feel brave enough to risk it, instead he waved as he walked over to his car.

Chapter Fourteen

Yet again Bella tossed and turned all night, the nugget of information Dave had given her subconsciously processing itself, jolting her into half-wakefulness at regular intervals throughout the night. Blearily she woke at 8 a.m. as the alarm shrilled at her, and though the temptation was to roll over and try to go back to sleep, she knew it wouldn't do her any good, in fact it would probably make her feel worse.

She dragged herself tiredly downstairs, pulling her thin white cotton dressing gown around her as she went, and switched the kettle on. What was it that was bothering her? There was something niggling at the back of her mind and she couldn't retrieve it, no matter how hard she tried. And what was it that Dave hadn't told her? She knew he was holding something back about Rupert, but what? And how could she find out? Yawning expansively, she made a cup of tea and filled a bowl with muesli. Surely there was something she could do to find out?

Reflectively she took herself off to church. No divine intervention or inspiration came to her whilst there and, no matter how hard she delved into her mind, nothing came to her that afternoon. As the sky turned grey and the thunder began to rumble again in the distance, she withdrew inside and flopped onto a sofa, but not before she had switched the television on. She flicked from channel to channel and despite there being so many, no programme particularly appealed to her. Eventually she settled on the Antiques Roadshow and - like most people - watched it in the hope that there would be that one big find, the little old lady who turned up with something she'd kept a pot plant in believing it to be a worthless piece of crockery, and then finding it was some rare piece worth thousands of pounds. It was only as the credits rolled that Bella took note that it had been filmed in the precinct of Salisbury Cathedral.

'Oh course!' she cried, 'how stupid of me! If Rupert grew up in Salisbury then I might be able to find out something about him there. All I have to do is go to Salisbury - surely there must be some records somewhere? Maybe a local newspaper that he might have been in, giving a little titbit of information which can't be found on the internet, perhaps I could find out where he went to school? Possibly even track down an old school friend?'

Filled with renewed enthusiasm she got out her laptop and spent the next two hours researching Salisbury and tracking down a bed and breakfast she could stay in. She gave them a call and, yes, they had one room available from Monday for three nights. Bella booked it and hastily went upstairs to pack a small bag with enough to keep her going for four days if necessary. If it proved to be fruitless she could always come back after one night, but if not she might stay there a little longer. Her packing was interrupted by the phone ringing.

'Hello?'

'Hi Bella.' It was Mia. 'How are you?'

'Great thanks,' she replied, trying to keep the excitement out of her voice. If Mia knew what she was up to she might try and talk her out of it. 'How about you? Nice weekend?'

'Good thanks. What about you?' They chatted amiably for a while until Mia got to the point of why she'd phoned. 'Do you fancy a trip out somewhere this week? Tunbridge Wells, or down to Rye, or wherever you want really?

'I'd love to, when were you thinking?'

'Tuesday?'

Bella hesitated. 'Friday would be better. Thought I might have a few days away.'

'Oh? That's sudden isn't it?'

Bella searched desperately for a plausible explanation as to why she'd suddenly decided to go away. 'Totally,' she replied, 'surprised myself actually. I was just watching the Antiques Roadshow, this week it was in Salisbury. I've always fancied going there but never been. Got on the phone, booked a B&B and I'm off tomorrow for a few nights - might be one night, might be two or three. Of course I could get there and realise it was a big mistake,' she wittered on.

'Oh,' replied Mia puzzled, it seemed rather out of character for Bella to be so impulsive. 'Everything is all right isn't it?'

'Absolutely. Probably regret it in the morning, but it seems like a good idea at the moment.' She kept her fingers crossed.

'Well, have a lovely time won't you. So Friday for a day out then? That should be fine, I'm pretty sure that there's no tennis on this Friday because of the village fête, but I'll have done my bit the day before and I'm busy helping out on the day itself. Shall I pick you up, say 10 o'clock?'

'Perfect. I'll look forward to it. See you then. Bye.'

'Bye.'

Bella felt a twinge of guilt at not having been completely honest with her friend. She pushed away the little niggling doubt which was starting to stir within her. Was she doing the right thing digging around?

Determined to get a good nights sleep and make up for the terrible one the previous night, Bella went to bed early and was relieved, and refreshed, to wake up at 7 o'clock and realise she had slept through. Washed, dressed and ready to go, she didn't bother leaving the house until 9 o'clock as she knew both the motorways, particularly the M25, would be so busy with rush hour traffic that it would be futile. She hoped that by the time she hit the motorways the traffic would be starting to calm down and clear, though knowing full well how hit and miss it was.

Bella topped up her car with fuel at the petrol station on the Monhurst Road and, armed with a bottle of water and some fruit to snack on in case she got stuck in traffic, she set off on her journey to Wiltshire. Unfortunately the M25 lived up to its reputation as being Europe's largest car park. As usual there had been an accident and, whilst that in itself had not particularly blocked the road - just a brief temporary closure of one lane - it was the rubberneckers slowing down to have a good look which added to the delay. Muttering a lot, Bella, who loathed sitting in traffic, drummed her fingers impatiently on the steering wheel as if by doing so the traffic would magically clear.

Three and a half hours later she eventually drove in to Salisbury, a trip that should have taken about two hours on a good run. She followed the instructions carefully to the Bed and Breakfast and prepared herself for the stereotypical, in her belief, type of person who ran those sorts of establishments, her preconceptions convincing her that it would be someone in their mid to late sixties, over-permed and coloured hair, lashings of make up, suffocating perfume and clothes that should only be worn by a girl in the first flushes of youth.

The house itself looked promising. It was old brick, double-fronted and neatly kept with not a net curtain in sight. It was down a quiet leafy road not far from the centre of Salisbury and had parking for several cars on the drive, she'd been informed that she was more than welcome to park on it. Bella took her bag out of the car and, though it was far too early for their normal check-in time, she had been reassured that it would not be a problem as the booking Bella had made covered a cancellation which had included the Sunday night and no one else had subsequently been booked into it for that night.

She rang the doorbell and waited. Eventually Bella could hear the tap, tap, tap of footsteps getting closer and braced herself.

'Ah, you must be Mrs Sparkle,' cried the woman welcomingly.

'Yes,' replied Bella, slightly taken aback as the woman greeting her was in her early forties and casually dressed in a pair of jeans and well cut white shirt, her red spirally curled hair was clasped casually to the nape of her neck by a simple, silver clip, and her feet were shod in a pair of blue espadrilles.

'Come in. Here, let me take your bag. Come through, I was just feeding the baby.'

'Oh, sorry. I didn't mean to interrupt.' Bella felt embarrassed now at having turned up so early.

'Don't worry. As I said on the phone, it's not a problem. Would you like a cup of tea?'

'Oh, thank you but no. I'll put my things in my room and then go into Salisbury if that's okay.'

'Sure?'

Bella nodded, looking at the rather cute baby – a boy she thought, but it was hard to tell – who was sitting in his high chair waving a spoon around and banging it on a bowl, the contents of which seemed to be all over his face and hair.

'Excuse Archie, he does like to try and feed himself, but he's not terribly good at it yet. Are you chicken?' she laughed, tickling him under the chin which made him laugh even more.

Bella's heart twanged with sadness. She had so wanted a baby. It wasn't Archie's fault that he was such a cutie, every baby seemed cute and, though she was okay most of the time, sometimes it hurt her heart more than she could bear. She could feel the tears prick at her eyes.

'You okay?' The women was looking at her concerned.

'Fine. He's so sweet, babies always make me go all soft. I'll leave you to it, you've got your hands full.'

'You're in the Spire Room, top of the stairs turn left. If there's anything you need please let me know. There's a sitting room for guests: it's the door at the bottom of the stairs, there's tea, coffee, milk, sugar and a kettle in there, help yourself.' She handed her the key.

'Thanks. See you later.' Bella walked to the stairs, picked her bag up - which was where the woman had left it - and climbed up two flights to the top of the house. She

202

opened the door on the left and found that she was in a large, airy room in the roof of the house.   The ceilings sloped and there was a double bed, dressing table, wardrobe and a comfy looking armchair.   The walls themselves were pale yellow, and the bed linen was a sparkling, crisp white, the armchair co-ordinated with the theme in a white and soft yellow check.   She peaked into the compact bathroom and found a small bath, basin and loo - all white, fresh and spotlessly clean.   Bella sat on the bed to test the firmness of the mattress, convinced that it would sag heavily in the middle, but was pleasantly surprised to find that it was firm and even all over.   Last but not least, she went to the dormer window and looked out.   There was a spectacular view over to the top of the cathedral spire; no wonder it was called the Spire Room.   Pleased with her accommodation, Bella freshened up, unpacked, and quietly slipped out of the front door to go and explore the city.

She wandered along in the hope that she was going in the right direction, following instinct and the mental map she'd worked out from looking out of her bedroom window towards the cathedral.   Speeding up and after a brisk fifteen minutes walk, shops began to appear and eventually Bella arrived in the Market Square.   Temporarily distracted by the shops, she wandered in and out of them, particularly enjoying the well-equipped kitchen shop but restraining herself from purchasing.   She continued to stroll around, taking in the ancient architecture, and came upon the River Avon which meandered through the city.   She stopped to watch the ducks with their ducklings, who were by now not so little and trying bravely to strike out on their own, much to the despair of the mother duck who kept having to swim round to rescue one or other of her offspring.   Bella smiled as she observed them, she didn't know what it was about ducklings - or for that matter any baby bird or creature - but she found them irresistible and couldn't help but stop and watch, so sweet and adorable.

Her walk took her through the rest of the centre of Salisbury until she could see the cathedral looming large in the distance. The ancient arch opened up into a beautiful precinct. Stunning houses edged the lawns of the cathedral which looked majestic in its stature. Bella stood in awe looking up at the architecture which was even more stunning and beautiful in real life than in any picture or television programme she had seen. Not able to resist, she paid and went in to the breathtaking building. Slowly she strolled her way around the ancient building and, despite the number of tourists inside, she could feel a strong and overwhelming presence of God. For a while Bella sat and gazed around her, her thoughts drifting to Hugh and then to Dave, reflecting on the conflict she felt within herself. When she walked out of the cathedral, she felt a calmness and peace within her that lifted her spirits, something she had not felt for a very long time.

Reluctant to leave such an historic and inspiring place, Bella wandered through the gift shop and into the café, which was light and bright, the glass ceiling provided a magnificent view upwards to the exterior of the cathedral. The café itself was packed, and not just with tourists, there were a few mums bringing their children in for a drink after school and other people who were obviously local residents, at least from what Bella gathered as she overheard snippets of conversation. She purchased a pot of tea and a luscious looking, and very generous, slice of sponge cake which was filled with fresh cream and raspberries. Spying an elderly couple preparing to leave from a small table to one side of the café, Bella weaved her way across to it.

She tucked in to the cake which melted delightfully in her mouth. Bella almost moaned out loud, it tasted scrumptious. Having munched her way hungrily through half of it, she sat back to sip tea and deliberated on the fact that she had not done a single thing to help her in her quest to discover more about Rupert. But where to start? She really didn't have the faintest idea. In her rush to get to Salisbury Bella hadn't come up with a plan of how, or what, she was going to find out whatever it was she needed to know, even if there was anything to discover.

Perhaps the library, she pondered? Or maybe the local paper? Still, she was enjoying herself and Salisbury was a very beautiful place. Glancing at her watch, she realised that it was 5.30 p.m - too late she assumed for the library. But what to do? Go back and sit in her room all night? She strolled out of the cathedral precinct and eventually turned right, looking in the shop windows as she went, most of which were now closed. She came across the cinema which was still in an old building in the centre of the town. Decisively she checked to see what was on and bought a ticket for a romantic/comedy film starting in ten minutes time.

It was a light-hearted, non brain-taxing film and she enjoyed the fact that it took her mind off Rupert and everything else that was going on in her life. A couple of hours later she reappeared blinking in the glowing evening sunshine, her stomach rumbled, reminding her that it was well past its normal feeding time. As she'd noticed some restaurants around and off the Market Square Bella ambled back and settled on the pizza restaurant which was located directly on the square.

There was one tiny table left and Bella sat down, suddenly feeling very alone as she looked at all the couples engrossed in one another, and the groups of friends gathered together having a fun night out. She sighed miserably and ordered herself a glass of house white, garlic bread and a pizza with tomato, mozzarella, rocket and parmesan. Feeling conspicuous by her singleness, she fished around in her bag, found a leaflet on the cathedral and studiously read it from cover to cover several times throughout her meal. She ordered another glass of wine and felt herself relax and feel a little less lonely as it absorbed its way into her. Draining the last few drops, she paid quickly and hurried out, self-consciously feeling as though dozens of pairs of eyes were looking at her and judging her – sad woman, can't have any friends if she's eating alone, and such like.

It was half past nine by the time she got back to the B&B. Lights were blazing despite it still being light outside. She knocked on the door and the friendly woman opened it - she must remember to ask her name - Bella scolded to herself.

'Hello. Have you had a nice time?' she enquired letting Bella in through the front door. Bella could hear a couple of older children arguing in the distance. The woman grimaced. 'Sorry about that. Don't know what's got into them today, ever since they got back from school they've been bickering.'

'Poor you. Must be very wearing.'

The woman smiled and laughed. 'I've got used to it, but some days I feel like pulling my hair out! I've just put some fresh milk in there,' she indicated to the sitting room, 'or perhaps I could do you a hot chocolate or something?'

'Thanks. That's very kind of you but I think I might just go to bed, it's been a long day.'

'You shouldn't be disturbed up there. But let me know if they make too much noise for you! Breakfast is between eight and nine o'clock. Sleep well, see you in the morning.'

'Thanks. Good night.'

How on earth does she manage to stay smiling with all that racket going on? Two older children, a baby and a bed and breakfast to run - it was a tall order. Bella wondered whether her husband helped out. She was impressed, sure that there was no way she would be able to do everything that the woman juggled. Sadly there would be no chance of her ever being in that position, despite being a similar age to the woman who ran the B&B, Bella felt that at the age of forty-two - apart from the fact that she was not currently in a long-term relationship - her fertility would be diminishing by the month, making it unlikely that she would ever have one child, let alone three.

Sinking into a deeper gloom as each step took her up to her room, Bella felt isolated and completely alone. If she disappeared nobody would really care, she dwelled self-pityingly and morosely. All she saw around her in life were couples and families happily being together. In reality life wasn't like that, but tonight she had her rose-tinted spectacles on. Bella ran herself a deep bath and poured in some of the rose bath oil which was in a large bottle by the side of it. She sank into the steaming, bubbly, fragrant tub and lay there contemplating upon the negative aspects of her life, the peace and contentment she'd felt earlier in the cathedral having evaporated. After half an hour she stepped out, feeling decidedly flushed and hot. It had been a mistake filling the bath with such hot water on a warm evening, particularly considering that she was at the top of the house where all the day's heat was rising to. She flung the bedroom window open and, making sure that the towel was wrapped tightly around her, she stuck her head out to cool down, a bit like a dog sticking its nose out of a car window.

She attempted to read but couldn't concentrate, then thought about phoning Mia or maybe Dave, but decided it was too late in the evening to do so. Flicking the light off, she sank into the extremely comfortable bed and went straight to sleep. However, two hours later she was wide awake wriggling and twisting, trying hard to go back to sleep, feeling sticky and hot as she shifted around trying to settle. Finally, as a clear, gentle dawn started to break, she drifted off and was only woken by a slam of the front door. A quick glance at her clock told her that it was half past eight. Leaping out of bed she swiftly washed and dressed not wanting to miss breakfast, quickly tying her long hair up into a loose knot as she ran down the stairs, following the tantalising smell of cooking bacon.

Breakfast was served in the room on the opposite side of the hallway to the sitting room. Four tables were occupied, with a fifth laid and waiting for her. Bella's misconceptions about bed and breakfasts' took a further educational turn. The tables were not occupied by geriatric pensioners noisily shovelling and slurping down their food, but instead there was an eclectic mix of people. A young couple were gazing gooely into each others eyes. A middle aged couple: both well rounded, with plates piled so high that it was obvious as to why they were the size they were. A lone gentleman, dressed in a smart business suit and an older American couple were pouring over their guidebooks to Salisbury and the surrounding area. All glanced in Bella's direction as she entered the room and gave her a cheery "hello". Bella smiled and reciprocated.

At that moment the owner, looking as fresh as a daisy, came hurrying back into the breakfast room. 'Good morning,' she said, 'sleep well?'

Bella nodded. Had she not had so much churning through her mind she was sure she would have slept beautifully, so it was therefore irrelevant even to hint at a bad night's sleep.

'What would you like for breakfast? There are cereals, yoghurt and fruit over there if you'd like to help yourself and juice too,' she indicated to a table that was prettily laid out and laden down with food, 'and I can do any sort of eggs you'd like, also there's bacon, sausage, mushrooms, beans, hash browns, tomatoes.'

'Oh thanks, it certainly smells delicious so, um, please may I have scrambled eggs, bacon and a few mushrooms, not too much, just a small plate, thanks.'

'Tea or coffee?'

'Tea please.'

'English Breakfast, Earl Grey, Darjeeling, Camomile, Peppermint, Green?'

Bella was impressed at the choice, she'd guessed - incorrectly - that it would be "builders" and no choice. 'Um, English Breakfast please.'

'Toast? White? Brown? Granary? Sourdough?'

Bella laughed. 'There's so much choice. I think white for a change please.' Sensible granary bread would have to

209

wait for a few days. There was nothing quite so delicious as white toast lathered with butter, inspiring memories of childhood breakfasts, and for that very reason Bella tended to refrain from buying white bread because she knew she could eat the whole loaf in one go. The woman, whose name she could still not recall, though sure that she had been told it, trotted off to cook Bella's breakfast. Bella in turn got up and helped herself to a small bowl of muesli, a sprinkling of freshly sliced strawberries with a dollop of natural yoghurt on top, and a glass of freshly-squeezed orange juice. Sitting on the wide windowsill were a couple of newspapers, which Bella assumed were there to be read, so she picked up a copy of the Daily Mail and munched as she read. Her pot of tea arrived and a few minutes later a plate with a perfect quantity of scrambled eggs, crispy bacon and mushrooms. Surreptitiously squirting some ketchup onto her plate, she ate her breakfast heartily. The other guests started to drift away and soon she was left on her own. Her spirits had risen by merely being in the presence of other people, now she was starting to feel deflated and the fullness of her stomach made her remember, guiltily, the diet she had broken yet again.

The woman unobtrusively and efficiently cleared the tables around Bella and started putting away the food from the breakfast table. Bella poured herself another cup of tea and pondered upon her course of action for the day. Her thoughts were interrupted by the woman asking if she could clear her breakfast dishes away.

'Of course. Thank you, it was delicious. By the way, sorry, I can't remember your name?'

'Trisha, didn't I say when you arrived? Sorry about that, I'd lose my head if it wasn't screwed on properly! What have you got planned for today?'

'Oh, er, probably just do more sightseeing in Salisbury I would think,' Bella replied cautiously.

'Well, there's no rush, take your time over the rest of your tea, have a lovely day and I'll see you later. Archie's about ready for some more food,' she grinned as the wail of the infant could be heard to crescendo in the distance.

'Thanks. See you later.' Bella continued sipping her tea, feeling totally uninspired as to where she should start with her search for information. Popping upstairs to clean her teeth, she took her bag and car keys, checked the weather – brilliant blue skies and sunshine again – and quietly took herself downstairs and let herself out of the front door.

The sun felt warm and pleasant on her as she strolled back in to Salisbury again. This time resisting the temptations of the shops, she walked purposefully across the square to the library, which was housed in an unattractive, low-rise, relatively modern (compared to the prevalent ancient architecture) building. She pushed the door open and walked around in the hope that something would leap out at her and inspire. Of course it didn't so she went to the desk and whispered to the librarian that she needed some information.

'It's okay,' she replied 'you don't have to whisper,' dispelling the old tradition that you weren't allowed to make a noise of any kind, let alone breathe, in a library.

Bella blushed. 'Sorry.'

The middle-aged woman with short slightly greying hair, wearing a navy dress which looked as though it had gone out of fashion twenty years ago, smiled at her. 'Don't worry, you can talk at a normal volume here, that's all I was trying to say. Now what sort of information are you after?'

'I'm not sure really. Local news from about thirty years ago would be good, perhaps local papers?'

'Hmm, what sort of news? Anything in particular, or just general from about that time?'

'About one particular event.' She moved to one side, to allow a couple of young mums with their offspring to check their books out.

'What was that particular event? Oh hello Gladys, how are you?' She interrupted her conversation with Bella to greet, Bella assumed, her colleague who must have been the wrong side of sixty and walked with the higgledy gait of someone in dire need of a hip replacement. The woman was small and rotund, with tightly permed hair which had a faint orange tinge to it. Her lips were smothered in a bright orange lipstick which clashed beautifully with her orange and black patterned short-sleeved dress from which protruded chubby arms with loose-hanging flesh squeezing out around the edges of them.

Bella tried not to stare at the vision, who was talking ten to the dozen as she tucked her bag under the counter and straightened herself out ready for work.

'Hello?' Bella realised that the librarian was talking to her.

'Oh, sorry. What did you say?'

'I was just saying that Gladys here might be able to help you.'

Bella smiled. 'Really? That would be fantastic.'

'Tell me what you need to know and I'll see what I can do,' beamed Gladys at her.

'Okay. I'm trying to find out about someone called Rupert Ireton who lived here around thirty years ago. I believe that something happened, which might well have been in the local news, and I'm trying to find out what it was,' she finished and thought it sounded feeble.

'Thirty years? That's a long way back. Don't know how much we'd be able to find out. Have you tried the internet?'

Bella was amazed that this woman even knew what the internet was. 'Yes, but I didn't get anywhere.'

'I didn't live here thirty years ago. Moved to Salisbury twenty years ago otherwise I might have remembered.' She looked thoughtful. Bella stood patiently feeling any hope of finding something out slipping away from her.

'Tell you what though, that journalist might remember.'

'Which one?' asked the other librarian.

'Oh, you know. That chap who was in the papers a few years ago. Got some sort of recognition for all the work he'd done. What was his name?' she tapped her crinkled fingers on the surface of the desk.

'Don't remember anything.' commented the other one.

'Got it! Bert Burstow.'

'Who? Never heard of him.'

'Bert Burstow, you must have heard of him?!'

Bella watched as the two of them launched into a lengthy discussion as to whether or not the other librarian knew who Bert was. She was getting impatient now, it was taking for ever to get any information out of them and, additionally, they were being constantly interrupted by people borrowing and returning books.

'So, where could I find this Bert Burstow?' Bella eventually interrupted. The librarians both looked at her in surprise, again having forgotten that she was standing there.

'Well now, that I don't know,' replied Gladys.

Oh, for goodness sake, muttered Bella inwardly.

'But I think Daisy will know. You hold on here while I give her a call.' Gladys disappeared off to make a phone call, returning fifteen minutes later.

Instinct warned Bella that Gladys wouldn't be capable of making a short phone call, and she was right.

Gladys looked triumphant. She handed Bella a piece of paper. 'I knew Daisy would know. I thought to myself, if anyone will know, it will be Daisy, and I was right! That there is the address of where Bert is currently residing. I think you're more likely to get the information you want direct from him than spend hours trawling through microfiche of old newspapers.'

Bella clutched the piece of paper tightly between her fingers. 'Thank you so much for all your help. I really appreciate it,' she said with feeling.

'Pleasure dear. Good bye, and good luck.'

'Bye.' Bella hurried out of the library and read the scrawl on the paper. It gave the address of a nursing home. Leafy Lane Nursing Home to be precise. Uh oh, that means he's either very old, very ill or both. Her sudden high was not quite so high, fearing that Bert would not be able to remember what he had had for breakfast, let alone what happened thirty years ago. She felt in need of a caffeine fix and ordered herself a cappuccino from a local coffee shop, she sat outside on the pavement at the junction where the road curved away as it met the pedestrian area. She watched the hustle and bustle of people and cars as she sipped her coffee and hoped fervently that she would at least make some sort of progress with her information-gathering by the end of the day. Taking a last swig of coffee, she walked down the pedestrian area to the tourist office, which was housed in one of the many ancient stone buildings of Salisbury.

She waited patiently whilst those in the queue in front of her, tourists (both overseas and UK based), were dealt with until it was her turn. She asked for a local map, as she had forgotten to bring her road map of England, and for directions to the nursing home. On the off-chance, she enquired whether they had a telephone number for it. The helpful woman tapped away on her computer and swiftly produced the number which she scribbled onto a piece of paper for Bella. Thanking her, Bella left and blinked as she walked back out into the bright sunshine.

It occurred to Bella that they may have visiting hours at the nursing home or perhaps one could just turn up. Rather than having a wasted trip, she phoned and ascertained that, as the residents would be having their lunch in about half an hour and then most of them had a post lunch nap, it would be best if Bella postponed her visit until around 3 o'clock. So what to do until then? Impatient to get to the home and speak to Bert, she reluctantly admitted defeat and resolved to explore the city a little more.

Seeing a bookshop she wandered in, whiling some time away as she rifled her way through the vast selection of books. Inevitably if she walked into a bookshop she always came out with a book, it was impossible for a bookworm like herself to resist, but on this occasion she could not concentrate and the appeal of a freshly-printed, pristine book, did nothing for her. Turning left out of the shop, she ambled back up in the direction of the cathedral and walked the full perimeter of the precinct, endeavouring to engross herself in the historical atmosphere of the cathedral and the many buildings around it, but that did little to distract her. For the umpteenth time she checked her watch and groaned, it was still only half past twelve. Decisively she walked up to the cathedral café for some lunch and was taken aback to see such a long queue outside it. The food really must be good, she thought - the cake certainly had been the day before - and sure enough it was. Bella settled on the chicken, which was served with a creamy mushroom sauce and a selection of fresh vegetables. She added a sparkling mineral water to her tray and paid. The queue coming in was still just as long as when she had arrived, and the tables too were full. She hovered for a few moments until she saw a small table being vacated in the furthest corner, near the gift shop.

Lunch was as delicious as it looked and met expectation. Feeling her blood sugar levels restoring themselves, she felt some semblance of humour returning. Bella relaxed slightly and tuned into snippets of conversations floating around her, as always a fascinating insight into the lives of other people. Squashing her desire for a pudding, she left and strolled back to the B&B to collect her car. It was a good half an hour's walk at a slow pace to the house, so by the time she arrived it was approaching 1.45pm. Itching to get going she started her engine, having reviewed the directions and ignoring her satnav, set off. Eventually, despite several wrong turns, she arrived at the nursing home at 2.15pm - had she not gone wrong so many times she would have been even earlier. It was far too early to go in and she resigned herself to sitting in her car until it was almost 3 o'clock. Bella sank back in the seat and closed her eyes. A gentle breeze wafted in through the open window but the warmth of the sun beating through the windscreen sent her drifting off to sleep. With a jolt she woke up and looked around her, feeling disoriented and momentarily wondering where she was. She gave herself a moment to come to then glanced at her watch. It was 2.55pm. Putting the window up and grabbing her bag, she hopped out of the car and gave her loose beige linen dress a little shake to let the air circulate and refresh her.

The front door to the nursing home was open and there was a small reception area off to the right-hand side.

'Hello?' called Bella.

A girl in her late teens appeared from the office behind the reception desk. 'Can I help you?'

'Yes. I phoned earlier. I'd like to see Bert Burstow please.'

'Are you a relative?'

'No. Gladys at the library in Salisbury suggested I talk to him. If he's up to it,' she added.

'I think he's in the garden. Come with me, I'll show you.'

She led the way down the hall towards the back of the modern brick building. Bella had expected some dilapidated Edwardian building that was in desperate need of attention, but instead the nursing home had turned out to be brand new. The smell, however, was worse than Bella had expected. The aroma of overcooked mince, mixed with a musty disinfectant smell, combined with what Bella thought of as the stench of approaching death, made her shiver and she breathed through her mouth in an effort to keep her nostrils clear of the unpleasant odours. They continued past a room which had groups of chairs clustered together. Some of them were occupied by antique looking beings, a few chatting, some sleeping - it was everything that scared Bella about old age.

They stepped through some French doors and out onto a spacious flagstone terrace. A large expanse of neat lawn was edged by several highly colourful boarders.

'Nice gardens,' commented Bella.

'We have a full-time gardener - we believe that having somewhere pleasant to sit or to look at helps our residents and it certainly brightens the place up. We've even got a vegetable garden. Residents can go and help out if they feel up to it, and even though most of them can't do very much they seem to enjoy the fact that they have the option and benefit, both physically and mentally, from being out-side in the fresh air.'

'Good idea.' Bella was impressed.

'There's Burt, over there,' the young woman pointed across the pristine lawn to a well established willow tree where there were half a dozen decrepit residents occupying chairs in the shade.

'Thanks.'

Bella strolled across the expansive lawn to the group of elderly people, who were clustered together, and braced herself for meeting Bert.

'Ooh, who have we got here?' warbled an elderly woman whose hair was so white that you could see the pinkness of her scalp shining through. She peered up through rheumy eyes at Bella. Bella smiled.

'Bert?' she asked questioningly at the only two men sit-ting with the group of four women.

'That's me. At least I can still remember my own name,' Bert chuckled. The others cackled with him as this was obviously some kind of "in" joke.

'That's more than can be said for old Violet over there,' added the other man, whose blue eyes had faded over time and were now ringed with white, hinting at a high cholesterol level. They all looked over at Violet who was a tall, willowy woman, younger than the group who were seated. She had a wispy dress on that floated around as she danced from side to side, her arms positioned, held by an imaginary partner, and deep in discourse with whoever was - or rather wasn't - there. Is this what it will come to, worried Bella. Will I be having conversations with imaginary people? Will the ageing process treat me cruelly? Will the younger generations show disregard and disrespect?

'So, you wanted me then?' asked Bert, snapping Bella out of her musings. Bert was shrivelled and shrunk, as though he'd been put into a washing machine at the wrong temperature. His skin was yellow and heavily wrinkled, and his teeth were obvious by their absence, other than three which were dotted about and such a dark, dirty, yellow colour that Bella could only conclude were a result of a lifetime of chain smoking. As if on queue, he let out a chesty, phlegmy cough which, in general, seemed to be symbolic of smokers, then spent a while wheezing whilst he recovered. The group looked at her expectantly, making her feel rather as though she were an exhibit in a zoo and she was today's entertainment.

'I went to the library this morning. I've been trying to get some information. Gladys there said that you used to work on the local paper. Quite a celebrity by all accounts, commended for all your work,' Bella felt flattery - much deserved by all accounts - would be a good softener to the conversation. Visibly she saw him grow a little taller, and his chest appeared to puff out in pride.

'Well, I don't want to blow my own trumpet but I am a bit of a legend in the journalistic world,' he grinned toothlessly.

'Oh, be off with you Bert! You were a local hack. It's not as though you were working on one of the big nationals,' piped up the white-haired old dear.

'Shows how much you know!' retorted Bert.

Bella stepped in quickly, fearing that the good-natured bickering would descend into a group event and she'd find it tricky to steer the conversation back in the direction she wished to take it. 'Anyway, she seemed to think that you would be able to help me.'

'Try me. I used to be able to remember everything, absolutely everything.'

'Pity you can't now! You're just like the rest of us. Go on, tell us what you had for breakfast,' goaded the blue-eyed man.

Bert folded his arms across his chest defensively. 'Shan't,' he replied like a truculent child.

Bella sighed. It was going to be a long afternoon. Persevering, she continued. 'It's about something that may or may not have happened thirty years ago.'

'So, if it didn't happen, how's he going to know whether it did happen and he's forgotten about it or whether it didn't happen and he can't remember that it didn't happen?' asked a petite woman who was sitting on the periphery of the group and had so far remained silent.

'Good point. How will he know?' added the white haired old dear.

'Just let the lady talk and then we will see,' snapped Bert. 'What's your name?'

'Bella,' she replied.

'I've got a granddaughter called Bella. By the way my name's Muriel,' introduced the white-haired, pink-scalped old dear holding out a gnarled arthritic hand for Bella to shake.

Bella took it gingerly, afraid to inflict any additional pain in the proffered hand, and felt the bones underneath the paper-thin skin.

Bert's interest had been stoked. 'Come on then Bella. Ask away.' He liked a challenge and he knew that even if he couldn't remember his friends would, sadly, not be able to remember Bella's visit by the morning.

'I'm trying to find out about someone called Rupert Ireton.'

'Why?' interrupted Muriel.

'Give it a rest Muriel, let her finish.' Bert rolled his eyes at Bella conspiratorially.

'He grew up in Salisbury, I believe, and something happened thirty years ago. I'm sure it did. I don't know what, but whatever it was it was bad enough for him not to have any kind of contact with his family afterwards.'

'Lots of people lose contact with their families,' murmured the blue-eyed man, who'd introduced himself as Jack whilst the others were arguing. He looked sadly at Bella and she felt a twang of pity for him. 'Like my family. Never come and visit. Lucky if they remember my birthday.'

There was a morose and reflective silence. Bella hesitated to interrupt but there seemed to be a growing number of reflective silences, she reasoned that they would have plenty of time for those after she'd left.

'He was fifteen when his family lost touch.'

'Oh poor love!' cried Muriel. 'Fancy being abandoned by your family. Poor little love. How cruel some people can be.'

'That's true enough.' There was a general nodding and murmuring at this.

Bella studied Bert who had remained silent. She willed his brain to work, for the cobwebs of old age to blow away and his mind to come back at full throttle. He pursed his lips then sucked the few teeth he had, shook his head and twisted his hands.

'It rings a bell, but I'll be blowed if I can remember why.'

'Why don't we all put our minds to it?' suggested Jack. 'Most of us were living in the area thirty years ago.' They nodded and gazed off in different directions. Bella couldn't be entirely sure whether they were thinking, or had actually gone to sleep with their eyes open. Each one of them must be at least eighty years old she thought, probably nearer ninety or more.

'That was the year before the Silver Jubilee year that was.'

'What was?'

'Thirty years ago, 1976. The year after was 1977, the Queen's Silver Jubilee.'

'Oh that were a good year it were. Do you remember the street parties? What fun we had, the children all dressed up, streets closed.'

'You got a real sense of community then, not like now where everyone is intent on looking after themselves and not giving a stuff about anyone else,' added Jack bitterly.

'Times have certainly changed. And not for the better, you mark my words,' added Dorothy.

Oh please, prayed Bella, please let them focus on Rupert and not have a reminisce about the good old days. But she was out of luck, the conversation wound its way through the seventies, then the eighties, then the nineties and into the twenty first century. She sat down on the grass, resigned to the fact that it could take all afternoon. Half an hour went by and cups of tea and some biscuits were brought out to them. Bella gratefully took the cup offered to her and sipped as she waited for the conversation to run its course, part of her fascinated by the tales they were telling.

'Didn't he do something bad?' Muriel suddenly piped up making the others halt their ruminations.

'I think you're right Muriel. There's definitely something.'

Bella sat up eagerly, hoping she was on the edge of a breakthrough.

'Something to do with a car as I remember.'

'Got it!' cried Bert triumphantly. Bella held her breath expectantly. 'He was the one who nicked his dad's car and went joyriding.'

So that was it, under-aged driving, stealing a car, no wonder he wanted to keep it quiet. But in this day and age would he really be vilified for such youthful stupidity?

'Pity it didn't stop at that though,' Bert shook his head sadly.

'What was it? What did he do?' urged Bella eagerly.

'He couldn't drive, thought he could like any cocky young teenager. Problem was he lost control, hit a child.'

'Oh no!' Bella's hand flew to her mouth. She had a horrible feeling in the pit of her stomach that there was worse to come.

'Poor child died. Rupert was locked up. Family moved away, never heard anything about them after that.'

Bella sat there stunned. Rupert had killed a child? And now he had been killed himself. There had to be a connection.

'What age was the child?' she asked.

'Ten. A boy. Tragic it was, tragic. Whole community was rocked to the core, and as for the child's parents well, I don't know how they coped, can one ever truly recover after the death of ones child?'

'Poor little lamb,' whispered Muriel, a tear running down her cheek.

Bella gulped back her tears as she remembered the devastation of her miscarriage. But to have given birth and loved and nurtured your child for ten years, then have him so cruelly ripped away from you... She couldn't bear to think about it, it made her heart ache so much she had to stop.

'That's so sad, so terrible,' she shook her head.

'Certainly was. Rupert didn't do it on purpose, it was a dreadful accident, but one that shouldn't have happened anyway,' continued Bert. 'Those were the types of stories I didn't like covering, particularly when they involved children.'

'What was the name of the little boy who died?' asked Bella quietly.

'Charles. Charles something, can't remember his surname.'

'Me neither,' added Jack. The rest of them sat in silence for a few minutes, reflecting and trying to remember, but they couldn't.

'Didn't he have a brother?' added Jack.

'No, it was a sister wasn't it?' said Muriel.

'Sorry I just can't remember,' Bert said apologetically.

Bella smiled and touched his hand. 'Thank you anyway. You have helped me a great deal.'

'Why did you want to know?' asked Dorothy.

'Rupert died in a car accident recently. Except that the police don't believe it was an accident. I wondered whether there was something in his past which might be connected to his death, tenuous though it may be.'

'Well I'm sorry to hear that. Despite what he'd done, it's tragic he's died too young, be it deliberately or otherwise.'

There were murmurs of "dreadful", "shocking" and the like. Bella seized the moment to leave.

'Thank you again, I must go now. It's been lovely to meet you all,' and she really meant it, the elderly seemed to be overlooked by society and yet they had a lifetime of experience and knowledge to offer and shouldn't be dismissed as so often happened.

She wandered reflectively back across the lawn, and turned to wave at them before she entered the house. In their own ways they waved back. She felt sad, not just about what she'd discovered but for all the residents there, this was no doubt where they were going to die. How depressing it must be to enter such a place with the knowledge that the next time you leave it will be by coffin. Bella sat for a moment in her car gathering her thoughts before driving back to the bed and breakfast. It was now five o'clock and she got ensnared in the rush hour traffic and, despite not getting lost this time, pulled into the B&B over half an hour later. What she really wanted now was to be at home surrounded by her own things. Funny how her rented cottage felt like home, despite there being few of her own possessions there. She knocked on the door and waited for Trisha to answer it.

'Hi,' her cheery face greeted Bella.

'Hello. I'm sorry Trisha but I'm going to check out now, I need to get home.'

Her face clouded. 'Is everything alright? Are you okay?'

'I'm fine, thank you. I just need to get back. I'm happy to pay for the nights I've booked, I know it's an inconvenience me departing early.'

'Nonsense, it's fine. Don't worry.'

Bella hesitated, feeling guilty at leaving her in the lurch. 'At least let me pay for tonight. It's so late in the day it's exceedingly unlikely you'll get anybody else to take the room for the night.'

'Well, alright then, thank you.'

They sorted out the payment and Bella nipped upstairs to pack her things. She bade farewell and popped her bag into the boot of her car. She felt she'd made the right decision and, despite driving home in very slow evening traffic which took her four hours, she felt her mood lift as she drove into Monhurst and parked outside her cottage. Dropping her bag in the hall she switched on the lights, feeling weary and mentally, physically and emotionally drained. Walking over to the answer phone she pressed the button and listened to two messages from Dave which made her smile, particularly at his second message where he made a joke of her paying him back for not returning her calls previously. It was half past ten, too late to phone and, as much as she wanted to talk to him, she was too tired and needed to get straight in her head what she'd say anyway. Without a doubt she was sure that Dave knew about Rupert's past, that must have been what he was withholding from her. She gulped down a couple of glasses of water to re-hydrate and munched on an apple as she ran a deep, bubbly bath. Throwing the apple core out of the window, she stepped into the bath and sighed as she sank down, feeling the tension in her muscles start to ebb away.

Chapter Fifteen

Bella slept in late the next morning and the first thing she did upon getting downstairs was leave a message on Dave's answerphone. She pottered about and whiled away the day, not doing much physically, but allowing her mind to continue to process the information she had received yesterday, attempting to tease out what the connection could be. Who was Charles' brother or sister, assuming he had one? What was the surname? And was there a connection? Or was it completely irrelevant? What if Kit were the brother of Charles? That would make sense. Her heart raced as everything seemed - to her - to slot into place. What more of a reason could you need to blackmail someone? Out of guilt, as well as fear, Rupert would have paid up, she was sure of it. Surely Dave must know? What if Kit had changed his name?

Desperate to speak to Dave, she left another message on his answerphone asking him to call her as soon as possible. This must be the answer. She'd solved it! She was convinced of it. Maybe Rupert had finally refused to pay Kit any more money. Maybe Kit was asking for even larger sums of money. Maybe Kit needed the money urgently and in a fit of rage killed Rupert?!

The day dragged on as Bella waiting impatiently for the phone to ring. Perhaps I should phone him at work? She felt a bit uncomfortable at the prospect of doing so but told herself she was being ridiculous, surely Dave would want to know what she had discovered? If he already knows then so be it, but if he doesn't he will definitely want to know. Nervously she picked up the phone and dialled the station number, but it transpired that both Dave and his sergeant were out. She left a short message asking him to call, just saying that she thought she had some information relevant to the case. Her stomach was in knots and she found it impossible to eat anything. Why on earth couldn't he hurry up and phone? Surely he had his mobile with him and his colleagues could contact him? And why didn't she have his mobile number?

At eight o'clock there was a knock on the door. Who on earth is that, she thought crossly flinging the door open. It was Dave. Her demeanour changed and she hurried him inside.

'There was a message at the station saying you needed to speak to me urgently?'

'I've found the missing link!' she cried.

'Really?'

'I know who killed Rupert!' her face shone with excitement.

'You do?' he raised an eyebrow, feeling rather dubious at her assertion.

'It was Kit!' She eagerly looked for confirmation on his face.

'Kit?' He looked puzzled.

How dense could he be? He was supposed to be the detective! She sighed and led him into the sitting room.

'Yes, Kit.'

'But why do you think that?'

Triumphantly she told him her theory. 'So you see, he had the perfect motive for murder.'

Dave nodded sagely. 'I can see that.'

'But?'

'There is no evidence to suggest that Kit was responsible for Rupert's death.'

'But I've just given it to you!'

'What you've given me is a theory, a plausible one,' he hastily added in order to appease her.

'But it must be him. It all fits.'

'Not quite. Kit's twin brother was not called Charles, he's not changed his name, and the paint on Rupert's Range Rover does not match the paint on Kit's silver Porsche.'

Bella felt instantly deflated but defiant. She was convinced her theory and the connection was correct.

'However I think you may be right on some level.'

She looked up hopefully.

'I do believe that somehow Kit found out about Rupert's past, either by doing his own research or perhaps Rupert told him many years ago when they were picking grapes. I think that could be a possible explanation as to why and what he was blackmailing Rupert about. But I do not believe that he killed him.'

Bella had been so sure. She'd found out Rupert's secret and had been convinced that Kit killed him. She felt rather foolish and very embarrassed. How could she possibly have thought she could solve the case? And how insulting it must seem to Dave.

'I would appreciate it if you could not go around doing your own detective work. It's best if you leave it to us.'

That was her told. She flushed with embarrassment.

His face softened, and he went and sat next to her, putting his hands on hers. 'I don't want you getting hurt. You may unwittingly uncover something that whoever killed Rupert doesn't want coming out. I don't want anything happening to you.'

That freaked her out. Irrationally she worried that whoever killed Rupert had her in their sight, that she was their next target How on earth would she now sleep at night?

'You don't think I could be being watched do you? Someone waiting until you've gone and then get me?' She shivered in fear.

'No, I don't. You'll be fine. But if you keep digging around you never know. I care about you and I don't want anything to happen to you.' He smiled at her and changed the subject. 'Are you going to the fête on Saturday?'

'Oh absolutely, particularly as it's going to be held right on my doorstep.' The fête was always held on the village green which was right outside Bella's cottage.

'I'm working most of the day. How about we go to the evening barbecue together?'

'That would be nice. Why don't you come here about 7pm. Mia and Fred are going to park on the drive, so squeeze your car in behind theirs.

'Great. I'll look forward to seeing you then. Now remember, no digging about! Leave it to us, okay?'

She nodded, but knew that if some titbit of information came her way she wouldn't be able to resist. She bade him farewell and closed the door behind him. Her stomach was no longer crunched and churning but rumbled in hunger so she poached some salmon and made herself a salad.

The day of the fête dawned cloudy and ominous. Fortunately the marquees had been put up on Thursday so - despite the torrential rain on Friday - setting up for the event had been able to go ahead without any delay. Bella had enjoyed her trip to the ancient town of Rye with Mia the day before. The rain had kept a few of the tourists away but it was still heaving with them, and who could blame them? The cobbled winding streets and general ambiance of the town was very special, it was like nowhere else Bella had visited before and she made a resolution to go back once the peak summer season was over, and the town had recovered a bit from the onslaught of visitors.

She peered out of the back bedroom window looking for signs that the weather was going to clear up, but there were none. It was just typical, she thought, week after week of gorgeous weather and the one day it was really needed it did this. Perfect weather would attract more people and hence raise more money for the village so gloomy and wet weather would not have the desired effect. She pulled on a pair of jeans and slipped a thin red sweatshirt over her t-shirt, the first time in weeks she'd needed an extra layer. She hugged her morning cup of tea to her in an attempt to take the chill off. Perhaps if I go for a cycle it'll get me warmed up she contemplated? Peering out of the back door, dark grey clouds hung heavily but it hadn't started raining. She decided to risk it and scurried out. Half an hour later she was back - hot, panting and with rosy cheeks - as Bella put her bike away there was the pitter-patter of rain followed by a torrential downpour as she ran to the front door. She dried off and flicked the kettle on to make a cup of coffee. Feeling refreshed after her cycle, she settled down with the newspaper she'd picked up on the way back, and wrapped her hands around the steaming mug. The best thing she could do now was not to venture out, competitors had started to arrive with their entries for the various competitions taking place. They would be judged that morning, and the winner announced that afternoon during the fête. Bella knew that once the constant flow of traffic had temporarily ceased, it would just as soon start up again as the helpers arrived, and a little while later the massive, she hoped, invasion of visitors would start, cars would be parked everywhere, up the lanes, in the car parks, anywhere where there was a spare slot. Bella had been warned by Jennifer what to expect, it was the same every year, anyone who lived in the village was considerate but many of those visiting from the surrounding areas seemed not to care about where they parked, or what damage they caused. Fences had even been knocked down in previous years, but the organisers now put a strip of red and white striped tape outside each house in an attempt to prevent this. There would be worse this evening apparently. After the barbecue it would be likely that a select few, who had been drinking all day and all evening, would add unmentionables to the front gardens which would additionally have been littered with beer cans, bottles and other rubbish during the event.

About eleven o'clock Bella was interrupted by a knock on the door. It was Mia and Fred.

'Got time for a quick coffee before you hurry off to do your bit?'

'Love to but we can't. The cat threw up all over the kitchen just as we were leaving so we're behind schedule. See you later though.' They hurried off in separate directions to perform whatever allotted tasks they had been allocated.

Bella made herself another cup of coffee and sat in the window seat of the sitting room watching the frenetic activity that was going on in preparation for the grand opening at two o'clock. She saw Jennifer hurrying down the lane and waved; she waved back and came up the front path.

'Hi, how are you?' asked Bella opening the door.

'Fine thanks. How about you? Haven't seen you in what seems like ages.'

'Fine too thanks. Got time for a coffee? Just made one,' she raised her mug.

'Just a quick one. It's frantic out there.'

'I know I've been watching. It must take so much organising.'

'I understand that as soon as one fête is over they start planning the next. Thanks,' she said taking the mug from Bella and following her into the sitting room.

'I had to tell you,' Jennifer's eyes glistened excitedly, 'I saw Kim this morning. She had a visit from that Inspector - the one you know - yesterday, and guess what?'

Bella had a feeling she knew what was coming, but wasn't going to volunteer any information in case she made the wrong assumption and revealed something she wasn't supposed to. 'What?'

'The photograph. It was Kit. Rupert and Kit knew each other years ago!'

'Ah,' she replied.

'You don't seem very surprised?'

'I had a feeling it would turn out to be him. A gut feeling, you know.'

'Yeah. But what I want to know is why did they pretend not to know each other at Sophie and Harry's party? Weird, huh?'

'It does seem a little strange. Did Inspector Ormandy say anything else?' she enquired cautiously.

Jennifer pursed her lips. 'No. I think he asked Kim lots of questions but didn't give any explanation.'

'What sort of questions?' Bella's curiosity was peaked.

'Stuff like, what did Kim know of his family? Did she know anything about Rupert's life before he settled here? That sort of thing. Really just going over what they've already asked her.'

'Hmm.' What's he up to, thought Bella.

'Hmm, what? Do you know something?'

'I was just thinking that's all. Actually, are Sophie and Harry coming to the fête?'

'They're parking at my house. Don't know what time though. Why?'

'Well, I wonder if Ariadne has mentioned anything about Kit in passing to either Sophie or Harry, you know, about his past? What he was doing in Australia?'

'I don't know. Good point, I'll ask them. I wonder if Kim has mentioned the photo to them?'

'Don't think so. Think she was just going to keep it between you, me, her and Mia until she knew more.'

'Okay. Well I'll have a word and let you know. Intriguing isn't it?' she giggled. 'Best be off, thanks for the coffee, see you later.'

'Yes. Bye. Thanks for letting me know.'

What about Ariadne though? The thought suddenly struck Bella, she'd been so busy concentrating on Kit, that she'd dismissed Ariadne completely. What was her background? Bella knew she went to school with Sophie, but did Ariadne have any brothers? Could she be involved? Or did she know about the blackmail? In her head Bella heard Dave's voice reminding her not to dig about, but she banished it from her mind. She wasn't digging she was just enquiring, helping Kim, she justified to herself. Having convinced herself that she was doing the right thing, she made herself a sandwich then went to inspect her wardrobe, to make her choice for her night out with Dave. A further inspection of the weather revealed that blue sky was attempting to break through and the sun was starting to peek in and out from behind the clouds. She laid out another simple, pale blue, cotton dress with a tie waist; additionally she laid out a pair of navy linen trousers, long sleeved navy linen top and thin, pale pink cashmere cardigan, just in case the weather didn't warm up enough. Slipping into a casual, cream cotton skirt and a lime green polo top, she slid her feet into a pair of beige deck shoes and trotted downstairs. Bella opened her bag, retrieved some money from her purse, put it deep into one of her skirt pockets and picked her keys up - she was intrigued to see what the fête would be like and didn't want to miss the start.

The locals weren't wrong about the traffic, it was backed up in all directions and there was a lot of honking of horns going on. Volunteers in fluorescent jackets were waving people in the direction the flow of traffic should be going, the problem was being caused by those who thought they would take a short cut and nip in and park somewhere else, this in turn was causing problems with the traffic patiently waiting to get directed to a parking space.

In order to allow as many people as possible to witness the start of the fête, it was opened a few minutes late. Children ran around screaming with excitement and a local brass band played a mixture of popular and traditional tunes. The village green was packed with people, and more were arriving. Bella strolled round admiring the stalls. She'd expected stall after stall to be full of junk - cheap plastic stuff sold at ridiculous prices, but purchased by the vendor at a pittance, thus making a substantial profit. But she was wrong, every stall was different and of good quality. Additionally there was the traditional tombola, Punch and Judy, coconut shy, cake stall, guess the weight of the cake, guess how many smarties were in the jar, Splat the Rat and so on, as well as stalls selling local goods and produce. Handmade wooden items, pottery, honey, apple juice, jumpers, jams and preserves. Bella purchased a pot of lavender-scented honey, a bottle of apple juice and a couple of jars of jam. Living on the doorstep of the fête meant she could pop home, leave them inside the front door and then lock up again. She'd been advised to keep her windows and doors all locked, unfortunately it was inevitable in this day and age that there would be opportunists who would use this event for their own purpose i.e. petty theft and burglary.

Next Bella joined the stream of people heading into the marquees, which had just been opened up; the winning entries displaying a "first", "second" or "third" card beside them. She admired the multitude of floral displays, then moved on to the vegetable section. A great debate was going on as to whether the right decision had been made regarding the allocation of awards. Bella smiled - it was nice that, temporarily at least, people were only worrying about the results, rather than what was going on in the world in general. Next was the cake area, her mouth watered at the sight of them, such a waste not to be able to eat them she mused as she eyed up the delectable display in front of her. After the jam and chutney section was the last, and perhaps the sweetest, of the entries – the children's miniature gardens. It was obvious that some of the children had had a huge amount of assistance from one or other of their parents, as there was no way some of the perfectly produced gardens in the five and under category could possibly have been created by a five year old. It was blatantly apparent to anyone - except the parents involved it would seem- and the judges were shrewd enough to award prizes appropriately, with the first, second and third prize going to the ones which basically looked like a pile of soil with a few twigs, and had inevitably been put together entirely by the child without parental assistance.

Her taste buds having been woken by the sight of the competition cakes, Bella wandered off in search of the tea tent. She knew there was one, as some of the group were making cakes for them. She bypassed the Pimms tent, preferring to wait until this evening before drinking alcohol, not wanting to be tipsy or drunk by the time Dave turned up. Patiently she queued and chose a large sponge cake stuffed with fresh cream and bursting with raspberries. People were sprawled on the grass eating which didn't appeal to Bella, fearing that damp grass on a cream skirt would leave an annoying stain. Instead, she noticed that there was a chair free at one table and went to enquire as to whether she could sit there. Settling herself down, she tucked into the cake. Before long the table was vacated and she was on her own and sat back to watch the maypole dancing the children from the village school were going to perform. Despite the real sense of community and togetherness, Bella felt a twinge of being an outsider, surprised that it bothered her so much as she had originally planned to stay for just 6 months.

'Mind if I join you?'

Bella turned and shielded her eyes against the sun. It was Florence. 'Please do. It's lovely to see you. How are you?'

Florence settled herself and placed her cup of tea and plate of chocolate cake on the rickety wooden table. 'I'm fine thanks. How about you?'

'Very well thanks. That cake looks delicious,' she observed as Florence took a mouthful, sorely tempted to buy a piece for herself.

Florence licked her lips. 'It is. Very moist and very chocolaty. Have you found much to keep you occupied?'

'Oh yes. I never seem to stop. There are so many places to visit round here and I've hardly got to any of them yet. I'm absolutely determined to get to Sissinghurst next week.'

'It is beautiful there, so tranquil and the gardens are magnificent. You know that it's closed on Wednesday and Thursday?'

'Thanks. I've got a leaflet on it. I think I'll go on Friday morning if the weather is good.'

'I'm sure you'll have a lovely time. What do you think of the fête then?'

They chatted amiably for a while and had refills of tea. Eventually Florence rose to go and Bella, feeling guilty about hogging a prized table and chair for so long, got up too, bade farewell to Florence and continued strolling around. She waved to Mia and Jennifer who were busy on a stall and paused to watch the children's running races. Deciding it was time for yet another cup of tea she ambled back to the tea tent and, despite the temptation, managed to resist having any more cake. As the afternoon drew on the crowds started to thin, another couple of hours and they would start to swell again as the evening crowd came in for the night's merriment. Feeling weary, Bella went over to an empty table and chairs, but before her bottom could hit the seat she was interrupted.

'Like to join us?'

Sophie and Harry were sitting on the next table with Jemima, giggling as usual and slapping her hands on the table, excited by the noise they made and eager to make the cups, saucers and plates rattle some more.

'Thanks, how are you all?' Bella made some cooing noises and faces at Jemima which made the little tot laugh even more enthusiastically. 'She's so sweet.'

Harry and Sophie glowed with parental pride. 'Thank you. We think she's pretty cute, but then we'd be a bit biased,' laughed Harry.

'Are you enjoying the fête, Bella?' asked Sophie.

'I'm really impressed. Some of these fêtes can be dreadful, which makes me wonder why they're held, but this one is really nice. All villagey and with local produce and products too which is a nice touch.'

'Several years ago the fête was becoming a bit tacky, full of all the rubbish you're talking about. After a great deal of debate and deliberation, the committee eventually decided to take action, taking what was perceived at the time as a big risk. They decided that only local small businesses, or individuals, would be able to have a commercial stall, all of them being vetted and checked out prior to a stall being confirmed, and that no plastic or tacky mass-produced products not made in this country would be allowed at the fête. Of course there was an uproar, a lot of people thought the committee were mad to take the decision, fearing that it would be the demise of the village fête - particularly given that fêtes in general seemed to be dwindling, and visitor numbers decreasing, thereby not making them profitable or worth all the effort of organising them. Though the first year after the new policy change was not quite as successful as previous years, it has picked up every year since and now, it is far more popular and profitable than it has ever been, and has a real community spirit about it. I gather there's now a waiting list of craftspeople and local businesses wanting to have a stall here, I think it's become a good marketing tool for them,' said Harry.

'I agree with you, if we took more care to buy locally and to support our local businesses, it would surely be good for them and us. It seems to make sense to me,' commented Bella.

'Oh absolutely, we agree with you,' replied Sophie.

'Room for another?' asked Jennifer pulling up a chair. 'Has Bella told you?'

'Told us what?' they looked at Bella then Jennifer.

'About Kit?'

'What about him?'

'You know how at your party Kit was introduced to us all, because none of us had met him before?' They nodded. 'Well he knew Rupert many years ago.'

'Really? That's strange, why didn't they say?'

'Maybe they didn't recognise one another after such a long time?' suggested Sophie.

'Possibly, though I bet they did. But why did they hide it from us? Are you sure you didn't know anything?'

'No, definitely not. It was the first time Kit was introduced to us.'

'What made you think there was a connection?' asked Harry.

'Bella discovered a picture on the internet. It had what we thought was a younger version of Rupert and Kit so we took it and showed it to Kim, but she'd never seen it before and had no idea whether they had known each other or not. Kim then found a photograph of Rupert taken a few years ago which was the spitting image of one of the people in the photograph Bella found. So Kim then asked Bella to mention it to Inspector Ormandy, as Bella knew him from when he trained with her late husband.'

Harry and Sophie sat with open mouths whilst they listened, astounded at what had been going on and that they were blissfully unaware of.

'Why didn't you just ask Kit? I would have given you the number,' Sophie looked a little hurt.

'Oh Sophie, we didn't want to upset you. If it turned out that it wasn't Kit in the photo then the matter would have dropped. And Kim wanted to keep it quiet.'

'But how did you come across the photo Bella?'

Bella, who had been sitting feeling uncomfortable during the exchange, hesitated; she really didn't want them thinking she was a nosey old snoop.

'I suppose Rupert's death hit a chord with me. You know, reminded me of the death of my husband, and well, I don't know really,' she shrugged her shoulders. 'I was just fiddling around on the internet and this photo came up. I didn't know what to do. I didn't want to do anything behind Kim's back, and I hardly knew any of you and I definitely did not want to upset anyone. Anyway, I showed Jennifer and Jennifer didn't know anything and she suggested we show Kim and well, Jennifer's told you the rest.'

'I wish you'd come to me. I could have just asked Kit outright or asked Ariadne, she would know or if she didn't she would have asked. Could have saved Kim getting involved,' replied Sophie.

'Sorry,' said Bella meekly.

'Come on, don't be hard on Bella. Besides, if he didn't want anyone to know that they knew each other it's unlikely he'd have told you, isn't it?' said Jennifer logically.

'Maybe.'

'So what did the police say then?'

Jennifer reiterated what she'd told Bella that morning. Bella sat quietly, praying that they wouldn't ask any further questions. Questions she knew the answers too, but wasn't allowed to reveal.

'I'm going to phone Ariadne when I get home and find out what Kit has been playing at. Why on earth would she want him, as her part-time boyfriend and full-time agent, if he's not going to be honest with her?'

'I'd be careful Soph,' warned Harry, 'you don't know what you might be stirring up.'

Too right, thought Bella.

'I know, but she's a good friend and I've known her long enough.'

'I'd do the same for Mia,' added Bella, seizing the moment, 'I've known her for so long, since we were at school together.'

'Exactly!' replied Sophie looking pointedly at Harry.

'I expect you had fun with Ariadne when you were younger. Did she have any brothers or sisters? I bet they were jealous of the way she looked!'

Sophie laughed. 'She didn't always look so stunning. When we were at school, she was decidedly average, but always had a certain presence about her. But no, she didn't have any brothers or sisters, so there was no sibling rivalry.'

'I thought she had a brother?' queried Harry.

'She did, he died when he was young.'

She what?! Bella's ears pricked up.

'That's so sad. What happened?' asked Jennifer, echoing Bella's very thoughts.

'I don't know really. Wasn't something she or her family talked about and I didn't ask.'

At that moment Jemima let out a large belch and vomited all over Harry's knees. He mopped it up as best he could, but it had soaked through his shorts.

'Looks like we'd better go,' he rolled his eyes and stood up, strapping his daughter deftly into her pushchair.

'See you later?' asked Jennifer.

'No, worse luck. Couldn't get a babysitter, everyone seems to be busy coming to the barbecue.'

'You could bring her. You have before.'

'I know, but she's been a bit of a madam about bedtimes recently so we're trying to keep the continuity and get her back into a routine. I fear that if we bring her out tonight all our hard work over the last few weeks will have been wasted. Sorry.'

'That's a shame. I can't believe for one minute she'd be a little madam about anything!' Jennifer grinned and raised her eyebrows.

Sophie laughed. 'See you soon. Bye.'

'Don't forget to let us know what Ariadne says,' called Jennifer after her. 'Be interesting to see if she knows anything,' she muttered aside to Bella.

'Hmm,' replied Bella non-committally. 'Think I'll go too, see you later at the barbecue.'

'Bye, yup, see you later.'

Bella hurried home to scribble down the snippets of information whilst they were still fresh in her head. The fact that Ariadne had had a brother who had died before Sophie knew her meant that he must have been quite young when he died. Maybe Kit had inadvertently told her about his time with Rupert in Australia? Maybe she was in on the blackmail too? Maybe she deliberately brought Kit down to spook Rupert? Maybe she'd planned it all along, waiting for her revenge, biding her time? Bella was eager to tell Dave, but decided to sleep on it. After her humiliation on Wednesday night, she didn't feel she could bear another dose of it, besides it was his night off, they were going to have fun, and there would be no work-related talk.

So consumed was she at writing, from memory, everything down - from the day of Rupert's death to the present day - that when she had finished it was almost half past six. Panicking that she only had half an hour to get ready, she ran up the stairs, threw her clothes onto the bedroom floor and jumped into the shower to rinse off the stickiness that had crept up on her as the temperature had steadily risen during the afternoon. Quickly she towel-dried herself and slipped into the pale blue dress she'd laid out earlier, deciding to take the pale pink cashmere cardigan with her as well just in case it cooled down later on. Hair brushed up into a twirly knot at the back, tendrils whisping around her face, she admired the silhouette it gave her long slim neck; mascara and a touch of pale pink lip-gloss later and she was ready. Her pale pink toe nails peeked out from the toes of her wedge heeled suede soft pink shoes, so pale that they could almost be cream. Satisfied with what she saw, she took the empty miniature cream beaded shoulder bag downstairs and placed lip-gloss, keys, handkerchief and cash into it, just about managing to squeeze it all in.

Punctual as ever, Dave arrived spot on seven o'clock. Bella could smell wafts of hot barbecue charcoal coming over from the green as she opened the door to let him in. She led him through to the kitchen, where she silently admired the freshly washed and brushed man in front of her, his pale cream chinos crinkle free and pale blue casual long sleeved linen shirt freshly pressed. His citrus aftershave floated over to her and she breathed it in deeply, it mixed well with her lightly floral and citrus perfume.

'You look lovely,' he smiled, 'a picture of summer.'

She blushed. 'Thanks. You're looking pretty good yourself. Have you had a good day?'

'Not bad thanks. But tonight not a word of work, promise?'

She grinned sheepishly. 'Promise, though I can't guarantee that the others are not going to grill you.'

'Fair enough. I'll be polite but firm. This is definitely out of business hours. Shall we go?'

People were thronging onto the green, the tantalising smells from the barbecue stimulating their taste buds; they were edging closer and closer, eagerly awaiting the signal that the food was ready, rather like vultures waiting for their prey.

Bella and Dave weaved their way through the crowds to the bar, which had been set up in what had been the competition marquees. Dave waited patiently as people jostled one another trying to get the attention of the bar staff, eventually he managed to purchase a couple of large plastic beakers of Pimms and squeezed his way back through to the entrance of the marquee where Bella was waiting. The sun was still strong and the evening was a perfect temperature. Mosquitoes were starting to appear, juicy pickings for them this evening mused Bella.

'Here we are. Got there at last.' Dave handed her the drink. 'Cheers!'

'Cheers,' she responded, touching her plastic beaker against his.

They chatted comfortably as they wandered around through the milling crowds. Food had started to be served, but there was such a mass of people queuing that they decided to wait for a while, instead nipping back to the emptying bar tent to replenish their drinks. Eventually they joined the queue, Mia, Fred and Jennifer passing them with laden down plates.

'Want to join us?' asked Fred.

'Er, thanks. See you in a bit.' Bella wasn't sure whether Dave would want to sit with her friends or keep her all to himself. 'You don't mind do you?'

'Not at all. I naturally assumed we'd bump into your friends, besides it'll be nice to catch up with Mia and Fred, it's been a long time.'

Bella felt a mixture of relief and disappointment. Relief that he wasn't rejecting her friends, but illogical disappointment that he didn't want her all to himself. To her delight the evening turned out to be relaxed and great fun and, despite Jennifer trying to prise the odd piece of information out of Dave, there were no really awkward moments. Bella had thought that Kim might turn up but she didn't and Bella assumed she had opted for a quiet night with Seb. She hadn't dared ask Dave any more about them, working on the assumption that no news was good news, and additionally the fact that neither of them were currently residing in jail seemed a good indicator that they were both off the hook. Before she knew it the party was winding down and people were drifting off, Dave escorted her back to the house but only came in for a brief moment, his excuse being that it was so late he needed to get some sleep as he had to work again tomorrow, despite it being Sunday.

Chapter Sixteen

Bella pottered around the house for the next few days, leaving her notes scattered on the kitchen table so that she could dip in and out of them, hopeful that at some point they would make more sense to her and that there would be a grand revelatory moment. She went out on her bike each day, which helped her mind mull through the sequence of events, but found no clarity. She was convinced that she was missing something, and this was added to by the niggling sense that there was a piece of information locked away in her brain that frustratingly she couldn't tease out. Bella went through the motions of everyday life, but was so distracted by Rupert's death that each day seemed to merge into the next. By Friday Bella decided that she had spent more than enough time on the case and needed to snap herself out of her current malaise, and, as the weather was bright and sunny, she kept her promise to herself and went to visit Sissinghurst Gardens and Castle.

Being a member of the National Trust, she waved towards her car sticker stuck next to her tax disc, to indicate that she was a member and therefore exempt from paying the car parking fee. The helpful volunteer gave her a map and information, and she went and parked her car in the car park which was filling rapidly, even though it was only eleven o'clock. Presenting her membership card in the ticket office resulted in a paper ticket being given to her, she showed this to the volunteer at the entrance to the castle and entered with great anticipation.

Bella wasn't disappointed. As she walked through the archway she was greeted by an expanse of lawn and an imposing tower with stunning views to the distance. Carefully she studied the map she'd been given, and decided to go clockwise round the gardens. The riot of colour was magnificent and she knew it must take many man hours to care for and nurture such beautiful gardens. Within the gardens she went into the library which was lined with fascinating books, and then walked through the Delos and into the White Garden which was exquisite in its array of white flowers and plants though sadly the beautiful canopy that had been covered in white roses was going over.

She was very taken with the wild flowers and grasses in the orchard, the bees buzzed happily and the white beehives made it look so quaint. Perfection, she sighed happily. Bella took the opportunity to sit for a while on one of the benches and to just enjoy and absorb the calmness and peace that the orchard gave her, despite the number of tourists milling around. Lost in her thoughts she didn't notice the person sit down next to her and it was only when she heard a quiet "hello" that she realised anyone was there at all.

'Oh! Hello!' she replied in surprise. It was Florence.

'Sorry, did I interrupt your thoughts? I'll go if you like?' She looked quizzically at Bella.

Bella felt irritated but she couldn't identify why, perhaps because she'd been enjoying the peace and tranquility, notwithstanding the visitors. 'No, that's fine,' she replied.

'It is beautiful here isn't it?'

'Magnificent. Mind you, I've only seen a fraction of the garden so far, it's amazing that it's so peaceful despite all the visitors.'

'I know. It's a great place to come and think.' They lapsed into a contemplative silence for a while, absorbing their surroundings.

'Charlotte!' Bella yelped out loud making Florence jump.

'What?'

Of course! She knew there was a nugget of information missing. What a fool she'd been! She'd been so fixated with trying to discover whether the boy who had died had had a brother or sister that she had blanked out the information about the name of the person who was mentioned in Rupert's will. Giving her brain the opportunity to drift and relax had released the piece of information she'd been trying to tease out all week.

'Charlotte Willingham. I forgot! How stupid of me.'

Florence was looking at her in a peculiar way, not surprisingly thought Bella, she probably thinks I've gone mad.

'Who?'

'Charlotte Willingham. She's the woman mentioned in Rupert's will.'

'His will?' she repeated faintly.

'Yes. But of course you weren't there at tennis, at Kim's house,' explained Bella, momentarily concerned that she'd let out a big secret, then relieved to remember that she hadn't as the others had been there too and Kim had been quite open about it. 'Yes, Rupert has left a chunk of

251

his estate to a Charlotte Willingham. The only problem is no one knows who she is.'

'Really?'

'Mmm, yes. I think Kim's solicitor is on the case, but I don't know whether he's found her yet.'

'So why does it concern you?'

'Well it doesn't really. I just wish for Kim's sake the police would hurry up and find out who killed Rupert.'

Florence looked confused. 'I don't understand.'

As the photo was now public knowledge Bella explained what had been discovered, but kept everything else to herself.

'Oh. So you've been doing some detective work yourself?'

'Um, not really, no, er, maybe. I don't know, I suppose I was just trying to help,' Bella replied evasively.

'So why did you shout out this Charlotte person's name?'

'Something had been bugging me and then the name popped into my head.'

'So what are you going to do now?'

Bella frowned. 'Hmm, not sure. Probably do a search on the internet, I don't know why I didn't think of it before. Perhaps something will come up.' Her mind was running through the options. Charlotte Willingham must be the sister of Charles. She must be, and somehow I've got to be able to find out if they are related. Could Ariadne be Charlotte?

'I'm sure the solicitor would have thought of that. And besides these things are best left to the police.'

'True. But aren't you intrigued?' Bella looked at her curiously. Florence's eyes were flat and dull and she still looked exhausted, work must really be taking it's toll on her.

'Not particularly. I mean, you've no idea what the connection is between Rupert and this person?'

'You're right, but I'm sure it won't be long before the connection is made.'

'I feel like walking round the rest of the gardens,' said Florence changing the subject. 'Care to join me?'

'Why not.' Bella picked up her bag and they strolled companionably through the orchard to the herb garden admiring the moat walk as they past. Up the lime walk, round the cottage garden, through to the rose garden and across the tower lawn. Bella found the gardens, and their individuality, breathtaking. She wanted to take her time, but Florence seemed in a hurry; when she suggested going up the tower to admire the views Florence declined making Bella, out of politeness, miss out on something she'd been looking forward to. Still, it was a good reason to return soon. Hoards more people were arriving as they came out, it had been a wise move to come early.

'Fancy lunch?' suggested Bella, eager to try out the restaurant. She was never disappointed with a meal at a National Trust property. Each one created their own dishes, nothing fancy but good wholesome fare, and they used as much local produce as they could.

'How about lunch at my place? It looks as though it might be getting crowded in there.'

Bella looked doubtfully at the restaurant, from what she could see through the glass it seemed relatively quiet. But she was flattered to be invited to lunch and didn't want to be rude.

'That would be nice. Thanks. Whereabouts are you?'

'Not far from the village. Tell you what, why don't you follow me, it'd be easier than me giving you directions.'

'Okay.'

Bella dutifully followed Florence's blue Honda CRV along the Monhurst Road and off down a couple of country lanes. They then went down a narrow overgrown driveway which wound along the edge of a small wood, subsequently opening up into a clearing by a small, detached, tumbled-down looking cottage. Bella got out and could hear nothing but the birds singing, it was a truly isolated and tranquil spot.

'No noisy neighbours here then!' she joked as Florence unlocked the front door.

'No. Nice and quiet. Just how I like it. Come in.'

They walked into a tiny entrance hall. Bella noticed the peeling paint and unmistakable smell of damp. The stairs were uncarpeted and scruffy looking, which matched everything else in the house from what she could see.

'How did you find this place?' she asked politely, following Florence into a small dark kitchen which held units that had seen better days; there were doors hanging off, a drawer with no front to it and an ancient looking electric cooker standing in the corner.

'I contacted a few local farmers to see if they had any farm cottages they might want to sell. This one came up.'

'And do you enjoy living here?

'Oh yes,' she replied with the first bit of real enthusiasm Bella had seen in her.

As far as Bella was concerned this house was not fit for human habitation. She shivered, the warmth from outside was not penetrating inside and she wished Florence would unlock the back door and open a few windows to let the warm air flow through to ease the musty smell and dampness within.

'Have you got much garden?' she asked, hopeful that Florence would take her outside and show her.

'No.'

Oh well, that didn't work and what was up with Florence?

'You okay?'

'Fine. I've got some salad and some quiche, is that okay?'

'Lovely. Thanks. Can I do anything?'

'No you're fine there.'

Bella stood uselessly to one side of the kitchen. 'Mind if I sit?'

'Please do.' Florence suddenly smiled at her. 'Coffee? Tea? Something cold?'

'Coffee please.' She felt in need of warmth, her bare arms had goose bumps on them and her legs were following suit. 'You going to tennis later?' Tennis was being held later than usual; at four o'clock today.

'No,' Florence shook her head, 'I'm going to be busy.'

'That's a shame. Maybe next week then?'

Bella gratefully took the mug of instant coffee, which had been offered, and clung onto it as though it were a hot water bottle. She watched as Florence deftly cut and chopped tomatoes, cucumber, radishes, celery and lettuce for the salad, admiring the knife as it slid with such ease through each item, reminding Bella that she really ought to buy some decent kitchen knives.

When lunch was ready Florence sat across from Bella at the small, beaten, wobbly wooden table.

'Please. Help yourself,' offered Florence handing Bella a chipped white dinner plate.

'Thanks.' Bella scooped up some salad and a slice of homemade leek and potato quiche. 'This looks yummy,' she commented, referring to the quiche, 'do you like cooking?'

'When I have time, I'm usually so busy. But it's a lot cheaper to make food and you know precisely which ingredients have gone into it.'

'True. Half the time the stuff you buy at the supermarket is full of additives and preservatives. This quiche really is delicious,' she added.

Florence sat quietly eating her lunch. Bella wondered what was wrong, maybe she's regretting inviting me for lunch, she pondered.

'What made you decide to move to Kent?' Bella did her best to make polite conversation.

Florence shrugged. 'Fancied a change of scene and a job came up at the local surgery. Kent is a lovely county, a bit more built up than I thought it would be, but there are still some lovely pockets of rural countryside.'

'It's pretty here. I've settled in really well, which I wasn't expecting'

There was another awkward pause. Perhaps I should have stayed at Sissinghurst mused Bella, maybe I've unwittingly said something to upset her? They finished their meal in silence. By now Bella was desperate to make a quick exit, and get into some warm sunshine and fresh air, the house was feeling very oppressive.

'That was lovely. Thank you. Well, I'd best be off. I've got a few things that need to be done before tennis.' She rose to go. Florence leapt up.

'Oh, no, don't go yet. Have a cup of coffee or tea. Please.'

Bella felt a twinge of guilt and didn't want to be ungrateful. 'Okay, thanks, just a quick coffee then. Thanks.'

Florence cleared the plates into the sink and ran some hot water into it, washed the chopping board and knife up and left the plates to soak whilst the kettle boiled. Bella's eye was caught by a scrap of newspaper peaking out from a pile of post and papers, which was crammed onto one of the work surfaces. It was about Rupert. Why had Florence kept it? The house wasn't particularly tidy, but it looked carefully cut out, as though she'd specifically wanted to keep this article. Bella became more convinced it was because Florence had been having an affair with him and took it as confirmation that she had been. She dived in feet first.

'So... what did you think of Rupert?' she asked.

Florence spun round and eyed her suspiciously.

'Why do you ask that?'

'I just wondered. You must have seen him up at tennis. Did you get on with him?'

'I met him for the first time at Sophie and Harry's party, not before.'

Hmm, in denial and obviously been sneaking around with him, concluded Bella to herself. 'And what did you think of him then?'

'I thought he was an arrogant, self-centred, drunken idiot!' she snapped.

Oh dear, maybe he dumped her. 'I see. Er, could I use your loo please?'

'Upstairs, second on the left.'

Relieved to get away from Florence for a few minutes, Bella carefully negotiated the rickety stairs. Was that first or second door on the left she wondered when she got to the top of the stairs? She pushed the first door cautiously open and peaked in. Bella frowned, and walked in to what was definitely not the bathroom. The wall was plastered in newspaper cuttings, there was a decaying old garden table filled with scrapbooks. She opened one up quietly and peaked inside; the blood drained from her face. Every single newspaper article was about Charles Willingham's death - so that was his surname - detailing from when the accident happened, to the outcome of the court case. Bella tried to make sense of what she was seeing, alarm bells going off in her head at full volume. Despite her instinct to leg it down the stairs and out of the front door as quickly as possible, her legs wouldn't move. She picked up another scrapbook. This time it was filled with articles all about Rupert. Little snippets from over the years. It couldn't be? Bile rose in her throat and she turned to run. As she did so, she screamed as she saw Florence blocking her exit.

'Er… Sorry… I couldn't remember which door you'd said. I'll just pop to the loo now if I may?' She tried hard to steady her voice and hide her shaking hands.

'I don't think so.' Florence closed the door behind her.

They stood there in silence eyeing one another, each with a different motive.

'So, you've seen my collection?' said Florence eventually. Bella nodded nervously. 'Not bad eh? It's taken years, but it's been worth the wait.'

There was a weird look in Florence's eyes and Bella knew that the person in front of her had lost the plot a long time ago. How could she not have seen it? Florence seemed so normal.

'Why?' croaked Bella.

'Why have I got such a collection? That's quite easy really. I knew from the moment my brother was killed by that murderer that I'd get my revenge. No one was going to take my brother away from me and not pay for it.'

'But your name's Florence, not Charlotte, and your surname is Petipas.'

Florence laughed. 'You're so stupid. Petipas is my married name, and Florence is my middle name, first name is Charlotte. You can imagine how surprised I was when you yelled out my name earlier!'

'Why use Florence?'

'I didn't want there to be any chance of anyone recognising my name and putting two and two together, I didn't know how much Rupert had told his wife or his friends about his past. It was perfect and legal, continue with my married name and use my middle name. Easy.'

What am I going to do, whimpered a terrified Bella to herself. How can I get away? She watched as Florence went over to a large, faded, colour photograph of a young boy of about ten. She stroked it tenderly.

'Oh, Charlie,' she murmured, 'how I've missed you.' Her head snapped round. 'I worshipped him, he was my everything. I was only five when he died. It shouldn't have been that way,' she snarled vehemently.

'Why don't we go down and have that cup of coffee you've made. You can tell me all about him? I'd like to hear about him. Really, I would. He sounds like a really super person, I would have loved to have had a brother like that,' she tried to smile in a sympathetic and encouraging way.

Florence stared at Bella, eyeing her up. 'Okay.'

'I need the loo first.'

'I'll wait.'

She followed Bella out of the room to the bathroom. Bella slipped in and closed the door, her heart hammering and her head swimming. She hurried to the window and flushed the loo to disguise any noise made in attempting to open it - hoping she could squeeze out and jump - but the window, swollen by damp, wouldn't budge. Frantically she pushed as hard as she could.

'Hurry up,' snapped Florence from the other side of the door.

'Coming,' called Bella, still frantically pushing and shoving the swollen wood, but it was no good, she concluded that it had to have been nailed shut. She washed her hands and took a deep breath, trying to calm herself down.

'Downstairs then,' ordered Florence, when Bella appeared.

'I'm a bit chilly, I'll just get my jumper from the car, and then you can tell me all about Charles,' Bella casually commented as she put her hand on the front door handle, turned and pulled. It was locked.

'Into the kitchen,' snapped Florence.

Maybe the back door will be open? How can I distract her? Bella thought frantically, as she sat as instructed at the table and grasped the mug proffered, tightly.

'So. Tell me Flor... Charlotte. What was Charles like?'

Florence's eyes softened as she spoke of her beloved brother, until she reached the part about his death, then a steely glaze came over them. Bella knew that it could only have been Florence who had killed Rupert. Somehow she had to get away from her.

'Perhaps you could show me some more photographs of him?'

Florence hurried into the next room and then upstairs, Bella seized the opportunity and leapt up, grabbing the back door handle. It too was locked, where was the key? Frenetically she searched, until she heard Florence coming back. She flung herself back into her chair, attempting to regain a calm composure, doing her utmost not to rile Florence. There seemed to be no way out. Patiently she looked at every photograph, attempting to make encouraging, friendly, noises.

'They're lovely. Do you have any more? What about photographs of you and him?'

Again, Florence disappeared upstairs, secure in the knowledge that there was no escape for Bella. Bella quickly grabbed her mobile and started to write a text. She got as far as "help" then heard Florence coming, she pressed send to the first number that came up, which happened to be Mia's. Unfortunately Bella was not quick enough and Florence saw it and snatched the phone off her.

'What were you doing?' she snarled.

'I was going to check with Mia to see if she needed a lift to tennis,' Bella lied.

'You won't need this!' Florence threw it onto the ground and stamped on it, the tiny silver phone shattered, shards flying across the floor of the kitchen. Bella gulped.

'I think I'd better be going.' Bella stood, randomly hoping that she might still get away.

Florence roughly shoved her back onto the chair.

'Oh, no you don't. You're not going anywhere,' she spat.

'But why?'

Florence smiled manically at her. It seemed to Bella that as every minute passed Florence spiralled further down into her delusions, losing a grasp of reality.

'If you go, you'll tell that Inspector boyfriend of yours. I've got away with it, and I'm not having you ruin it. If what you say about Rupert's will is correct, I shall walk away with a lot of blood money and will then disappear. No one will ever find me. But you could ruin it, and I can't let that happen. I've spent years planning this. Why do you think I moved here? Because I wanted to? No chance!' she spat, spittle flying out in all directions. 'I moved here because it was the next stage in my plan - get myself settled in, be a pillar of the community, and what better way than being a local nurse eh? I hated it, dealing with all those whingeing, moaning, sick people, but I knew the long-term goal would be worth it.'

Bella was starting to shake violently as her body went into shock. Florence meant to kill her, and her mind was so fuzzy with terror that she couldn't work out what to do, how to escape - desperately she tried, whilst Florence continued to rant and rave.

'The look on Rupert's face at Sophie and Harry's party made it all worthwhile. He knew. I hadn't spoken to him by then, but he knew who I was. I look so like Charles, there was no way he could not see the resemblance,' she grinned to herself enjoying the pleasure of the memory. 'It freaked him out, I could see that. It was so delectable, I could barely stop myself from moaning in ecstasy,' she licked her lips. 'It was so easy. I'd followed him for

262

weeks, knew what he did, when he did it, and with whom he did it. He'd been following Kim for weeks, he knew she was having an affair with Seb and every time she went to see Seb, Rupert came back the same way, and he always stayed the same length of time outside Seb's house. All I had to do was time it to perfection. I knew he'd been drinking, which would make it so much easier. All I had to do was drive in the middle of the road, the look in his eyes when he realised, in that split second, what was happening, what was about to happen, was incredible, he knew he was going to die, justice was finally done for my darling Charles.'

What a freak! How insane! How could anybody be so evil? Terror coursed through Bella's veins. To plan something for so long, to be so obsessed, she wanted to throw up.

'But getting rid of me won't help. If you let me go, no one will be any the wiser, and you can disappear as you planned. I won't tell anyone,' Bella pleaded.

'Wouldn't you?'

'No. Honestly I wouldn't. Let me go now. They'll wonder where I am if I'm not at tennis. Mia's expecting me. Let me go and I promise I won't say anything,' she pleaded and looked beseechingly at Florence.

Florence seemed to consider this, then gazed contemptuously at her. 'You're like all the others. You won't keep your promise.'

'I will! Honestly I will. I'm good at keeping secrets. I know so many.'

'And what secrets might you have?'

'I know stuff about the case. I know how someone else can be framed for Rupert's murder.'

This sparked Florence's curiosity. 'Go on.'

'Kit was blackmailing Rupert. The police are suspicious, I'm sure he could be put in the frame,' Bella said eagerly, desperate to say anything which would get her away to safety.

'I need to think.' Florence paced up and down, rubbing her head, her knuckles white from the pressure, muttering to herself.

'It would work,' encouraged Bella.

'Shut up!' screamed Florence, 'I need to think.'

The minutes ticked by. Each minute feeling like an hour. Bella dared not move. Barely daring to breath as she waited to see if her plan would work. Florence continued with her pacing, becoming more and more agitated. Bella checked the clock, two hours had passed. Surely they would have missed her at tennis? She prayed fervently that somehow Mia had got her text and sounded the alarm. But why would she? And she had no idea of knowing where Bella actually was. Tick, tick, tick went the clock, Florence seemed lost in her own little world, talking incessantly to herself. Six o'clock came, then seven o'clock. Bella, by this time drenched in sweat from fear, became more and more desperate. Out of the corner of her eye she thought she saw some movement outside. She peered intently but could see nothing, she must have imagined it.

Explosively there was a crash. Bella screamed. Florence grabbed her and the knife on the draining board simultaneously, and forced the sharp blade against Bella's throat. Bella's heart pounded frenziedly, exploding in her chest cavity, she daren't move - one slip and that would be it, Florence had her in a vice-like grip.

'Police! Put down the knife.'

Though Bella couldn't see all around her, she could feel the presence of marksmen, poised and ready to shoot. Please God, not me. Please let me go, she prayed. Sweat poured off her in torrents and yet her body felt like ice.

'Put the knife down Florence. Let Bella go.' Dave's soothing voice was music to Bella's ears and her knees went weak with relief knowing that he was there, despite knowing that reasoning would not work with Florence. Sanity had left her a long time ago.

He continued to talk calmly, soothingly, quietly, persuasively, attempting to persuade Florence to voluntarily drop the knife and let Bella go. Bella's pulse raced more the tenser Florence's body got. Suddenly, and for some inexplicable reason, Florence shoved Bella forward. Bella stumbled and hit the kitchen wall, smacking her head against it. Behind her there was a thud. She turned and screamed. Florence had slit her throat and lay bleeding to death on the grubby kitchen floor. Bella threw up as she was bundled out of the room. All around her there was manic activity as paramedics and police swarmed into the building. But nothing could be done to save Florence. Bella was left sobbing, shaking, overwhelmed with shock in the arms of Sergeant Swart.

Chapter Seventeen

Bella woke groggily the next day and sat up feeling bewildered and woozy in her bed. Next to her, in a chair, was Mia fast asleep with her mouth open and snoring gently. Bella smiled then frowned. What was she doing here? Her head was so muzzy, she shook it, trying to clear it, and quietly got out of bed and went to the bathroom. She splashed cold water on her face and then looked at the unrecognisable face peering back at her in the mirror. Hair greasy and wild, face pale, ink-dark circles under her eyes, a purple-black bruise on the side of her face, red welts at her throat. She screamed as she had a flashback of turning around and seeing Florence's body bleeding to death on the floor. Mia burst in through the door.

'You okay?' she asked breathlessly, her heart pounding as she recovered from being shocked awake by Bella's scream.

'Did it really happen?' Bella whispered.

'Come here.' Mia put her arm around Bella and guided her back to bed. 'Sit tight, I'll go and make a cup of tea, then we can talk.'

Bella sat there feeling shaken and nauseous, it was starting to come back to her. The whole nightmare in technicolour. Despite it being another scorchingly warm day outside, she shivered and tucked the duvet right up under her chin.

'Here. Take this.' Mia handed her a mug of tea and sat down in the chair clutching her own mug.

Bella gazed miserably into her steaming tea for a while.

'Did it really happen?' she asked again, even though she knew the answer.

'Yes. I'm afraid so.'

'And Florence? Did they save her?' Again she was sure she knew the answer.

Mia shook her head. 'No. She died quickly.'

'If the police hadn't turned up, she would have killed me. I tried everything I could to get her to let me go, I hoped I'd come up with a plan, but I think she was just using the time to work out what she would do with me, how to dispose of my body,' she shuddered.

Mia wiped tears from her eyes, it didn't bear thinking about. She couldn't imagine life without her best friend.

'How did the police find me?'

'I'm not sure. Inspector Ormandy turned up at the tennis club looking for Florence, he was on the way to her house when he remembered that she usually played tennis with us on a Friday. When he turned up, we were puzzling over your text. At first I didn't think much about it, but when you didn't turn up at tennis I started to worry. Anyway when he came looking for Florence I mentioned it to him. He shot off like a startled rabbit and said that if you turned up, I needed to contact him immediately. Well, we then all started to worry frantically, but we had to stay at the tennis club in case you arrived. Jennifer went back and knocked on your door and looked through the windows

267

and went into the garden. When she reported that you weren't there I really started to panic. It seemed like an eternity sitting up at the club, none of us felt like playing tennis. We waited until half past six then I phoned Inspector Ormandy and told him that you still hadn't arrived and you weren't at home. He said he was fairly sure where you were and that we should all go home. None of us wanted to disperse, so everyone came back to my place, checking your house again on the way. I kept trying your mobile, but it would ring and then go to answerphone.'

'Florence saw me use it. I didn't think the text had gone. She threw it on the floor and stamped on it.' Bella sipped the hot tea, not noticing the sweetness from the sugar Mia had spooned into it, as Mia continued.

'It was a couple of hours or so later that I had a phone call from Dave,' she reverted to using his first name, 'to say that you were safe but could I go to your house and stay with you overnight. We were mystified by this, but the others went home - apart from Jennifer who dropped her car at her house and walked down to join me. I let us in as I had the spare keys and switched a few lights on, we waited and waited, eventually a police car arrived with you in it and Sergeant Swart escorted you in. They'd contacted the on-call doctor who arrived shortly afterwards and gave you something to help you sleep.' A vague memory of this stirred in Bella's mind. 'The sergeant gave us an edited version of what had happened, we were absolutely stunned and horrified. Anyway, they've had a policeman outside all night and Jennifer and I were told not to contact the others as Kim needed to be told what had happened. Jennifer stayed for a while, then she left and I've been with you ever since.'

Bella tried to absorb what Mia was telling her. It sounded like a work of fiction, something you might read in a novel, not something that could happen in a small village in Kent. If she hadn't gone poking about trying to find out who had killed Rupert, this might never have happened and Florence might still be alive. She whispered this to Mia who shook her head.

'You don't know that Bella and, from what you said, it sounds as though Florence was   incredibly mentally unstable and could easily have killed herself anyway. Besides, even if she hadn't, she would have spent a large part, of her life - if not the rest of it - in a mental institution or possibly prison. I suspect it's unlikely she would have been fit to go to trial.

'What a waste of a life. Waste of several lives. You don't consider, do you, what the consequences of your actions might be.   I mean, when something happens, you would never imagine what the ripple effect might be, that the ripples could continue for years to come. Like a stone being skimmed on open water - which in this case was Charles' death - and the ripples kept spreading out for years, encompassing the lives of many other people: Charles's family - particularly Florence - Rupert's family, Rupert himself, Kim. It goes on. How do we know that what we do now won't result in tragedy in thirty years time?'

'You can't think like that Bella. Nobody knows what's ahead, that's life. You can't predict the future. Charles's death was a terrible and tragic accident. Rupert didn't mean to kill him, he was just a foolish young teenager who thought he was having some fun, but it all went horribly wrong, no one could have predicted what would happen.

What Florence did was different, it was planned, pre-meditated, she deliberately set out to kill Rupert.'

'Yes, I know that, but if Charles had not died, this wouldn't have happened.'

'Maybe not. Maybe his death triggered something within her, or maybe she was genetically disposed to be the way she was. Maybe she would have found a reason to kill someone else. It's all speculation, she's dead and we will never know.' Deliberately changing the subject, she said. 'Let me get you another cup of tea and some toast.'

'I don't feel hungry.'

'Maybe not, but you've got to eat. Dave will be here soon. You do know that you will have to give a statement at some point, don't you?' she said gently.

Bella nodded miserably and disappeared under the duvet to try to forget. When Mia arrived back with the tea and toast, Bella picked at a couple of pieces whilst Mia stood sternly over her, determined that Bella would eat at least a little of the toast, which she eventually did. Reluctantly, Bella got out of bed - quite happy to stay there for ever - and got dressed. A little while later Dave turned up. Mia made them some coffee and left them in the sitting room together.

'How are you?' he asked tenderly.

'Okay, I suppose. Though I can't get my last sight of Florence out of my head.'

'It should fade eventually, but you had a major trauma yesterday. I wanted you to go to hospital to be checked over, but you flatly refused.'

'Did I?' She couldn't remember.

'Oh yes. You left me in no doubt that you weren't going to go,' he smiled at her. He made her feel safe.

'How did you know it was Florence?'

'Eventually we tracked down a car body shop about forty miles away, where a blue car had been repaired and re-sprayed. The owner said the woman wanted it done in a hurry and she didn't mind paying extra for it to be done quickly, and she paid cash. The name was Charlotte Willingham. Anyway, with a bit of old-fashioned detective work, we discovered it was Florence yesterday afternoon. It was only when Mia told me about your text that alarm bells started ringing and I became concerned about your safety. I knew that you couldn't resist poking about, trying to find out what had happened to Rupert, and my gut feeling was that, somehow, you had discovered who Florence actually was. The rest you know really.'

'I was so relieved that you turned up. I knew she was intending to kill me. I tried to persuade her that Kit could be framed for Rupert's death, and for a little while I really thought that she was going to go for it, but as the hours passed my hopes dwindled. I'm sure she was just biding her time, trying to work out how to dispose of me.' Bella shuddered at the memory. 'I guess I'll have to make a statement?'

'Yes, you will. You told me everything last night but you were not in very good shape, not surprisingly. There's no rush, take a day or two to recuperate.'

She didn't remember telling him anything last night, but most of what happened after Florence killed herself was a blur.

He took her hand. 'I was so worried about you. I don't know what I would have done if anything had happened to you.' He kissed her hand tenderly.

She smiled wanly at him. 'I'm glad you don't have to find out.'

They sat in a companionable silence for a little while until Kim popped into Bella's head.

'I assume Kim knows?'

'Yes. I informed her last night.'

'How did she take it?'

'Shocked. Devastated. She's not just lost a husband, but a friend - or someone she believed to be a friend - too, a friend who had deliberately set out - and succeeded - to murder her husband. I'm sure she'll want to talk to you when you feel up to it. You're the one person who will be able to answer all her questions. I can only tell her the facts as I know them, whereas you were there, the only one who heard-first hand from Florence, her twisted perspective.'

'I guess so.'

'It will probably help to talk about what happened anyway. Bottling it up won't do you any good.'

'No, I suppose not.' The last thing Bella felt like doing at the moment was talking to Kim, or anyone else for that matter, but experience had taught her, from Hugh's death, that there would be a time and a place when it would feel right, and that it would indeed help her and probably Kim too.

Chapter Eighteen

A week later and still Bella could not bring herself to go out of the house. The horror of what had happened was as vivid and fresh in her mind as if it had happened a few minutes ago. She knew that she was being irrational in fearing that something similar might happen to her again if she left the house, but there was also the element of fear about what people were saying about her, the fear that they were holding her personally responsible for Florence's death, that she was to blame. Despite Mia's insistence that everyone she came across saw Bella as a heroine and not the criminal, Bella did not feel reassured. In her head she knew she was being irrational and she knew that Mia wouldn't lie to her, but she couldn't shake the thoughts from her head. Mixed in with the jumble of emotions was also the fear that she might bump in to Kim, and with that she would have to go over again what had happened on that terrible day. By hiding herself away she didn't have to face reality or Kim.

Though the sun was out the warmth - which had most people in t-shirts and shorts - did not permeate into Bella, who was wrapped up in a thick fleece and still feeling chilled to the bone. She clutched her cup of coffee tightly to her in an effort to warm herself up and stared blankly at yesterday's newspaper which Mia had dropped off, along with a few supplies. The ring of the door bell made her start and she narrowly missed spilling burning coffee over her lap. She didn't move, hopeful that whoever it was would go away, but the bell rang persistently. Bella's heart started to race in panic, as again and again the bell rang. Eventually she got up and walked to the front door, slipping the security chain on before she opened it.

She peered round the edge of the door and saw the petite figure of Kim standing on her doorstep, her brow was wrinkled in concern.

'Bella, how are you? Are you alright?'

'Er, fine.'

'Can I come in?' she asked gently.

Bella sighed. The moment she had dreaded had arrived. Perhaps it would be better to get it over and done with. She closed the door and slipped the security chain off, reopening the door a moment later, fearful of what Kim might say to her, convinced that she would be angry with her.

Kim stepped in through the door and gathered Bella up tightly in her arms. Startled, Bella burst into tears. Kim smoothed Bella's long, unkempt, straggly hair away from her face, then hugged her again, pushing the front door closed behind her with a shove of her foot. They stood there as Bella cried and howled, as the tide of terror of that day flooded from her, as she finally let go and released the inner pain she'd repressed. As her sobs receded, Kim led her through to the kitchen and sat her down at the table, then busied herself making them both fresh coffee.

Bella dabbed at her sore face and blew her nose on some kitchen roll.

'Sorry,' she murmured.

'For what?' replied Kim without turning around.

'For doing that. It's you who's upset. You're the one who has lost your husband.'

Kim glanced over her shoulder and shook her head. 'I've had weeks to mourn Rupert, and part of me always will. We didn't have a perfect marriage, far from it, but I did love him for a long time. But you are the one who has gone through the most unimaginably horrific ordeal. I can't begin to truly comprehend how terrible it was for you, and in some way I feel responsible.'

Bella's jaw dropped open. 'You? Responsible? That's ridiculous!'

'No it's not. I was married to Rupert and it was his actions in his past that caused Florence to do this, so in a strange way. I feel like it was partly my fault.'

'Absolute rubbish!' cried Bella vehemently. 'There's no way that any of it has got anything to do with you. You're the victim in all this.'

'And so are you Bella. No one is blaming you for what happened.' Bella looked startled. 'Mia told me what you've been thinking, and there is not one person who thinks it's your fault that Florence killed herself. They have nothing but admiration for you, for what you did. How on earth could you have known that Florence would do that? I think that if she hadn't killed herself then, she would have done so at the next opportunity she had.'

Bella looked uncertainly at her.

'Really Bella. Everyone thinks you're a heroine. You helped solve Rupert's murder. You found out who was responsible, and for that I will be eternally grateful. I cannot imagine spending the rest of my life not knowing who had killed him. You've given me peace of mind.'

'But the police discovered who had killed him.'

'You got there first, and if it hadn't been for you looking in to things, then maybe they never would have. Here,' she handed her a mug of coffee, 'and Sharon at the shop sent these up for you.' Kim handed her a thick pile of glossy magazines and today's newspaper.

'Wow, thanks. That was kind of her.' Bella felt a flicker of warmth ignite inside her.

'And these are from the delicatessen, with their compliments.' Kim unpacked a brown paper carrier bag, which was packed full of delectable salads, a portion of cooked lobster, a crisp lemon tartlet, and a large box of organic dark chocolates.

'Gosh! I can't believe it, that's so sweet and kind.' Bella felt touched, and reassured, and also slightly foolish that she had thought they might all turn on her.

Kim placed the chilled food into the fridge, and suggested they go outside and sit in the garden. Bella carried the box of chocolates out and tore of the cellophane, her appetite suddenly showing a flicker of interest in food. She offered them to Kim, who took a moment to choose one filled with a dark chocolate mousse, while Bella chose one with a champagne truffle filling. They sat in companionable silence for a minute, before Kim cleared her throat nervously.

'Would you … Would it …?' her voice trailed off.

'Would I what?' Bella glanced at Kim and then comprehended what she was trying to say. 'Would I mind telling you what happened? Is that what you'd like to know?'

276

Kim nodded. 'If you don't mind. I really don't want to upset you any further than you have been, but it would be a such a help if you could tell me, not just of that dreadful afternoon, before that, when you found out the awful truth about what happened when Rupert was younger.'

'I don't think Rupert meant to kill that child. From what was said to me, I believe it was an accident. And it changed the course of his life for ever.'

'I agree. Rupert was many things, but he wasn't a cold-blooded murderer.'

Bella started to recount what she had done, and what had happened, the tears flowed not just from Bella but from Kim too. After she had finished, and Kim had asked all the questions she needed answers for, they sat in silence, each feeling a sense of peace coming over them. It was time to attempt to start to move on, no matter how hard it might be.

Chapter Nineteen

Two weeks later Bella had started to get back a semblance of the routine into her life in Monhurst. She had been embarrassed, but flattered, by all the attention and praise she had received when she had eventually ventured out of the house. Even now, people were still complimenting and praising her about it. She had gone with the others to Florence's funeral. Despite what Florence had done it had seemed the right thing to do. She had no family, no other friends and, in her crazy mixed up head, they had been her friends. It had always been about Rupert.

Bella was determined to have a good evening on the Saturday night three weeks after Florence's death. Tonight was the surprise party for Cressa, organised by Jack to celebrate their twenty-second wedding anniversary. Bella had been invited, and also had the option to bring a plus-one, so she'd asked Dave. In fact, it was Kim who suggested she bring him, reassuring her that there would be no awkwardness, that, in fact, Bella would be doing her a favour as she was unofficially going to be there with Seb.

Bella spent quite some time getting herself ready. She'd even gone as far as having her hair highlighted and cut that morning and spent the afternoon painting nails and relaxing. Looking at herself in the long mirror, she admired the slimmer her, in the pale pink silk wrap dress she'd purchased. Ironically, Florence's death had put her off eating and she'd lost quite a few pounds in the preceding three weeks.

Prompt as ever, Dave knocked at the door and smiled appreciatively at her when she opened it, complimenting her on how beautiful she looked. She glowed in response and admired his chinos, beautifully cut navy jacket and blue and white, wide-stripped smart shirt, and spotted blue and red silk tie.

The party was in the village hall so they didn't have far to walk. The hall was packed with friends and family of the couple. It had been meticulously planned by Jack over the previous six months, hence the secrecy and the cause for Cressa's concern with regard to the bank account. How shocked she would be when she found out the real reason! Bella grinned to herself. The champagne was flowing and delectable little canapés were being passed round. Jack had certainly gone to town. This would be followed by a five course sit-down meal, and a jazz band for dancing afterwards.

'Sssh, they're coming,' squeaked Mia excitedly. Henry and Emma, their two children, hid well out of sight and someone switched the lights off.

'I thought we were going out to dinner,' moaned Cressa in the distance, 'why on earth do we have to check on the hall on the way? Why can't you do it tomorrow?'

279

'Surprise!' yelled everyone, as the lights were switched on again.

And, for once, Cressa was at a loss for words. She burst into tears and hugged Jack so tightly it didn't look as though she'd let go. It was only when she was tapped on the shoulder by her children that she turned and let out a howl of excitement and clung on to them, tears pouring down her cheeks in delight.

'I can't believe you've done this!'

'It's taken a while,' replied Jack bursting with pride at his success, 'not quite the affair you thought it was, eh?' he joked.

Cressa, poked him in the arm and hugged him again, smothering him with kisses.

It was enough to make you weep. Bella felt all mushy inside, she caught Dave's eye who was grinning at her, he subtly squeezed one of her fingers tightly, and for a while she forgot all that had happened, and felt blissfully happy.

Out Now…

Dead Fit

Dead Fit unites, for the first time, Bella and Kitty as they strive to uncover the perpetrator responsible for the wave of deadly crime ricocheting through their respective Kent villages of Monhurst and Wynenden.

Can they do this before it's too late…?

Instagram @emelliotoffical

www.emelliot.com

Printed in Great Britain
by Amazon

32632352R00158